To Jac,...

The Narrow Sea

Best wishes
Uncle. Henry.

Hamish Morrison

PART ONE

14th day of June 1762 AD
The Manse of Langmuir

Sir

It is near a twelvemonth since we bade farewell to our mutual friend Willie Shaw. There's more than me remembers with deep respect the gracious elegy you made on that sorrowful occasion. As you made clear in your noble address Willie did more than anyone in the Parish to bind up the terrible wounds left by the cruel events of seventeen years ago.

In the twelve months between I am sure we have all been exercised, in our separate ways, to live up to the fine example Willie set us. It has been my especial honour to carry out your lordship's wishes in the matter of young master Mungo Shaw, Willie's grandson. As you know a place was secured for him at the Burgh School under dominie Guthrie. I have to report that he has exceeded all our expectations for he is to be considered for the Provost's prize for meritorious work. I have no wish to tempt providence, yet I judge he will be ready for the University at Glasgow in a year from now.

Your stalwart support of the family does you great credit, Sir, and is much remarked upon by the gentle folk of the Parish. The people are grateful too for your more recent acts of generosity in support of those poor families bereft by the smallpox which has lately come among us. May I express my deep gratitude on behalf of the whole Parish for your great and continuing generosity to us all?

I Have the Honour to be Sir
Your Humble Servant
Torquil Maclintock
Minister of this Parish

Sir Archie Crawford
Langmuir House

Chapter One

Ayr Burgh School was an elegant building set under the lee of Cromwell's Fort. Its austere facade was on a surprisingly grand scale and somehow seemed to embody the ambition and self-confidence of the citizens in that historic county town. For the most part the boys knew that their school was more than just a place of learning. They took pride in being there and willingly accepted the responsibilities required of them for good behaviour and hard work.

Of course there were always exceptions. Mungo Shaw lacked neither the diligence nor courtly manners demanded of him, but he would rather have been elsewhere, away at sea.

"Face the front and pay attention to me, Master Shaw," bellowed Mr Craig as he wrestled to explain the meaning and purpose of the subjunctive mood of some obscure Latin verb. Mungo was staring across the muir to the sea beyond. A fine brain was concealed behind Mungo's sparkling brown eyes and tousled dark hair. He was good at Latin and most other subjects too but he wanted to be up and away from all this book learning and to be making his way in the world.

It was the last lesson of the day and he planned to take a walk down to the harbour to see what ships might be there but as he was leaving the classroom a familiar voice called out to him.

"Hey Mungo, do you want to go up the river to see if we can get a fish?"

Mungo had befriended Graham Murray, a slightly built lad, on his first day at school. They got on well together but if he was honest Graham's sister Margaret was an important factor in their continuing friendship. She was a real beauty. Mungo had seen her often enough at the Kirk on Sundays but had never plucked up the courage to speak to her. It was maybe a long shot but angling for a trout with her brother might just end in a chance encounter.

The two boys soon despaired of taking a fish because the river was in a full spate after two days of heavy rain and that warm May afternoon was too bright for fishing. Graham, a thoughtful lad, was busy putting the country to rights with no more direction than the summer breeze. Mungo was more interested in the two figures coming towards them. Just ahead of them the turbulent flood speeded up as it passed between the grassy bank below the path and a gaunt outcrop of grey-blue whinstone on the opposite side. At the very narrowest part of the gorge Mungo suddenly said to Graham,

"Well, well, if it isn't Master Wallace!" Mungo's face took on a mirthless grin. Graham was instantly silent.

The swaggering figure of Charles Wallace was the last man Mungo wanted to meet that day, or any other day. During the past year at the Burgh School they had never exchanged so much as a civil word. Their shared hostility almost boiled over on several occasions but it never came to much more than over-energetic jostling. Mungo had always managed to restrain himself from a full-blooded fight.

His reluctance to engage was not for any want of physical courage. He was driven by a practical calculation. Mungo knew that even if he could beat Wallace in a square go - no foregone conclusion - he would still lose. After all, the school was run by the Town Council and Wallace's father was the Provost.

Even Mr Guthrie, the dominie, otherwise a good man, would have to favour the Provost's son over a farm boy like Mungo. Brawling was bound to get him turned out of the school with consequences too dire to think on. Old Sir Archie, the laird, who paid his fees, would be deeply disappointed. The Reverend MacLintock who sponsored his place at the Burgh School would surely condemn him to the stool of repentance. Worst of all, his widowed mother would be heart-broken.

These thoughts crowded Mungo's mind as he watched Wallace come ever closer. With just over a month to go before school broke for the summer, he was more determined than ever to prevent this chance encounter with Wallace from becoming a full blown set to. All the same his pace had taken up a more rhythmic cadence - defiant somehow. He knew it would be especially difficult to keep his distance from Wallace. The narrowness of the track would push them together. It would be best to avert his gaze and just ignore him.

At first it seemed that Wallace was also looking the other way but when they were just a few paces apart the focus of his cruel blue eyes became all too clear; he was staring at the anxious face of Graham Murray.

"Well Murray you're surely a long way from home," Wallace sneered "Your stuck-up sister is too good for the likes of me, is she? You're nothing but a dirty wee clype," Wallace barked, stabbing his finger into Graham's chest. "Don't expect Shaw to back you up either. He's full o' wind and piss," the bully continued.

"You just stay away from my sister," said Graham, in a vain attempt to face down the bully.

Mungo felt the rage growing within him yet he demurred. No good could come of this. He knew it was pointless but he tried to shame Wallace out of his hostile talk by ignoring him, 'Come away Graham,' he said, 'he's not worth it'

Just then Wallace's hand punched forward, knocking Graham's school books from under his arm and scattering them all over the river bank.

This cowardly assault on his slightly built friend snapped Mungo's tether. He elbowed Graham aside and with one almighty blow sent his fist into the very depths of Wallace's guts. He shocked himself with the ferocity of the punch. He had been in scraps for as long as he could remember but these were just tussles; about getting the better of some other boy. This time it was different; he really meant serious harm to Charles Wallace.

Wallace went down like a felled ox. Yet, badly winded though he was, he managed to raise himself to his knees and tried to get up.

"Pick up Graham's books, you horse's arse!" Mungo screamed at Wallace, moving in to strike again.

Wallace was alert to the danger and rolled to his left to avoid Mungo's enraged advance. This took him onto a part of the bank that was severely undermined by the fast flowing current. Suddenly there was a tearing and grinding as the turf gave way and crumpled under Wallace's writhing bulk. Down he tumbled until, with a loud splash and amidst cries of angered desperation, he was swallowed up by the flood.

The immediate result of this commotion was to put Wallace's companion to flight. It crossed Mungo's mind that he might have gone to seek reinforcements but his thoughts quickly returned to Wallace. He had disappeared!

The river was deep at this point. The heart-pounding excitement of the confrontation was now tinged with a hint of fear. Had he killed Wallace?

"Graham, can you see him," he yelled, "We can get down to the water off that ledge over there."

The two friends reached the ledge, more a kind of gravel beach, in a few seconds. God but it was quiet! For what seemed an age they saw nothing and heard only the gurgling of the flood. Then there was a sudden thrashing in the water, not six feet away. Charles Wallace loomed up and started to lumber out of the river, bedraggled as a drowned rat and his face a ghastly white.

At first Mungo was unsure whether to help him out or to hit him again. His murderous compulsion had abated but it was still some way short of compassion. As he stood wondering what to do Graham reached forward with a piece of driftwood. He held it towards Wallace to help him ashore.

As soon as he found his feet Wallace grabbed for the stick and with a mighty heave wrenched it clear of Graham's grasp. Lurching forward he jabbed the splintered end of the stick like a spear. He lunged at Mungo's head but missed, though not by much. Mungo was now much closer in and so able to counter with a hooking right hand that crunched into the bully's chin. Wallace reeled back. He seemed out on his feet but he shook his head fiercely until he regained his focus. Struggling to keep his balance with his feet slipping on the boulders below the surface he faced up to Mungo again.

"You miserable piece of cow's shite," Wallace growled as he repositioned the stick under his armpit, making it into a kind of lance. He aimed it straight at Mungo's face and launched himself forward with a cry of, "Die you swine!"

As he moved to dodge the point of Wallace's pike Mungo's foot became stuck in the mud. Now his shoulder was in the line of attack. He heard his shirt ripping as the point tore into his upper arm. The intense pain and the warm blood running down to his elbow might have finished a lesser man. But serious as the wound was, Mungo paid it little heed. He dragged his foot free of the cloying mud and launched himself straight at Wallace, wrapping his good arm round Wallace's throat. Now both warriors lost their footing and they tumbled into the margin of the river. Wallace grabbed for Mungo's hair and by degrees the two dragged each other to the deeper water. Before long both were submerged and this time in a stronger current. The shallows were now coloured with Mungo's blood. Graham had lost sight of them and was sure that one or both would surely perish.

Unable to breathe and gulping great draughts of the muddy river had weakened both boys. Wallace struggled free of the head lock and scrambled into the shallows. He got to his feet uncertainly. A wound had opened on his forehead causing a bloody wash on his contorted face. He was roaring like the wounded animal he had become.

"You boys are as good as dead," he shrieked as he staggered on to the little beach retching and spewing up water. Whatever his physical impairment Wallace's warlike spirit was still aflame and he took another swing at Graham. But he was weaker now and the blow went wide, the momentum of his swinging arm almost capsizing him. Graham was now worried sick about the fate of Mungo and ran frantically, back and forth, along the shingle bank casting agitated glances at the swirling water. At the same time a much-weakened Mungo was some 15 yards downstream trying to manoeuvre himself ashore, one-handed. In the deeper water he was out of Graham's line of sight..

Just then a cry went up from two men rapidly approaching along the path. A groggy Mungo his head just above the water heard them. He instantly remembered the lad who had run off and was worried that these men might be more of Wallace's henchmen so he kept close to the bank and out of sight.

Wallace was also uncertain about the allegiance of the newcomers. In his exhausted state he settled for retreat as the best option. He scrambled up the bank and took off at a kind of drunken trot in the opposite direction from the approaching men. As the two men came on Wallace could still be heard puking and cursing as he staggered off into the trees.

Even before the men got close they could be heard ranting and raging about the ill-bred behaviour of the boys. They seemed particularly angered by the damage to the bank where Wallace's impromptu immersion had taken place. By their air of outraged authority Mungo took them to be water-baillies. He called out as they came close and at the sight of bedraggled blood-soaked Mungo the two men reached down and dragged him on to the bank. Then one of them recognised Graham.

"It's young Master Murray," he said to his companion whereupon their demeanour changed completely. Mungo knew that Graham's people were wealthy – most of the boys at the Burgh School came from well-to-do families – yet he was surprised that mere recognition could cow grown men in this way. He was not to know that these men were actually employees of Graham's father. But Graham didn't know that either.

Straight away one of the men came forward to examine Mungo's injuries.

"Sit you down and get your breath," he insisted. "Now, where's a' this blood comin' fae?" he cleaned and bound the stab wound in Mungo's upper arm with some muslin he took from the creel he carried over his shoulder. "That's a gey deep wound, son," he said, "you be sure and get the surgeon tae take a look at it for fear it'll go rotten."

The second man was talking animatedly to Graham whilst setting a fire on the same gravel bank which had so recently been the battleground.

After ten minutes or so of good-natured, and respectful, conversation the Good Samaritans resumed their patrol. Mungo and Graham were left steaming quietly before the fire.

Their hearts were still thumping from their exertions and the high anxiety of the whole incident. Even so Graham was in a rather sombre mood. He had recovered those books which had not been carried off by the river but Mungo could tell he had something else on his mind.

"I don't think I should have told that baillie it was Wallace we were fighting," Graham ventured, "It'll be the talk of the town before night."

"It won't do much harm, though," said Mungo, "Wallace will be in no hurry to tell folk he got a kicking."

"Yes but his father – like as no – will make a stink about it," Graham continued, "and we'll be up before Guthrie for 'loutish behaviour' "

He was right of course; it was just as Mungo had feared all along.

"We'll just have to stick to the truth of it and hope that the dominie can square things away with the Provost," he said without much conviction. "I'm sure your family will be proud of you though; sticking up for your sister's honour and all." He grinned, trying to lighten the mood.

Graham said nothing, smiling back through gritted teeth.

"Hell!" said Mungo, suddenly clasping his good hand over his wounded arm. The baillie's dressing had slowed the flow of blood but had not stopped it.

"What is it?" put in Graham, anxiously.

"Oh just a twinge, not more," Mungo replied but his grimace told another story.

"We'd better get off home just the same."

"Aye I suppose you're right," Mungo said kicking the cinders into the river. He had felt better.

As they took the road Mungo had furthest to go; more than a mile and a half. He felt shaky and although he was still making steady progress when their paths parted, he began to wonder if he would make it all the way home. When Shaw Farm, his home, finally came into sight, tiredness began to sweep over him in waves. Still he ploughed on. Surely he could make the last half mile. He could no longer keep his train of thought for more than a second. His mind raced from his current concerns, to his earliest memories and then to all kinds of disjointed situations and ideas.

He knew he was staggering because the trees in the little wood below the house were coming at him like breakers on the shore. The tiredness was now replaced by bouts of dizziness then sudden feelings of elation. When he was through the wood he could see the house but the sky was getting dark. Even in his befuddled state he knew this was wrong for a May afternoon. After a few moments more the light was gone completely.

Chapter Two

"It was the old dog that found him," he heard his mother's voice say, or at least he thought he did. He was semi-conscious and not even sure where he was. "Ben doesn't stir himself for much nowadays. It would be about eight o'clock I heard him barking like a mad thing, down at the road-end," her voice went on.

"That was fortunate, Mistress," said the Reverend MacLintock – there was no mistaking *his* sanctimonious twang. The evening light was glinting through the small window in the gable and it dawned on Mungo that he must be at home in his own bed.

"We will give thanks for Ben on Sunday," the minister muttered. But where were these voices coming from? Mungo wondered.

"He'll be mending now, though?" the minister asked. They are in the front room, Mungo thought. Their voices must be carrying through the ceiling boards, my floorboards.

"It was three days before we could wake him then we had to shake him every few hours to make him drink. But today he took some stew though he was no better than half conscious," she said. "The poor soul must have lost an awful lot of blood. When we found him his face was the same colour as the stones in the dyke. I was sure he was dead." she sighed.

Who was she talking about? Mungo wondered, until the throbbing ache in his shoulder roused his memory. Just then a third voice spoke up. At first he could not make it out and again he wondered if he was dreaming.

"He was a dead-weight. I had to get Gregor Lamont to help us carry him home."

The resonant bass belonged to James Scott, the estate factor. He was noted for his assertive voice yet it did not seem to carry too well through the floor boards. The factor was a frequent visitor to the Shaw now the estate had taken

13

the farm in hand following the death of Mungo's grandfather. That was to be the arrangement till Mungo came of an age to take on the tenancy. In his semi-conscious state he wondered if Mr Scott's interest in the Shaw was only land management. He had seen the way Mr Scott looked at his mother. Jean was a slightly built but strong willed woman She was handsome rather than beautiful though her well-groomed hair and green eyes gave her a striking appearance. Her devotion to her son was absolute and any feelings she may have had for Factor Scott were surely secondary.

The factor seemed to be mumbling something about the school. He couldn't make him out and again drowsiness overtook Mungo.

"It was the matter of Mungo's schooling I wanted to discuss," said the minister. "Last week the Town Council approved the award of their special prize for practical subjects to Mungo. His outstanding attainments in book-keeping and navigation and his creditable performance in everything else except English put him ahead of all his fellows." In a brief period of lucidity Mungo heard the second part of the minister's account but decided he really was dreaming before drifting off again.

"What wonderful news," Jean exclaimed barely able to contain herself, "his grandfather would be so proud. He always knew Mungo was a clever lad."

"There is a problem though," said the minister in a pained tone. "It seems the Provost means to block the prize; not appropriate to reward one guilty of loutish behaviour, apparently."

Jean's elation quickly gave way to hurt amazement then seething anger. The factor's dander was up too.

"The boy must have his prize!" Mr Scott asserted. His voice was louder now and his tone higher. Mungo came to again. "If their brawling is to be punished then each boy must suffer the same penalty. It's outrageous for the Provost to favour his own lad in this way." Mr Scott was spitting with rage. "Taking away Mungo's prize would be a scandal."

Although he didn't quite understand, Mungo sensed Mr Scott was on his side and he slipped into a deep, contented sleep.

"Well it's all very difficult," the minister fretted, "Dr Guthrie rather agrees with you Mr Scott but I fear it's likely that the Burgh Council will side with the Provost. That will be difficult for the Kirk." His weasel words did not disturb Mungo's slumber any further.

* * *

Every day Mungo felt he was getting stronger and after three weeks abed he felt the need of some fresh air. His first attempts at getting to his feet were confounded by weakness and loss of balance. His loss of mobility was deeply shocking and he even entertained the horrified thought that he had become a cripple. He persevered, though and by the afternoon he had managed to walk the length of the room. The next day he was able to make it downstairs, much to his mother's amazement and displeasure.

After a few days walking round the farm he felt strong enough to go further. Only five days since he first rose from his bed he overcame his mothers objections and set off for a longer walk. .

The port had always been his favourite haunt for his only ambition was for a life at sea. There were few books at the Shaw but for us long as he could remember he was fascinated by 'The Travels of Lemuel Gulliver'. At twelve he left the village school and was put to work on the farm with his grandfather. It was hard graft. The farm overlooked the Firth of Clyde and every day he could see the majestic ships coming and going to and from distant lands. He was sure that life at sea had to be much more exciting than farming. Alas no one seemed to share his vision. The minister thought he should go to university, Mr Scott was sure he would make a fine farmer or even a factor like himself and his mother wanted him to be a clerk and, in time, a man of business. Mungo would have none of it; a sea captain was the only position that ever made any sense to him.

His agreement to enrol in the Burgh School had been a way of trying to square these competing demands on his future. When grandfather died, family, friends and sundry acquaintances advised him to take up all kinds of occupations. After seemingly endless discussion, debate and argument only one point of agreement ever emerged; a good education would give him freedom to choose his own way. Mungo eventually agreed with this assessment but only after he discovered that as well as all the usual subjects the Burgh School taught book keeping, navigation.

His fight with Charles Wallace had made him think again. He was sure that the incident would get him turned out of school. Since he was a reluctant scholar in the first place that prospect did not trouble him too much. He worried, though, about how his mother might take it. As for all that stuff about a school prize, he was sure he dreamt it. Certainly his mother had not mentioned it. He must now put all his efforts into getting away to sea.

He wondered too about the reason for his fight with Wallace. They had quarrelled that first day at school when Wallace had mocked him for bringing cheese for his lunch. In factMungo had offered to share his cheese with Wallace - whether out of generosity or sarcasm was not clear. At all events the other boys had cheered him for the way he stood up to Wallace. As time went on he realised almost no one had a good word to say about the appalling Wallace. But he was the Provost's son and what he lacked in fiendliness he made up for in arrogance.

Wallace had designs on Margaret Murray. Surely she did not return his interest? Mind you he was a good looking fellow – half a foot taller than Mungo with a fine head of blond hair. Still, Mungo wondered how Margaret would feel about him defending her brother against Wallace and, indirectly, standing up for her. How he hoped she would think well of him.

His mind was churning as he stood on the wharf staring out through the tall masts. He was surrounded by anchors, ropes, canvas and all the other paraphernalia of the harbour. School seemed a world away. The cries of the sailors and the harbour billies were muted only by the endless hum of the wind in the taut rigging. The quarrelsome seabirds moaned and sniggered as they foraged amongst overturned casks and burst sacks. This was the real world. But however hard he tried he could not see a way of getting a berth on one of these handsome ships.

"Whit are ye daein' here?" bawled a familiar voice from over Mungo's shoulder, "Ye're no feart ye'll fa in wi a bad crowd doon here at the harbour!"

It was Hughie Maclure: He and Mungo had been as close as brothers at Langmuir village school. Hughie came from Fisherton, further down the coast. He had boarded with his auntie in Langmuir village when his mother, father and elder brother were all away at the fishing. At the age of twelve Hughie joined his father's boat and Mungo went back to the farm with his grandfather. In the last four years Hughie had grown a little taller than Mungo. His face was fuller too. But the two boys still shared the same stocky build, black hair and dark complexion.

"Man but its grand to see you, Hughie Maclure!" cried Mungo in surprised delight. He had last seen Hughie at his Da's funeral two years back, but that was a day for hand-shaking condolence rather than back-slapping banter. "I suppose you are still at the fishing," Mungo beamed at his old pal.

"Well no exactly," the big fellow replied. "Oor boat was driven ashore in that bad storm last April. We all got off but she's stranded on the sands at Carrick Shore; maybe two miles from yer ain place at Langmuir," Hughie said. "I'm just getting odd days of work here and there; lumping fish, mending nets, anything at a'."

"You must be having a thin time of it, all the same."

"We never died o' winter yet! Brother Sandy is the skipper noo and he says we'll get her back in the water in another week or two. But whit aboot yersel, though?" said Hughie, his face brightening now into the broad smile that had always been his hallmark.

"Oh I'm at the Burgh School for a spell," Mungo said, kind of sheepishly, for it occurred to him that Hughie might find something odd about the notion of a sixteen-year-old schoolboy. "I'm studying the navigation," he quickly put in, "I'm hoping to go to the sea myself."

"Good for you," said Hughie not quite sure of how he should react. "I daresay you'll be my captain one o' these days." He grinned.

The two friends talked about old times, current gossip and what had become of mutual acquaintances. Mungo realised he had not really spoken so freely to anyone in a very long time. The family were always trying to rule his life. His school mates were an interesting bunch of lads, even quite amusing, but their world was not his. His old friend's earthy tales told in the broad Scots of their childhood gave Mungo a warm feeling.

After maybe a half hour of breathless talk and wild laughter Hughie brought them back to earth.

"I'm finished here for the day so I'll hae tae awa' doon the coast tae help wi' patching up the boat," Hughie said, almost apologetically. "Brother Sandy and Johnson the chippy are doing a fine job."

"I'll come with you. It's on my road home," Mungo said impulsively for he didn't want to part company, so soon, with his old friend.

"Aye nae bother, but it's a richt roon aboot road hame if ye ask me," laughed Hughie.

The stranded boat was nearly three miles away across the foreshore. It was slow going but since it was low water they were able to make short-cuts by rounding the cliffs, and wading through the burns. Even so Mungo worried that he might not be up to it. They sighted the boat about the middle of the day and Mungo's concerns about his fitness vanished..

Even at a distance Mungo found the sight of the derelict strangely moving. The closer they came the more it looked awe-inspiring to Mungo's eye. From maybe a hundred paces the stark white characters of the name '*VENUS*' on her bow were clear enough to read. In truth though she did not look much like a goddess, more of a prize fighter really; battered and bloodied but still ready to rise for the next round. She was resting on an even keel and the gash where the starboard bow had been stove in was now perfectly smooth. The pale new wood of the patch melded seamlessly into the rest of her darkened timbers. Her mast soared into the clear blue of the sky as if in some supreme act of defiance. Yet, as a caution, the black jagged rocks where she grounded lurked just a few feet away, like so many, disappointed, hoodie-craws.

"See wha I've brocht tae see ye," Hughie called out to his brother.

Sandy Maclure was only ten years older than the boys but he had already outgrown most of his hair. He had the look of a well-fed medieval monk as he peered over the boat's side and cast a quizzical look towards his brother's companion.

"It's never young Mungo Shaw," Sandy roared. "I've no seen you since ye were at the school wi Hughie. Aye up tae mischief wi' the erse hanging oot o' yer breeks! Quite the young man noo though."

Johnson the chippy did not know Mungo. He just smiled amiably at him as he made his way to the fire above the high water mark at the top of the beach.

"The Maclures are a' the same. Yer like the beggars; ye aye turn up at feeding time." The chippy took a wooden ladle and began to stir the contents of a black pot that was perched on some boulders beside the fire. "You're in luck, all the same. There's plenty broth for the four of us; my mate's awa mendin' a roof at the big hoose"

Sandy came down the ladder from the boat's deck and joined the other three beside the fire. All four began to sup their broth along with some oatcakes the chippy had heated on a flat stone by the fire.

"Well, whit dae ye think o' her, Mungo? She should be ready for the sea next week," said Sandy admiring the repair on his boat's starboard bow. "You'll surely come and help us tae float her."

"Mungo has a notion of the sea himself," Hughie announced to his brother.

"Is that a fact," he pondered. "Are ye looking for a berth along wi' us, young Mungo?" After his anguished thoughts of an hour ago, Mungo could hardly believe his ears. Fishing on the *Venus* was not the seafaring life he had in mind, but he had to start somewhere. Still he couldn't quite take it in and did not reply to Sandy straight away.

"Ony way its up to you," said Sandy, uneasy with Mungo's hesitation. "We'll be sailing a man short till father's ribs are haled up."

On their walk along the shore Hughie had told Mungo how his father had all but lost his life during the wreck. Old Rab had been trapped between the mainsail boom and the gunnel. For a while it had seemed he would have the life crushed out of him or he would be drowned. Hughie still did not know how they got him out. Despite this horrific tale Mungo's seagoing ambitions were undaunted. Indeed, he was anxious to know every detail of how the *Venus* had come ashore. The story was also a convenient distraction from having to decide on Sandy's invitation to join the boat.

"You must have been fishing very close in to fetch up on the sands?" he wondered aloud.

"Ah weel," said Sandy stirring the fire with a stick, "we wisnae exactly fishin'. We were runnin' a special cargo for the MacCullochs, if ye get my meanin."

"Oh, I see," said Mungo, though he did not get Sandy's meaning at all. "Still you'll be happy to get back in time for the herring."

"Aye," said Sandy, pleased that the conversation was back on easier ground. "I hear the Ballantrae boats have landed some bonny fish already." He stood up and surveyed the scene. Then he announced, "The top o' the spring tide will be at six o'clock a week on Wednesday so we'll need a' the help we can muster from aboot dinnertime onwards if we are tae catch the tide."

Mungo was already looking forward to the great adventure of re-launching the *Venus.* He could have talked on for the rest of the day but Sandy had more urgent matters on his mind.

"Hughie, you and Mungo'll hae tae earn your keep; awa up to the top road and fetch down the tar boiler."

For the next two hours the two lads wrestled the boiler and humped several large chunks of pitch down to the shore. The boat was the best part of a quarter mile from where the carter had set down the gear and materials. Carrying this load through the sand hills on such a warm day was very slow going. Mungo quickly realised that he was not yet as strong as he thought he was, but he persevered. He had not made up his mind about joining the *Venus* but he could not show any weakness to the Maclures, just the same.

The lads had to build a small 'U-shaped' stone dyke with the open end facing into the breeze. Then they had to manoeuvre the boiler on top of it. Next they needed to gather a large stock of firewood. All the while Mungo turned over the arguments for and against leaving school at once and going to sea. There was a worry about the lease on the Shaw. According to the agreement with the laird it would be open till he was twenty-one. If it became clear that he had lost interest in the farm, and he had, his mother might be put out of her home. Still, fishing aboard the *Venus* would only be a summer job he reasoned; just till old Rab was fit.

When they finished setting up and stoking the boiler the foreshore was clear of every last twig of driftwood. Mungo's mind was clear too.

"Skipper," he called over to Sandy who was standing under the bow caulking round patch with teased out rope. I would like fine to sail with the *Venus.*"

"Ye'll no regret it son," said Sandy bounding over to him and wrapping a large muscled arm round Mungo's shoulder. His embrace was warm but brought considerable agony to Mungo's wounded arm. As they say, though, 'worse things happen at sea.'

Chapter Three

Mungo wondered if Dr Guthrie had forgotten all about him as he sat on the bench outside the dominie's room. He had returned to school on Monday. Now it was Wednesday and he had not been summoned. There was plenty of talk amongst the boys about his fight with Wallace but from Dr Guthrie, not a word. The mystery of the school prize nagged at his mind too. Graham Murray was saying less than he knew. On Mungo's first day back Graham had sought him out to enquire about his injuries. As they talked he made some remarks about his father having a blazing row with the Provost but was as evasive about the cause as he was about the outcome. Anyway, Mungo was more interested to know what Margaret had thought of their battle at the river. Either she thought very little of it or Graham was saying even less.

Mungo had his own reasons for his meeting with the dominie. It was proper to ask permission to leave early though he had no idea what he would do if Dr Guthrie refused. He had, too, a morbid curiosity about what the dominie thought of the fight and whether there might be anything to this prize business.

As he waited his mind drifted to other things. He had hardly slept at all the night before, endlessly rehearsing the refloating of the *Venus*. This was easily the biggest event in his life so far, and he could not stop thinking about it for very long. Although he had been waiting only ten minutes he had already seen the whole event, at least twice, in his mind's eye.

"Come this way," a familiar voice ordered. Mungo hurried through the open door and stood bolt upright before the dominie's desk, his arms pressed firmly to his sides. Formality was everything at the Burgh School.

"You had something urgent to say to me, Master Shaw?" said the dominie in an expressionless tone which seemed to lower the temperature of the room.

Mungo had intended to introduce his request in a round-about way but this frosty reception caused him to abandon any attempt at diplomacy. He spoke to Dr Guthrie directly.

"I would like your permission to leave school before the end of term, sir; today in fact," said Mungo with a well judged combination of brevity, clarity and respect.

"Might I know the reason for your proposed early departure?" the dominie enquired, rather haughtily.

"Well sir I have a job for the summer and I must start right away. I plan to sail with the fishing vessel *Venus* tonight."

Amazingly this information seemed to improve Mr Guthrie's whole demeanour. Whatever Mungo may have been expecting it was not this visible relaxation in the dominie's attitude. He stopped short of a smile of course, though the dominie had every reason to permit himself at least a sigh of relief; if Mungo was away at sea the vexed question of the Burgh Prize would go with him.

"We have only three days to go until the end of term and you have less than half a dozen classes, so maybe your time will be better spent aboard your fishing boat. In any event I can think of no better summer occupation for the boy who came first in navigation."

Mungo did not know the reason for the dominie's new mood and he did not care. He was quietly ecstatic but a measure of restraint was necessary. Experience had taught him that in Dr Guthrie's presence no show of emotion was ever welcome.

"I am greatly obliged to you sir," Mungo said with the slightest nod of his head.

"Since you are to be absent on Saturday, I will review your progress now."

The dominie paused and sorted through the papers on his desk.

"As I said you have done particularly well at navigation and achieved distinction, too, at book-keeping. Your progress in the pure academic subjects has also been impressive although you seemed to do best in work related to your own practical interests. That is well and good but if you are to pursue your studies further then you must develop a more voracious appetite for scholarship.

"I only wish I could be complimentary about your performance in English. You seem to think that, as a proud Scot, you have no need of correct English in speech or writing.

"I will discuss my report, in detail, with the Reverend Maclintock and he will report to Sir Archie Crawford. I am aware that both these gentlemen are keen to see you progress to University. I can be optimistic about your chances of admission next year if we can deal with one other serious defect." He paused again and let out a deep sigh. "It is a matter of your character, Master Shaw. Your feuding with Master Wallace is the talk of the place. Indeed I was most concerned when you asked to see me this morning. Apparently Wallace suffered an appalling assault at Simpson's tavern last evening. Though why on earth he was in that den of iniquity I cannot imagine. Nothing to do with you I hope?"

This news aroused mixed emotions in Mungo. If someone had given Charles Wallace a hiding, that was a good thing. But it was a great pity that he had nothing to do with it. Of course, as in all dealings with Dr Guthrie, he kept these feelings and opinions to himself.

"No sir I was not even in the town last night. I was at home at the Shaw. The Reverend Maclintock was also there until after ten o'clock. I only returned to the town at seven this morning."

"I don't doubt you," said Dr Guthrie, now visibly relieved to the extent of shrugging his shoulders. "I am sure the serious injuries you sustained in your last brawl taught you a welcome lesson," he said, his piercing eyes searing right into Mungo's soul. "Well good luck to you and good fishing," he said, extending his hand. Mungo was almost sure he saw Dr Guthrie's lips curl into something close to a smile, but maybe not.

* * *

The project to refloat the *Venus* was the talk of the neighbourhood. The powerful combination of brain and brawn necessary to re-launch the stranded vessel was a matter of endless speculation and fierce argument all along the coast. Of course there was nothing too remarkable about refloating a beached vessel. It was common practice to run boats on to the beach every two years or so for a bottom scrape but the size of the *Venus,* and the ferocity of the weather that drove her ashore made the project altogether more problematic. She had been beached beam-on some way above the normal high water mark so manoeuvring the vessel was always going to require ingenuity as well as skill and power. Some had theories about how the float out might be achieved but many more thought it could not be done at all.

With less than an hour and a half to go before the top of the tide maybe a hundred souls had gathered on the raised beach above where the *Venus* was lying. No longer was she the broken derelict that had been driven ashore that April night. Now she stood proud, shored up by stout timbers and head-on to the ripples of the incoming tide. Her new rigging and furled sails gave her the air of an elegant lady about to take the floor for a stately waltz. There was not even a hint of the near fatal gash to her starboard bow. The *Venus* was so well prepared for sea she seemed ready to launch herself.

"Let us thank the Lord and ask his blessing on this re-born ship," cried the Reverend Maclintock's reedy voice, disturbing the quiet industry around the vessel and the murmuring of the spectators on the upper shore.

At his summons the work party around the vessel came forward and stood before the tussock of grass that the minister had commandeered as an improvised pulpit.

"If it's anything like his Sunday sermons we'll miss the tide," Sandy muttered darkly.

"Mair like the boat'll gang wi' oot us," said Hughie, whose faith in his brother's preparations was unshakeable.

As he walked forward Mungo saw his mother and James Scott standing in the crowd. They were talking with some animation to Rab Maclure, father of Sandy and Hughie. Mungo had a distinct sense of foreboding about this unlikely communion. He had not told his mother that he planned to sail with the *Venus* that night. Now she would hear it from Rab Maclure, a man she had never pretended to like.

His mother was very good at dealing with crises and dramas but she was impatient with plans she had not thought of herself, especially if she heard of them second hand. After the prayers he would go forward and make his peace.

The assembly listened to the minister's overlong recitation of the Maclure family history, followed by a rambling sermon on the importance of the fishing fleet before he finally got to the point:

"Let us praise God for all His goodness and ask His blessing on the good ship *Venus.* May He also watch over those who sail in her and keep them safe from the perils of the sea. So let it be."

For a long moment Mungo feared that the minister was going to lead them in the singing of psalms but his fears were groundless. Maybe Mr Maclintock had seen that the water was now a foot and a half up the stem of the *Venus*.

"Thank you minister," Sandy shouted, "and look lively the rest of you. She'll be ready to go in half an hour. Hughie and Mungo get the skiff into the water." No chance now for Mungo to talk with his mother. He waved wildly and gave her the broadest smile he could manage. To his delight she returned the greeting – and so did factor Scott.

Little had been left to chance. Since low water, two heavy horses had been pulling aside boulders on the launch path. Then a series of round-wood timbers were laid out. The horses together with all available manpower had eased the ship forward on these runners till her stern was below the high water mark. During this prolonged and arduous manoeuvre Mungo and Hughie had to reposition the cradling props as the *Venus* inched forward. Two long lines were then shackled to the stem post and laid out on the sand. The other main element was the kedge anchor. It was set 100 yards ahead of the *Venus* and secured to her windlass on a hundred fathoms of cable. The two fishing boats that were anchored off began to drift inshore on the tide.

"Right, Hughie," shouted Sandy, "You and Mungo get in the skiff and carry the lines out to the boats." The idea was that the two boats riding on their anchors would take the lines from the *Venus* to their own winches. This would provide extra traction during the launch as well as support for the critical first few yards afloat. It was unthinkable that the repairs to *Venus's* hull might leak but they would have to be checked as soon as the weight was off her keel.

Now that the operation was underway the atmosphere on the shore became acutely attentive and maybe a bit anxious. Mungo was aware that Sandy's whole personality seemed to change. His normally laconic and easy going manner was replaced by a crisp power of command as he organised the many hands required for a successful launch.

The first boat to take a line from the skiff was the *Trojan* from Maidens. The other line went to the *Heather* from Dunure.

When Mungo and Hughie had rowed ashore after passing the lines, Sandy called everyone together for a final briefing.

"Everybody has to be clear about what's happening and what their part is," said Sandy in a ringing tone almost free of his usual thick Doric twang, "I don't want folk working against one another."

Mungo and Hughie clambered on board the *Venus* and took up their position at the windlass. On three short blasts from Sandy's whistle they were to start hauling in the anchor cable until it was bar-taut. The same signal would carry to the boats offshore and they would start heaving in, to take up the slack on the lines fastened to the stem post. The men on the shore would be keeping the boat upright as well as taking the strain on the warps attached to the gunnels.

Once all the men were in their places it fell eerily quiet save for the low murmur of the onlookers, the screeching of some oystercatchers along the shore and the soft lapping of the water on the sand. Mungo was sure that Sandy's calculations were right but he knew that for others a question hung in the air. Would she lift clear on the tide? Sandy stood at the centre of affairs biting his whistle and twisting his head this way and that. Mungo could tell he was worried by the fluky wind. It was not a strong blow but the nearby cliffs might cause gusts from unexpected directions.

The suspense seemed unbearable until it was broken by three piercing blasts from Sandy's whistle. Within a matter of seconds all the lines were taut. Another minute ground by before the *Venus* began to move; first with just the trace of a shudder and then a small heave of her fore-ends. Sandy's whistle now made the pre-arranged long blast. Mungo and Hughie hauled away on the windlass for all they were worth. In the attendant vessels the same action was taking place as the lines fastening the *Heather* and the *Trojan* to the *Venus* fairly leapt out of the water as the strain came on them.

Under all this power, slowly but surely, *Venus* began to find her buoyancy and one after another her props fell away. Everything seemed to move quickly now, though in reality it was the best part of quarter of an hour from Sandy's long blast till the cheering from the shore confirmed she was well afloat.

After the stern was maybe twenty feet from the water's edge, Sandy took the skiff alongside to get on board to check for leaks. He was half way up the jumping-ladder when his worst fear was realised. A sudden gust of wind caught the flare of *Venus's* bow. Being light and floating high she rolled, heavily pitching Sandy into the water.

More seriously there was an ominous crack as the *Heather's* line parted. Realising the problem Hughie and Mungo hauled away on the windlass to compensate for the loss of support. The wind gusted again and the *Venus* began to veer, alarmingly, to starboard. To their horror the boys realised their anchor was dragging as the *Venus* drifted further to starboard. A mere hundred feet away lurked the same jagged reef *that* had holed her on the original grounding. Everyone was gripped by the danger and the crowd ashore fell silent.

The *Trojan* was now *Venus's* only life line. The wind was gusting more frequently. Sandy, soaked to the skin and despondent, could only watch from the shore whilst Hughie and Mungo looked back at him in fearful impotence.

Billy Ferguson was still in his first season as the *Trojan's* skipper but all eyes turned to him. He ordered his crew to hoist the foresail. "He's too close to the wind," Mungo fretted under his breath. In any case it was a fearful risk for if too much strain came on the line too quickly it would part like the *Heather's* rope and nothing would then stop the *Venus* from drifting down on to the reef.

At first the wind died back and the Trojan's foresail hung loose. When the next gust came it was the strongest yet. The boys could hardly bear to look – the strain would surely part the Trojan's rope. Mungo was so scared he felt his stomach turn.

Billy's plan was to keep the line taut and to spill the wind from the foresail if it came on too strong. It was a bold plan and it required equal measures of skill and luck. With all the arrogance of youth Billy knew he had judged the situation exactly. He carried it off to perfection.

After half an hour of backing and filling he coaxed the *Venus* out into the deeper water and clear of the danger. It was a feat of seamanship that many would speak of for years to come but at that very moment any residual doubt Mungo had about a life at sea vanished entirely. The relief at avoiding disaster was part of it but his dominant thought was a new ambition to be as good a seaman as Billy.

There was a new round of cheering and waving from the shore. Mungo could just make out his mother who seemed to be hugging Rab Maclure; elation indeed.   When Sandy finally got on board Hughie reported:

"She's dry as a bone, skipper, unlike yer guid self."

Chapter Four

The high drama of the float-out was soon replaced by the stark reality of the herring fishery. The chief quality required for a herring fisherman was a talent for doing without sleep. Not so long ago Mungo had argued that life at sea must be preferable to the long hours and backbreaking work on the farm. He had dreamed, then, of marching about the poop deck of some mighty square rigger with a telescope tucked below his arm. Nothing in these fanciful dreams had prepared him for the hard graft of life at the fishing.

The *Venus* was one of the largest fishing boats on the West Coast. Everything about her was dedicated to catching and storing fish. She was free of all but the most rudimentary comforts for her crew. There were bunks and a mess table in the focsle which, at a stretch, could accommodate about half the ten-man crew. Eating was always a crush and the men had to sleep anywhere they could find a dry corner out of the wind.

Hauling the drift net was as back breaking as any farm work. There was, too, a special knack in shaking the herring out of the mesh as the net came aboard. Mungo was slow to develop this skill so most of the time he had the arduous task of heaving the sodden net aft in preparation for the next shot.

They were fishing in Kilbrannan Sound at the seaward end of Loch Fyne. After the nets had been shot the first priority was always to snatch a couple of hours sleep. After being called for the haul, there was often half an hour or so whilst Sandy manoeuvred the boat into position. Mungo was ever eager to learn and in these quieter moments he would be deep in discussion with Hughie, who was enjoying his status as master's mate.

Mungo asked endless questions about the boat, the fishing and all the finer points of sailing and steering. He marvelled, too, at the dramatic scenery of the Argyll coast. It never got completely dark in these summer nights yet the sunrise illuminated the coast with an intensity that always astonished Mungo. Quite suddenly the deep green of the croft lands punctuated by the stark whitewashed croft houses seemed to leap out of the gloom and shock the senses. Being close to the shore the early sun also called forth a screaming chorus of seabirds and the offshore breeze carried a pungent draught of ozone that he had never before experienced.

"My father's people come from round here," he said to Hughie. "They're called Lachlan. That's my mother's married name. It should be my name too, but I've always been called Shaw."

"I think it would be fine to go and see my relations over there, one day," Mungo said gazing westward. "I wonder if they are anything like my folk in Ayrshire."

"I would nae think so," said Hughie. "We've been into Tarbert a time or two. It's a fine enough wee town but the folk are kinda queer. They're aye dressed up in heavy clothes. Faither said they used to wear kilts. But that was afore the troubles. And ye ken they don't speak Scots. They have a strange tongue; called Gaelic I think. The Heilans is a foreign country, man!"

"Come away lads," shouted Sandy, breaking into their rambling talk, "It's time to haul."

The drift net hung from floats on the surface and was held vertical in the water by sinkers along its foot. It was also Mungo's duty, when re-positioning the net, to ensure that these attachments were still securely in place. The gear was new and the fishing easy so there was rarely a problem. Still he had to stay alert, anxious lest he should miss something. The hard labour and the concentration wore him down. At times though, the boredom was even worse than the fatigue. But though the work was hard, the catches were good, so it rarely took more than two days to fill the boat.

Every other day they landed their catch at Greenock. There was a near insatiable demand for fresh fish from the rapidly growing population of Glasgow and its surrounding parishes. Many thought old Rab was daft to have sunk so much money in building the *Venus.* After her stranding these Wailing Willies were proved right, or so they thought. But now her landings were copious and the auction price was the best any one could remember. They were making money hand over fist. They fished flat out until the boat was full and then raced inshore to the market. This routine continued relentlessly day in day out.

Venus had been on the grounds for about three weeks. Their haul was the best so far even so the landing went quicker than usual. For all his shortcomings as a net handler Mungo was gaining great prowess as a derrick-man. Thanks to this new-found skill the crew were able to have extra time ashore to stretch their legs. After the catch had been landed everyone went to the tavern near the Customs House where they ate a big feed of ham, eggs and potatoes washed down with plenty of ale. That morning the Skipper rewarded Mungo's dexterity on the derrick with a glass or two of rum.

As they were finishing their food Sandy set his narrowing gaze across the room "I'm sure that's Tommy Kirkwood. He used to sail wi' oor faither when I started the sea. He's nothing but trouble, that yin!"

"Is that the same Kirkwood that stole Wull Ferguson's skiff?" enquired Hughie.

"Haud yer tongue Hughie. Naethin' wis ever proved. Any way it's time we wisnae here," said Sandy, pulling his bonnet down about his brows.

As they approached the *Venus* Mungo saw a knot of shifty looking men standing by her bow.

"That'll be some o' the local wee-boat men," said Sandy under his breath, "they're aye moanin' aboot something."

"Now you lads stay close and keep quiet," said Sandy, "I'll deal wi this."

Mungo held his tongue if not his balance; he was not really used to drinking rum.

As they got alongside, Sandy spotted an acquaintance within the group. "How ye daein Scottie," he said, offering his hand to the embarrassed youth.

"Were no here tae pass the time o'day, skipper," piped up a wizened fellow who Sandy took to be the leader. "A big boat like yours should nae be working here. You're fishin' day and night and you'll hae the Loch cleaned oot in nae time."

"Oh that canna be right friend," Sandy said in his most affable tone. "The Firth is full o' herring just now; plenty for everybody." He smiled broadly.

His conciliatory approach made no impression on the grim-faced delegation.

"Awa the hell hame tae Ayr," said the leader. "Yer kind's no welcome here."

Sandy knew all along that there would be no reasoning with these people. He stepped forward and took the wizened fellow's coat collar in his ham-fists.

"Whit dae ye mean 'your kind'?" he growled. "Awa and dae a day's work and stop botherin law abiding folk." He pushed the malcontent back into his gang with such force that two of his henchmen fell over and narrowly missed going into the harbour.

Before the others could retaliate, Sandy's crew closed ranks around him.

"Oh so the Maclures are law abiding folk, noo," said a voice from behind Sandy's men. It was the same Tommy Kirkwood who had caught Sandy's eye in the Tavern.

"I want no trouble wi you Tommy Kirkwood. You just keep oot o' it," said Hughie as Sandy kept his focus on his tormentors.

"Aye but I'll be 'ettlin tae have trouble wi you Sandy Maclure," Kirkwood taunted. "Ye think yersel the big man noo ye hae yer faither's boat."

One of the motley gang made to board the *Venus*. Hughie waded into the crowd and seized the would-be boarder's coat. Mungo was close on Hughie's heels and caught a crack in the eye from someone's elbow. In no time at all a full blown melee had developed. Mungo concentrated on covering Sandy's back as the skipper tried to get back aboard. He was quickly beset by two assailants, but his blood was up and he was soon giving better than he got.

There was maybe ten minutes of this rumpus before the shifty figure of Kirkwood re-appeared with two harbour officers. The sight of the officials quickly brought about a lull in hostilities. Mungo stood rubbing his fists, taking a gory pleasure in his handiwork. He had spread most of one man's nose across his face and the other was doubled up over a bollard, spewing into the harbour.

"These men are right," one of the harbour officers said to Sandy, "Ye've nae business tae be fishing here."

"Yer faither had a Fishery Board grant tae build that boat," Kirkwood put in, "You're only allowed to work south o'Campbeltown and that fishing disnae open till the first o' August."

"I know nothing about that," said the fishery officer. "All the same ye better sail at once. You'll not be allowed any more landings here."

Mungo could see from the slump in his shoulders and his startled expression that Sandy was mystified by Kirkwood's claims. Sandy's father, Rab Maclure, was a canny businessman who always kept his own counsel about his dealings. Sandy was well used to his old man's secretive ways and so was in no position to argue the toss about grants and licences. "Get aboard lads," Sandy shouted, "we'll fish where ever the hell we like and we'll no be bothered wi the likes o' you, Kirkwood!"

For all Sandy's fighting talk it seemed clear that they would not be back in Greenock for a long while. Yet, in keeping with his defiant tone the *Venus* set course back for the Loch Fyne grounds. It was also the course that made the best of the wind.

They fished all that night and up to the middle of the following day. They had done well for they were more than half full when Sandy set course back to the Cock of Arran. They were heading home for Ayr.

"I don't understand all this business about grants and permits," Mungo said to Hughie. "If we are barred from working out of Greenock will it not be the same at Ayr?"

"I don't understand it either but don't mention it to Sandy. He's still fair ragin' aboot yesterday," Hughie cautioned. "I can only think he has some plan in mind. That fishery officer at Ayr takes a powerful amount of drink so maybe Sandy thinks he can keep him fu' till the end of the season."

The two lads were still chuckling about the idea of Sandy pouring rum down the water guard's throat when Sandy called out, "It's time you learned some real seamanship, young Mungo. Ye canna learn the feel of a boat from books. Come here and take a spell on the tiller."

Mungo hurried aft and stood beside Sandy.

"Right, my lad," said Sandy. "We have to turn the boat through the wind to get on the other tack. It's no as difficult as it looks but ye hae tae ca' canny," he said, easing Mungo into the steering position. His first reaction was nervousness verging on terror yet he was soon reassured by how light the huge tiller was.

"I hold her head on yon white house, but when do I turn?" he asked Sandy.

"Just hang on to this course as long as you can, but don't put us ashore. I'll tell you in plenty of time. Learn to judge the wind by the feel of it on your face. Only look to the tell-tales on the mast if you're no right sure."

This was what a life at sea was all about. He instinctively picked up Sandy's instruction about how to feel the wind. As his confidence grew he began to look for signs that might help him to judge the tack.

"Don't let her get too close to the wind," Sandy called out. "See how the foresail is starting to lift." It was a timely reminder to Mungo that there was still much to learn.

"Right skipper," Mungo replied, easing off the helm a fraction. "Are we no getting too close in now?"

"Ready to go about!" Sandy roared to warn the crew on deck. "Now put your rudder hard over. She has to come right round to near enough the reverse course."

Half way through the manoeuvre Hughie ordered the crew to aft in the mainsail sheets. Now they were catching the wind on the other side. The tack was completed in just a few seconds yet it seemed to Mungo a majestic achievement. He had learned the principles in school and followed it through in his head every time he saw Sandy take the boat about. But tacking the ship, on his own, gave him a rare feeling of exhilaration.

"Well done, Mungo!" said Sandy. "It'll be the best part of two hours before we have to go about again. Just hold your course as near as you can to the north end of Holy Isle and don't get too greedy with the wind. Hughie'll keep an eye on you now; I'm away for a sleep!"

Mungo was not in the least worried at being left in charge of the *Venus.* Indeed he was already working out the best point to tack for the final run in to Ayr harbour. Hughie came to join him in the stern sheets.

"He must think a lot of you," he said to Mungo with a tinge of envy in his voice. "It was two years before the old man let me bring her round."

"Aye but I'm a lot older and a good bit bigger than you were when you started."

"Naw, he was just impressed by the way you sorted out yon Greenock lads."

They both had a good laugh and spent the next half hour re-fighting the battle that had only taken ten minutes. For an hour after that they reflected on the trip and speculated about being back in Ayr.

"Mind you don't go too early or you'll miss the harbour mouth on the high side," Hughie cautioned his helmsman. "There's a current that sweeps us to the north at this state of the tide. You'd better steer for the Heads of Ayr on your next run."

It was good advice and they didn't need to call Sandy till *Venus* was a mile south west of the harbour mouth and lined up for a straight run in to the pier. Mungo had been awake for almost twenty four hours yet he did not feel in the least tired.

There were enough buyers for their catch at Ayr but it was not the same frenzy as Greenock. They only made about three quarters the price per basket that they got the day before.

"Well, this'll no dae at all boys; it'll be a poor share efter the boat's cost comes oot o' it," Sandy said to his men after the value of the catch had been settled. "I'd better away and look for some more profitable cargoes." And he took off in the general direction of Simpson's Tavern.

"What does he mean by 'more profitable cargoes'?" Mungo asked Hughie.

"I think he means to run contraband," replied Hughie with a sardonic smile.

Chapter Five

Ailsa Craig had been a constant feature of the seascape for as long as he could remember but he had never seen it this close at hand.

"I can hardly believe the colours," he said to Hughie. "The Craig was always just a great lump of rock to us; a bonny blue colour in the summer and black as the devil's heart in winter."

"Aye it's braw at this time o' year," Hughie agreed, "wi the yellow on the broom and the heather turnin tae a purple haze. It's gye bare on the windward side, though. Just a million nesting birds and the stink that goes wi them."

He was right about the birds. All around gannets were diving from astonishing heights. It seemed they would never survive the impact yet they entered the water with barely a ripple. There were other little birds he had never seen before. Some were fluttering across the inky water below the cliffs and others swooping over the waves at high speed with great agility. The upper air was filled with more familiar gulls of various kinds. The constant din of shrieks and screams from these birds was amplified by the echoing cliffs. All the birds had mouths to feed and so did the men on the *Venus*. Since returning to Ayr the herring catches had been quite good but the prices were poor. The pay was little better than a bare subsistence. Standing off Ailsa Craig that August day, though, the *Venus's* crew were expecting a much more lucrative catch.

"I doubt she got held up somewhere. She was due here yesterday," said Sandy.

Maybe he was haunted by the memory of his ill-fated expedition back in April, or perhaps it was the late running of his new partner in this risky venture. Either way he was agitated and short tempered.

"What if she was caught by the Navy Brig," said Hughie, who seemed to be pessimistic for once but maybe his grin had more to do with dark humour than bleak prospects.

Sandy glared at him. "How many times dae ah hiv tae tell ye? Stop putting the wind up Mungo. Anyway there's naethin' illegal aboot carrying any cargo ye like; landing it's the offence."

It was a fractious riposte which reflected Sandy's anxiety rather than the law relating to the importation of dutiable goods.

Just then Mungo let out a yell, "I can see a sail away to the south west!"

Sandy took up his glass and, steadying himself on the backstay he peered, for several seconds, along the line Mungo was pointing.

"It might be the *Swan* right enough," Sandy announced. "Hughie could be half right, too. She was maybe tacking away for the Kintyre coast to dodge the Brig."

It took about another hour before the *Swan* was near enough to be sure. There was no point in the *Venus* sailing west to meet her. She was down-wind and the Brig might indeed be shadowing her. The business at hand could not be done in open water.

Whoever christened the old collier the *Swan* surely enjoyed a joke. Unlike her namesake she was black as night and could hardly be described as graceful. Sandy's only contact with the *Swan's* master had been that day a month earlier in Simpson's.   He hadn't been sure of the fellow at the time and that was another reason for his present uneven temper. The day after that first meeting with Captain Brady he had been contacted by a merchant's agent who had then set up this seaborne tryst.

"What happens now?" Mungo asked Hughie. He had not asked questions when Sandy had explained the plan because Sandy was grumpy and Mungo didn't wish to appear ignorant. But now he was worried that his ignorance would cause him to make a mistake.

"We'll go alongside her and take off the cargo. She'll carry on to Ayr and we'll land the stuff later tonight," Hughie replied in a rather impatient tone. As the *Swan* came closer everyone became more anxious.

"I know that," rejoined Mungo, sounding edgy too, "but how do we get alongside?"

"Nae bother. It's all in the timing," said Hughie striding forward to man the fore sheets.

"Mungo, go forward with Hughie and put out the fenders," Sandy ordered.

Two crewmen were stationed forward and two more aft to man the mooring lines. Three others were already in the hold making ready to stow the cargo. Everyone was now focused on his own particular task.

Sandy brought the *Venus* near enough to a standstill on the same heading as the *Swan* but maybe 100 yards ahead. The *Swan* then came on as if to overtake the *Venus*. When she was almost abeam her crew released the sheets and let her sails fly. Mungo was amazed at how quickly the *Swan* lost way. He was mesmerised by the whole manoeuvre. With a combination of Sandy's accurate steering and Hughie's working of the foresheets the Swan was suddenly alongside.

"Fenders, Mungo!" roared Sandy. In the nick of time Mungo positioned the heavy canvas pillows as near as he could judge to the contact point; *Venus's* newly repaired bows were spared any fresh damage and Mungo's favour with Sandy survived – but only just. The vessels were then secured together by head and stern ropes.

The *Swan* had unloaded her coal at Dublin and was carrying a part back-load of limestone. The extra hold space was taken by the special cargo Brady took on at Peel, on the Isle of Man.

"You were surely held up, Captain," Sandy shouted to his opposite number on the *Swan*.

"Aye, my mate broke his arm and we had to leave him in Dublin. Then another fellow took fever and we had to put him ashore at Larne. This old girl's a bitch to work without a full crew. Still here we are." Captain Brady's usual mournful demeanour was almost funereal that afternoon. His large head, which was completely hairless, glistened with sweat and his shoulders were hunched forward as if expecting an attack at any moment.

Sandy stayed at the helm whilst Hughie went aboard the *Swan* to count the barrels and bales before the transfer could begin.

"It's all present and correct, captain," Hughie reported.

"That's fine," grunted Captain Brady, "but I'm short-handed. I'll need help with the derrick to swing the cargo across," he complained, as if it was Hughie's fault.

"Nae bother," said Hughie, "Mungo's a dab hand wi the derrick." Then he shouted across to Mungo, "Come aboard here and mak' yersel useful."

"I'm obliged to you," the captain growled at Hughie.

Although he still had a way to go in mastering his seamanship skills Mungo was now the established expert on cargo handling. The absent mate and the man sick ashore in Ulster must have been the *Swan's* derrick crew for the hands on deck seemed to have little experience in that kind of work. Mungo was in his element and was soon swinging out the casks, two at a time.

Twenty casks of spirit, ten chests of tea and a dozen bales of expensive cloth were transferred in less than an hour. There was only one anxious moment when the vessels drifted out of the lee of the Craig and were suddenly wallowing in a heavy swell. But Hughie's skilful manoeuvring of the *Venus's* foresail cured the problem almost as soon as it occurred.

When the transfer was complete the relief was obvious on the faces of both captains. The edginess had gone and all was now broad smiles and cheery waves. They had both been acutely aware that as long as the vessels were lashed together they would have been easy pickings for an excise cutter or the navy brig.

"Well Mungo, if you ever need a new berth don't go by the *Swan,*" Captain Brady called to Mungo as he crossed back to the *Venus.*

"I'll bear that in mind. It's been a pleasure to work with you, sir!" Mungo replied.

As he watched the *Swan* pick up her course Mungo wondered what happened next but he was reluctant to ask. It was only about five o'clock so there would be at least another four hours before dark and they could land the cargo. Sandy set a course to the East and after sailing for an hour ordered the nets shot away just off Maidens Bay. Surely he was not going to dump herrings on top of this precious cargo, Mungo thought.

"We'll lie to the nets till it's time to go inshore," Sandy said as if to resolve Mungo's doubts. "Nosy navy folk will think nothing of a herring drifter fishing in these waters."

In fact the Navy brig did pass about a mile off an hour later and, as Sandy had supposed, it came nowhere near them.

"He'll catch up wi the *Swan* in about two hours," Sandy calculated out loud. "Brady'll be a happy man watching the excise officers picking through the big limestone boulders." The laughter of the crew was relief as much as amusement.

As the sun started to set over Arran, Hughie and one of the crewmen were splicing a light anchor and a marker buoy on to the warps of the net. They would return and haul the net after their other business was dealt with.

Then they set course to the north and passed close in by the cliffs at Culzean where the Earl of Cassilis was building his new castle. Mungo had heard that it was very grand but this close in and even in the half-light of the gloaming it seemed massive. Another few minutes on the evening breeze took them to the north end of Croy shore where they saw the twinkling lanterns of their reception party. The consignment was for a merchant called McCulloch who was famous in the district for being able to lay his hand on any luxury item his customers might require. His generosity was also well known. He had sent a gift of two bottles of French brandy and a dozen of claret to the funeral of Mungo's grandfather. McCulloch was also a noted Jacobite.

They could just about make out the men with their ponies on the shore. Four skiffs were also in the shallows at the water's edge. Mungo wondered about the wisdom of landing their cargo so close to the Earl's fine new house. It was well known that, down the centuries, the Kennedys had mainly prospered by helping themselves to the property of others.

"Right," said Sandy, "Strike the sails. We'll anchor up and drift as far inshore as we can on the anchor cable." Although the light breeze was offshore at this time of night there was still another three hours of flood in the tide – more than enough to put the boat about a hundred feet from the shore line. This arrangement gave them a way of hauling off quickly in case of emergency or more likely unwanted attention from the shore. There was enough breeze for the *Venus* to beat a hasty retreat, if that was needed, but the water stayed quite calm and all the skiffs were able to take full loads.

The whole operation was carried on in near silence and that only added to the excitement of it. Sandy had forbidden them to use one another's names during the landing. The few phrases uttered by the men, aboard and ashore, were brief and to the point. In any case few words were necessary. Mungo's precision in dropping the casks, chests and bales into the skiffs rarely required subsequent adjustment.

Everything was over in less than two hours. By eleven o'clock Hughie was piloting the *Venus* back to her nets.

As they stood by the tiller watching the beach disappear into the gloom Mungo turned philosophical.

"Smuggling is not what you would call a godly pursuit, is it?" he asked Hughie. Mungo was recalling the Reverend Maclintock's many fiery sermons on the subject.

"It's no smuggling," said Hughie, "It's free trading. No Scotsman should have tae pay English taxes."

Right enough Mungo remembered being taught that there would be no English taxes charged in Scotland if our Parliament agreed to the Union.

"But don't the English folk have to pay the same taxes as us now? It's all the one country," Mungo countered a little uncertainly. "How much are these taxes anyway?"

"I dinnae ken," said Hughie, "I've never heard o' ony yin payin' them."

Sandy had come aft and overheard the boys' discussion. "The main thing tae remember, young Mungo, is tell naebody nuthin aboot this nicht's work," Sandy said in a severe tone, "The sheriff's no a bit interested in the richts or wrangs o' taxes. The law is the law and the jyle's aye the same whether ye think yer guilty or no."

Mungo knew that 'free-trading' as Hughie called it was illegal but he had never heard of any one being put in jail for it.

"Keep a good look out," Sandy cautioned Hughie, "if you run ower oor ain nets I'll pit the twa o' ye in the jyle, masel."

Chapter Six

"That's a fearsome amount of money," Jean said as she watched Mungo tip out the contents of the little canvas bag. "You're Da would have taken the best part of a year to clear that much!"

Mungo had arrived at the Shaw, unannounced at ten o'clock on a warm but drizzly September forenoon. Jean was delighted to see him, of course, but was soon distracted by his sudden wealth.

"It's a tidy sum, right enough, but the fishing's been good and Sandy works us like beasts." Mungo could see that his mother did not completely accept his explanation but he didn't care. "Since when have we been bothered by having too much money?" he asked, giving her a roguish smile.

"Oh you're right enough about that. All the same I worry what you get up to when you're away. The Maclure's are good, kind people but they take awful risks and folk say that they're involved with the smugglers in some way."

Mungo stepped round this line of conversation.

"Well you needn't worry any more about the Maclures' bad influence," he mocked, "I paid off from the *Venus* this morning. Old Rab is back aboard now so they don't need the extra hand."

Jean was reluctant to express her delight at having her boy back home.

"How is Robert," she asked about the elder Maclure. "He seemed to have some trouble with walking and he coughed a great deal, that day you all re-floated the *Venus.*"

"He seems well enough to me. He met us when we landed at six this morning; roaring like a bull and strutting about the boat like an admiral. I think he'll be an even harder driver than Sandy."

"So what's next for our young Mungo?" Jean asked her son with an affectionate smile. "You know the Reverend Maclintock still has high hopes that you'll go to the University."

"Aye maybe one day but I mean to get back to sea as soon as I can. A few more good trips and maybe I'll have enough to buy my own boat." This prospect made Mungo's face light up whilst Jean's expression turned to stone.

"And who will take you to sea, if not the Maclures?"

Mungo became cagey.

"Well," he said in a confidential whisper, "When the old man came back this morning he said he has plans to buy a second boat. I'm sure he would make Sandy the skipper of the new boat so Hughie would become mate on the *Venus,* or the new boat. I'm sure there would be a berth for me in one or the other." He finished with a kind of flourish. Then as an afterthought he said, "It was all told in secret so not a word to a living soul."

Jean took a while to digest this. Surely Mungo had more ambition than the fishing.

"It'll be a while since you last ate," she said. "I can give you cake and cheese with some ale, if you would like it."

"That would be grand," he said and returned to the serious business of stacking his coins in small piles whilst his mother went off to the scullery.

This was the first time his mother had ever offered him ale. She generally took a poor view of the demon drink; so why did she have such a thing in the house? Jean brought the food and returned to her questioning about Mungo's immediate plans.

"You may have some time to wait before Mr Maclure is able to find a suitable boat," she mused. "I could certainly do with some help here since I bought the extra cows." Although the estate managed the farm Jean had grazing for her own cows and ran the dairy as a separate concern. By all accounts she was doing very well and her butter and cheese was much sought after at Ayr market.

"I'll certainly help as much as I can," Mungo volunteered, "but I'll only be here for a week – two at the most. I have an offer of a place on a coal boat working the Irish trade. She'll be in next week."

Jean found it hard to keep up with Mungo: one minute he was going back with the Maclures, now he was about to join the coal trade.

"And how did you come to get an offer of a place on a coal boat?" she asked with more than a hint of challenge in her voice.

Mungo thought quickly. "Oh it's a boat called the *Swan.* She's owned by Mr Murray. You remember; his son Graham was in my class at the Burgh School. I expect he spoke up for me to his father." The *Swan* was indeed owned by Mr Murray but neither he nor Graham knew anything of Mungo's arrangement with Captain Brady.

"The Murrays are a good family," said Jean by which she meant they were rich. "I know them from the Kirk, but not to talk to. They have a bonny daughter about your age; Margaret I think," said Jean, anxious to take something positive from Mungo's latest escapade.

"I only know Graham," said Mungo with some finality.

The conversation petered out as Jean took the dishes to the scullery. Mungo put his money back in his purse and left the table. He settled into Da's old chair by the fire and was soon asleep. Since going to sea he knew the value of sleep and missed no opportunity for a snooze.

He had been asleep for maybe two hours when he came to with a pleasant aroma from the stew pot filling his nostrils.

"You always made a fine stew," he said to his mother with unusual tenderness. "I often thought about your cooking when we were surviving on hard rations on the boat."

"Well the dinner's a wee bit special today," she smiled. "Mr Scott the factor is coming to eat with us."

Clearly Mungo had walked in on an assignation. He had been sure for some time that James Scott's interest in his mother was more than their shared duty for managing the Shaw. He did not know what to make of that. He quite liked the factor as a man and, as far as he could make out, Mr Scott liked him too. All the same he was nervous about his mother and the factor's growing familiarity with one another. It was neither a fear of being edged out of his home nor even the prospect of being displaced in his mother's affections. Mungo just had a feeling that something was not right about the situation.

"Welcome home, Mungo!" Mr Scott exclaimed, holding his arms wide when he saw Mungo. "You're looking well – I think you've grown an inch or two."

"Aye, maybe an inch," said Mungo smiling and returning the factor's greeting with an outstretched hand which the other shook warmly.

"Come away boys," said Jean, "I've made you a fine beef stew and some special bannocks." Mungo wondered whether he was meant to be the prodigal son or the factor's brother.

After they had finished eating Jean brought out her silver tea-kettle. Mungo couldn't help wondering where she came by the rich dark leaves in the infusion. Could they be from the crates he had been swinging in the lee of Ailsa Craig?

"It's fine stuff, this tea," said Mungo, "where do you get it?"

"There's quite a few houses with a tea kettle nowadays," his mother replied, "and Mrs MacCulloch always has a chest of it in the shop."

Mungo permitted himself a wry grin.

"There's very little the McCullochs don't sell," he smirked.

"Yes," said the factor beaming broadly, "I wonder who supplies them!"

Mungo suspected the factor knew more than he was saying so he steered the conversation towards more certain territory.

"You'll be starting harvest soon," he said to the factor, "will you have enough folk with just your own men and the neighbours?"

"Why, Mungo are you looking for a start?" The factor did not seem to be joking. "We never have too many hands at harvest."

"Well, James, I think the estate would find it hard to pay Mungo with all the money he's making at the fishing," Jean said without any trace of irony.

James, is it? Mungo pondered but the look in Jean's eyes told him that she and the factor had long since gone beyond friendship. It was an awkward moment with all three feeling more than they dared say.

After a few seconds that seemed like an eternity, the factor broke the ice.

"I'm pleased you are making a good living at the sea but just remember, the herring season will be over in a few more weeks. There will be little enough to do over the winter." Mr Scott made his observations sound like a sermon, "If you are not inclined to go back to your studies I think you would do very well as an apprentice estate manager." He seemed to be staring into Mungo's soul. The offer was deadly serious and it was not going to be easy for Mungo to turn it aside.

"I know it would be fine for me to have some experience like that," said Mungo choosing his words with unaccustomed care, "but when I'm twenty one I'll take over here and be right back as a tenant farmer. Da always said I should not get ideas above my station." Class consciousness was a notion Mungo despised but he knew others found it to be an unquestionable principle of civilisation. "Anyway," Mungo continued, "I'm leaving the fishing to join a merchant ship."

He explained his imminent appointment as spare hand on the *Swan.*

"I've had dealings with Mr Murray," the factor announced. "His new pit is very close to the boundary with our estate. We nearly finished up in the court over his thrawn-ness. Be very careful not to get the wrong side of Mr Murray."

"Mungo was very friendly with the son, Graham, at the Burgh school," Jean suggested, as if that fact might soften the factor's opinion of Mr Murray's business practices. The factor cast an amazed look to the heavens at what he took to be the naivety of Mungo and his mother.

"I doubt if I'll meet Mr Murray," said Mungo. "My master will be Captain Brady but if I ever do have any dealings with the owner I'll keep a civil tongue in my head and a firm grip of the rigging. Now, is there any more cake to go with this tea?"

The rest of the time went by in amiable banter between the men and the occasional reproach from Jean. When the talk had run out of steam Mungo excused himself and went outside. He sat for a while on a small hill above and a little apart from the house. He had a clear view of the whole Firth from up there. It was where he and his grandfather often sat after their supper, when the weather was fine. He chuckled a little to himself remembering Da's endless advice on farming and land improvement – he had just assumed that Mungo would, in time, take over the Shaw. While the old man rambled on, Mungo would be looking out to sea and musing to himself about the day he would have command of a square rigged ship. The way things had turned out he could surely have the Shaw if he wanted and he was well on his way to fulfilling his sea going ambitions as well. He felt very content as he came down from his perch, with his treasure now in a stout wooden box. He tucked his moneybox into the thatch and went back to the house for a whole night's sleep in a dry bed.

PART TWO

10th day of February 1763
The Harbour Office
The Port of Ayr

My Dear Mistress Shaw
It was a pleasure to renew your acquaintance at the market on Saturday last. I well remember meeting you and your father all those years ago when you came to the sale of the beasts after my own father died. I often think maybe I should have taken the old place on but I had my own life at the sea by then and my mother wasn't fit to work the land herself. As a contrast and by all accounts you are making a great success of the Shaw.

Your concern about Mungo is understandable but I hasten to assure you that he is in no way concerned in the smuggling. His ship, the Swan, carries coal from here to Dublin and fetches back limestone. They would have no prospect of running contraband in such a slow and cumbersome vessel. Smugglers are known to favour faster, manoeuvrable ships that can put into the smaller harbours along the coast.

In order to reassure you further I took the liberty of calling on Captain Brady. He is an old friend and an upright citizen. He thinks very highly of your son and has lately promoted him to be third hand which is to say next in command after the master's mate - an impressive achievement for a seventeen year old lad.

Thank you very much for the gift of butter and cheese. It is much appreciated by the whole Wilson family. Mistress Wilson hopes you will sup with us one evening when she can wheedle the secrets of cheese-making out of you.

Please be assured that I will take a special interest in Mungo's well being.

Sincere Good Wishes
I am, Madam, Your Good Friend
Abraham Wilson

Harbour Master
Port of Ayr

Mistress Jean Shaw
Shaw Farm
Langmuir

Chapter Seven

He had been on the *Swan* for more than a year and this was his seventh visit to Dublin. The Second City of the British Empire was a vibrant seaport that catered to every nationality and taste. This was just as well for the *Swan's* crew looked like Negroes when they were unloading coal and more like ghosts when taking on limestone. In the evenings they spent their free time at the ale houses around the harbour. Malone's Inn was their favourite haunt.

Mungo always looked forward to visiting Dublin for he had become tired of the Taverns at home. He had gained a name as something of a bruiser after the melee at Greenock and his earlier thrashing of Charles Wallace. Although this reputation was not entirely undeserved, it seemed to encourage all kinds of lowlifes and rough necks with something to prove to challenge him every time he set foot in an Ayr tavern. In Dublin by contrast he was just another 'Scottie off the boats'. He could drink and carouse until the wee hours every morning without so much as a harsh word from anyone.

The tavern women around Dublin's harbour were a special attraction too; although none came close to Margaret in beauty or elegance. Alas he had all but despaired of Margaret. Their difference in social class and his seagoing life made his prospects with Miss Murray completely forlorn. Still the Irish Colleens had their attractions even if Presbyterian Ayr would have been outraged by their immodest dress, never mind their bawdy talk and suggestive behaviour. Mungo was on easy terms with a number of these ladies and very close to one of them.

"Oh the Scotchmen are back again," Bridget called out from the taproom of Malone's Inn. She had a slim and proportionate figure rather than the buxom features that so many of the harbour belles boasted. Bridget was easily the prettiest girl in Dublin – in Mungo's certain opinion.

"Come away out here and give your best customers a real Irish Welcome," Mungo called out from the doorway.

"Six flagons of stout if you're ever going to get a song out of us," demanded Alastair, the oldest of the *Swan's* deck hands. Alistair was a highlander and spoke Gaelic. This made him a favourite with the country girls from the West of Ireland who made up most of Malone's staff.

It was the crew's first night ashore, on this trip. They had been heaving coal all day and the morrow was unlikely to be any easier. Between draughts of black beer to wash away the coal dust there was the usual chatter about the need to take an early night. In fact that was what was said every night but never once did the *Swan's* men get back aboard on the same day as they came ashore.

Mungo was taking his stout slowly. By the time the others had finished their third he was only half way down his second.

"Aye, aye," said young Robert – at fourteen he was the elder of the ship's two boys – "what's our canny Third Hand up to? Has he stopped drinking?" Then he addressed Mungo directly, "If you'd take your eyes off Bridget for a second you might be able to get your round in!"

The Third Hand's position, on board, was as a buffer between the officers and the crew. He was constantly engaged with the Captain and Mate in the general running of the ship and like them he kept a watch at sea. During the working day he had to organise and allocate the work amongst the hands. However his true status was indicated in the sleeping arrangements. The Captain and the Master's Mate had cabins in the deckhouse at the stern whilst Mungo and the rest of the crew slept forward in the focsle. Even so he had a position to maintain. Although he lived among the crew and went ashore with them he discouraged any over-familiarity.

For once, though, he did not bridle at the boy's cheek. He could chat with Bridget in the taproom whilst she filled their order. He hadn't seen her for six weeks.

"Have you missed me?" he asked with a melancholy smile.

"Sure and I'd have to be hard stuck to be waiting for the likes of you," she hit back, flicking her blonde locks over her shoulder and pursing her lips.

Mungo was not deterred by this show of petulance. It always happened on the first day back in Dublin. Anyway, this time he had brought her a gift.

"Well," he sighed, "you won't be wanting this then."

"Give it here this minute," she demanded, snatching the leather pouch from his grasp. Quickly she undid the drawstrings and let out a gasp of delight. "It's a beautiful brooch," she cried admiring it in the lamplight. Then, quite suddenly, she gave him a kiss, full on the lips, to roars of approval from the assembled company.

As he bent over to fasten the ornament to her breast she whispered in his ear, "I'm finishing up in another hour; I've been working since breakfast," and with a conspiratorial smile she added, "You can see me home if you like."

This was progress. The best he had ever managed before was a kiss and a cuddle in the shadows at the back of the taproom.

As he and Bridget left the tavern there was a riot of whistling and stamping but he paid it no heed. He was proud to be walking out with Bridget and quietly ecstatic at the prospect of a night of passion.

His ardour was undiminished when they were still walking half an hour later. He had no idea where they were going but he eased their embrace from time to time to try to get his bearings. He could see next to nothing in the dark, though, and after another half hour they were still

57

cuddled up together strolling through the soft drizzle of the black Dublin night.

"Do you come all this way home every night?" he asked her.

"No, I usually stay with Eimar. She has a room just behind the Customs House," she said rather defensively, "but tonight we're going to my mother's house." Sensing some disappointment in Mungo she added, "It's all right, she goes to bed early and sleeps like a top."

Just then she wheeled him round into a narrow lane and made her way up a few steps to the door of a small house. She had difficulty finding the latch and fumbled about in the dark. Just as Mungo was about to try a voice called out:

"Is that you Bridget?" Clearly mother's top had stopped spinning. "I thought you were never coming," said the tall woman, clad in nightclothes, who opened the door to them. "And who is this young man you have with you?" She ushered them in and soon they were, all three, seated in front of the dying embers of the fire by the light of two candles.

Even in the poor light the mother was immediately entranced by Bridget's new brooch. After some extravagant words of admiration she proceeded to interrogate Mungo. Who was he? Where was he from? A hundred other details of his life were laid bare. Bridget tried to stem the flood of questions but each time she spoke up she was sent on some errand – 'fetch turf for the fire,' 'warm a bowl of soup for Mungo.' So it went on and all the while his passion was evaporating.

"Have you always lived in this part of Dublin?" Mungo managed to enquire during a rare moment when the mother paused for breath.

"We have nothing to do with this God-forsaken place," she protested, "We are from Connemara." There followed a sad tale of how they had come to Dublin to make their fortune but the father took a fever and died after three years leaving Bridget and her mother to fend for themselves in the big city.

"Folk from Connemara speak Gaelic," he ventured remembering that some of the carters at the harbour were Connemara men. He supposed it was Gaelic they spoke for their tongue made no sense to him.

"Do you speak Gaelic?" the mother asked him.

"No, but my father's people were from Argyll, I'm told they speak it there."

He then related his own family history which seemed to give the mother a second wind. Having all but despaired of any amorous adventures Mungo became fascinated by the Gaelic lady's stories of her mystical homeland. He found her tales rather haunting and he wondered if Argyll might be like that. Bridget had restored the fire to a cheery blaze and returned from one of her errands with a bottle of whiskey.

Now the mother started to sing Gaelic songs which she encouraged Bridget to join in. To be sociable, Mungo managed a few verses of some old Scots airs. More than once Bridget cast a wistful smile to Mungo along with some whispered words of endearment. There was little point. The ever-present and now over-refreshed mother filled the room with her tales and anthems to the exclusion of all other sounds and sentiments.

She had held the stage for nearly two hours before she was interrupted by the sound of a muffled bell on the night air.

"Was that the midnight bell?" she asked.

"It must be about that time," said Mungo

"Oh well, all good things must end. I will bid you good night or I'll never rise in the morning." She made for the door, a little unsteadily, and still chuckling at her last story. "Bridget, you make up a bed for Mungo. He'll never find his way back to the harbour in the dark." As she reached the door she turned and smiled at him, "I hope you'll come and see us again, Mungo."

* * *

After such an unpromising start, Mungo's night ashore had exceeded all his expectations. He had not slept a wink but was not in the least tired. Indeed he was back aboard a good hour before the hands turned to, and in a very good humour. In the galley a very drowsy boy was stirring a large pot of porridge but before he could even greet him, Mr Cross, the master's mate, emerged from the officer's cabin.

"The captain wants to see you before you turn to," he said in a tone that was much too severe for that hour of the day. "Your tally was three ton short yesterday. We had the agent round here just after you all pushed off ashore. He was raising hell with the captain."

Mungo was speechless for a time and then, very deliberately, he said, "I don't understand that at all. I worked the derrick myself. We filled sixty-two cart loads."

"That's not the way the agent sees it. If you hadn't been in so much of a hurry to get ashore to your strumpet you might have done a full day's work."

He couldn't decide whether it was the accusation of laziness or the insult to Bridget that angered him most. Either way Mungo could have happily knocked the mate's head off, there and then. But he had to keep calm. It was a lesson Sandy had drummed into him after the brawl at Greenock.

The mate wasn't liked amongst the crew though, in a way, Mr Cross was in part responsible for Mungo's rapid promotion. When Mungo joined the Swan, the Third Hand was a man called Iain. Iain was competent and well respected by the men During Mungo's second trip there had been an altercation between Mr Cross and Iain but

Mungo never found out the details. When the ship returned to Ayr the Third Hand paid off and Captain Brady gave his place to Mungo.

Mungo was seething as he made his way forward to get the tally book from his locker in the crew's quarters. He met Alistair coming up from the focsle hatch.

"You've got a queer face on you for a man who's just spent the night with the bonniest lass in the town."

"Trouble with Mr Cross," Mungo snapped. "He's saying yesterday's landing was short."

"That's not right," Alistair was visibly shocked. "In all the years I've worked this trade we never put out as much coal as we did yesterday."

Mungo just shrugged as he took Alistair's place on the ladder and went below to get his book.

He hardly ate any breakfast. He just kept going over his figures until he was called to the captain's cabin. The discussion with the Captain did not go well. Mungo found it difficult to make his case because of constant interruptions from Cross. He had shown his tally book to the captain who seemed surprised and impressed by the neat, orderly way the loads had been recorded. The standard of the record had knocked some of the wind out of Cross's sails too and he became fractious as well as garrulous.

"Shaw could have written anything he pleased. Just because it's written in a fair hand doesn't make it right."

"All the same, I'll hang on to this, Mungo," the captain said waving the tally book. "I'll show it to the agent when he comes back."

Mungo was not willing to leave it at that. To his way of thinking important matters had to be put right straight away.

"You see, Captain, if Mr Cross is right, that we unloaded less than the quota, then the coal will still be there, in the hold," he argued calmly, "but I know for a fact we put off fifteen and a half tons so we must find out where the three tons went."

"You just leave it with me," the captain said, "I'll get to the bottom of it. Now away the pair of you and turn to or we'll be short today as well."

It was progress of a sort but not the outcome Mungo wanted. He felt depressed and just for a moment he wanted nothing more to do with the *Swan,* her cargo and Dublin. Then he reminded himself that the *Swan* was Mr Murray's ship. He would see this rotten business through till the bitter end.

Chapter Eight

As Mungo looked back towards Dublin, her grand buildings looked grey and forbidding in the failing light. The weather and the deepening gloom combined to intensify Mungo's sense of depression and foreboding. It wasn't just a fear of what lay ahead but a realisation that his selfish preoccupation may have cost him the affection of Bridget.

Unloading the *Swan's* cargo of coal and taking on her backload of limestone had taken a full fortnight. Usually it took ten days. In all he had spent four nights ashore with Bridget but latterly they had become awkward in one another's company. Bridget found it hard to cope with his obsession about the missing coal. At first he had felt sure that someone had miscounted and it could all be squared away. But, as time went on, matters got worse. It was hard to see how so much coal could have gone missing on the short haul from the harbour to the agent's yard. When the final tally was taken it turned out that another three tons, six in all, were missing. He was so wrapped up in what he took to be his own problem that Bridget began to avoid him when he came into Malone's. The worst of it was that Mungo had hardly noticed the changes in Bridget's attitude towards him until now, when it was too late.

Cross was on watch as the *Swan* picked her way eastward along the southern edge of the Howth peninsula. Mungo had already eaten his supper and was standing-by to take over for the early evening dog-watch. Once they were clear of the headland the fair wind would give them straight run, just east of north, right up to the North Channel. Off Corsewall Point they would alter another half point and that course would carry them all the way home.

"If this breeze holds," Cross said to the captain, "we should make Ayr in two and a half days."

The usual time for the passage was four and a half days but that gave a generous allowance for contrary winds and heaving to in the hours of darkness. The delay to investigate the missing cargo meant that they would have to try to make up time. The owner, Mr Murray was anxious to take advantage of the high winter prices in Dublin. He was committed to another consignment before the end of the year. Of course that plan was laid before anything was known of the current irregularities amounting to the loss of one tenth of the shipment.

"Aye, but we wouldn't want it blowing any harder than this or we'll meet crossing traffic in poor light," said the Captain. "Mind you it's a pity to be missing our wee bit extra from Peel this time."

On their return voyage it was their normal practice to short-load the limestone and take on contraband from the Isle of Man for delivery to merchants in Galloway or Carrick.

"I'll be taking the second dog and the middle watch?" Mungo asked.

"Aye," said the captain, "Mr Cross will take the eight till twelve and I'll take over at four. That should see us through the night."

"I'll away for my supper then," Cross said, tersely. "You have the ship!"

Since the business of the lost coal relations between the mate and third hand had sunk from formal to frosty.

Mungo took over the watch and the captain and mate went below to the deckhouse for supper. The steering position on the *Swan* was on the deck above the after accommodation. The arrangement was much superior to the layout on the *Venus;* a wheel rather than a tiller and a commanding position with better visibility. Even so night passages required an extra man forward to look out where the helmsman was unsighted by the sails.

Life at sea aboard the *Swan* was very easy-going compared to the hard graft and frenetic activity on the *Venus*. Most nights at sea the hands on the *Swan* could be assured of at least four hours sleep – usually six – in a dry bunk. The deckhouse back aft had a stove where the ship's boys took it in turns to cook. Weather permitting they had three hot meals a day, whereas three a week would have been high living on the *Venus*.

Yet for all its creature comforts Mungo found the *Swan's* routine boring. It lacked the excitement of life on the *Venus*. Every haul of the nets had been a moment of high drama; bone-crushing effort followed by elation or despair at the size of the catch. The only real drama on the *Swan* was the loading and transfer of 'special' cargoes from the Isle of Man. On this trip even that excitement was denied.

Aside from the boredom, Mungo was surprised at how much he missed his friend Hughie. They went back a long way together. To Mungo, the *Venus* had seemed like an extension of their community at Langmuir. They understood each other's humour and moods. By contrast no one on the *Swan* had Hughie's sense of fun – or his forthright views on every known subject. The captain of the *Swan* was an Ulsterman and the mate was Manx. They barely spoke the same language as Mungo.

The two hour dog watch was quiet with little to disturb Mungo's thoughts. The clouds had cleared and the moon was beginning to rise over the Isle of Man. Moon-light was always a blessing, except when landing contraband.

"I'll take her on now," said Cross from behind Mungo's shoulder.

"Is it that time already? I've nothing much to report. That'll be Drogheda," he said, indicating some pinpoints of light off the port beam. "I'll just go forward and give the look-out a shout."

As he walked to the fore end he wondered what was going on in Cross's mind.   He was certainly involved, in some way, with the theft of the coal. In Mungo's mind theft was the only word adequate to describe its disappearance. His accusation that the short tally on the first day was due to slackness of the unloading crew had been shown to be nonsense. The figure for the final discharge proved that and raised the further conundrum of how an additional three tons came to be missing. These thoughts continued to buzz in his mind as he went below to his bunk.

"Time to rise, Mr Shaw," young Jamie's voice piped through the creaking of the timbers as the *Swan* wallowed uneasily in the long swell. Jamie was the younger of the ship's boys and always stood watch with Mungo.

Mungo had slept soundly. In the seconds before waking though he had an odd dream; he thought he was back in the Shaw. He was a bit confused, at first, by Jamie's voice. The confusion did not last. By instinct he rolled straight out of his bunk and into his boots. It was midnight and time for him to take the middle watch.

"All quiet?" Mungo inquired as he came on deck.

"Yes, though we had a bit of a close call an hour ago. A big three-master came up on our starboard bow. She was going at a fair lick and held her course till she was less than a cable off,' Cross reported; his flat tones and slight slur seeming to underplay the dramatic event.

"But if he was on starboard, we should have given way! Did you call the captain?"

"There's not much you can do with this old girl in that situation," Cross sighed as if to say, 'there was nothing the captain would have done differently'.

"Did you get her name?" Mungo demanded

Cross did not respond directly.

"You'll have to keep your wits about you these next few hours, Mr Shaw," he droned. "There's often fishing boats getting under your feet as well as crossing ships coming from England to Belfast."

Mungo paid no attention to Cross's patronising advice. He had been standing middle watches off the Irish coast for more than a year. He knew what to expect. He was troubled, though, by the mate's admission that he had failed to call the captain when, by his own account, the *Swan* had been in very real danger. It was possible, of course, that Cross was exaggerating; trying to inflate his own importance.

"I want to stand a bit further off the shore," Mungo called out to the watch on deck. "Stand by to re-set the main after I've altered." This was Mungo's less than subtle reproach to the mate for drifting too close inshore. "I'll keep us out of harm's way," he called after Cross, with ill-concealed irony.

As the night went by, it turned colder. Mungo took out the rum jar. It was nearly empty but it should have been filled before they sailed. Could this explain Cross's apparent lapse of judgement and his odd style of speech? More likely it was just an oversight by the cook whose responsibility it was to fill the jar. He must not let his dislike of Mr Cross unbalance his own judgement, he told himself.

He took a swig of the strong spirit and the warm afterglow reminded him of his dream about the Shaw. Mungo had only been back to visit his mother once since the summer and maybe that was on his conscience. His thoughts then flitted here and there, the way they do in the quiet of a wakeful night. Somehow he came back again to Cross. Had Cross caused the previous third hand to be put ashore? Was he trying to force him out too as a way of covering his tracks? If it came down to a choice of who to support the captain would have to support Mr Cross. Just like Dr Guthrie had to favour Charles Wallace.

He was wrestling with these conundrums when he felt the wind change. It was going round towards the south and freshening.

"Jamie," he bellowed and almost immediately the young lad came trotting up to the wheel. "You hold her steady. I have to help the others to reset the main."

The boy was only twelve or thirteen and was plainly delighted to get his hands on the wheel.

"I'll keep her steady, Mr Shaw," he said, although the wheel was a good foot taller than Jamie.

After five minutes of easing out the sheets, taking in reefs and adjusting the stays Mungo came back aft. The boy had been as good as his word and handed the wheel back with the course exactly as Mungo had left it.

"Will you take a drop of rum, Jamie," Mungo asked the boy. "Just to warm you up, mind?" Jamie took a mouthful of the powerful spirit with an audible shudder but a second later there was a visible glow about his cheeks.

"Don't get too fond of that stuff. It causes nothing but trouble," Mungo told the lad, in his sternest tone. "Now away below and see if there's any soup left in the pot." It crossed Mungo's mind that he might have his own ship by now if he had started the sea at the same age as Jamie.

For the rest of his watch the wind continued a moderate blow with strong gusts from a variety of directions between south and east. Mungo was constantly on the wheel whilst the watch on deck were kept busy trimming the sails to hold their course without getting too near the Irish shore. They also saw a few other ships but none so close as to cause alarm.

"Not a bad morning," the captain said arriving on deck a good fifteen minutes before the end of Mungo's watch. "The wind seems a bit changeable all the same."

Although he was not due to go off watch for another few minutes he made his report. The captain, who would be taking over for the four hours till eight o'clock, liked to keep the morning watch.

"Seeing the sun come up is the only way I know I'm alive," he said staring at the still black sky over Man. Then he turned to Mungo and said, "You're a fine seaman Mr Shaw and a smart lad too. But take my advice, cast your eyes beyond this narrow sea. There's a whole wide ocean out there where you can make your fortune."

Any other time Mungo would have taken this for the compliment and sound advice it was but, in his current state of mind, he was suspicious. Was he being prepared to take the blame for the stolen coal?

He was still trying to work out the captain's meaning when the time came for him to go off watch.

"Hang back a while. We need to settle this business of the missing cargo."

Mungo's heart missed several beats. He wanted nothing more than a clearing of the air but he was very, very apprehensive about what might be in the captain's mind.

"The plain fact is that the Irish agent is only going to pay for the coal delivered to his yard. Mr Murray will be very unhappy. I need a story to tell him or we'll all be lifting our gear."

Mungo did not respond straight away. He let the captain's words hang on the breeze for quite a time. At last he said, "Only two things are for certain. First, the total unloaded on the first day was three tons more than ever reached the agent's yard." He paused to be clear about his next statement. 'Second, because everything was double checked on the second day, then that missing three tons was never loaded at Ayr.'

It was now the captain's turn to pause and he took a while. Several times he seemed on the point of saying something but the words did not come. He went forward and steadied himself on the shrouds all the while shaking his head. At last he found his words. 'By the agents way of it your tally book is wrong, According to him you put out twelve carts short.' There was another long pause. Then the captain said very deliberately, 'We were definitely three ton short in the lading bill or if the agent is to be believed six ton in all. Somebody is a stranger to the truth in this whole miserable business'

The Captain's analysis did not resolve anything. Mungo was still under suspicion but still convinced his version of events was correct. The idea that he had somehow misappropriated three tons of coal was laughable. He was depressed but determined. There must be a logical explanation and since Cross was responsible for loading the cargo at Ayr he must have an explanation for at least half of the conundrum.

After he came of watch Mungo went to his bunk. He passed a sleepless two hours but then to his surprise he was summoned back on deck.

'The way I see it I only have half a story,' the captain said, 'I must now rouse Mr Cross so I would be obliged if you would take the watch.' Mungo had never seen such an expression of anger and determination on the captain's usually placid features. Breaking off his watch seemed to suggest he had made a decision but he gave no inkling of what it was.

Chapter Nine

"So you're Mungo Shaw," said Mr Murray, "Captain Brady has told me all about you. I'm deeply obliged to you for smoking out that rascal Cross. It seems he's been working his fraud ever since he joined the *Swan*. It seems he was in league with the merchant's agent in Dublin as well as a crook here in Ayr. They should all be hanged for it but it we don't have enough evidence to be sure of a proof," he sighed and made an exasperated grimace. "It was just as well he took off when Brady confronted him." He paused from his embittered tirade and looked Mungo straight in the eye. "It took courage to stand your ground through this rotten business. Many another young lad would have just paid off the ship and walked away."

"I've always been taught to keep a fair record of important business. It helps to avoid disputes later on," Mungo said with some formality and just a hint of pride.

"When Captain Brady told me your name I was sure you were the same Mungo that was in our Graham's class at the Burgh School, the year before last."

"I was indeed, sir," Mungo confirmed. "I hear Graham did very well, finished up dux of the school, I believe."

"Aye the lad did us proud. He's been apprenticed to the Law in Edinburgh; working for the Lord President, no less," beamed the proud parent. "But what about yourself,Mungo? Graham used to tell us you were such a clever fellow; very good at the mathematics, top of the class for book kccping and a dab hand at the navigation too. All the same I hardly expected to find you working on one of our coal boats."

"Well, sir, I've always been set on a career at the sea and I learnt early on that you have to take your chances when they come. The *Swan* was too good an opportunity to miss. 'If you see a stick cut it', as the old hands say."

Tom Murray had the kind of hard-grained features that seemed to say 'coalminer' yet he had started out as a farmer's boy, like Mungo. Thirty years of hard graft and even harder driving, with some astute dealing thrown in, had brought him a vast estate and a grand mansion by the River Ayr.

When Captain Brady had told Mungo that Mr Murray wanted to see him he was sure it would be connected with Cross's misdeeds. All the same he was a bit apprehensive because of Factor Scott's warnings about Mr Murray's fierce temper. Sitting in the drawing room of Blairadam House – they had smaller fields at the Shaw – Mungo was completely reassured. He thought Graham's father was a fine man. His vast wealth had given him every comfort and luxury but none of the airs and graces Mungo had expected.

"Good for you young man; I don't much care for folk who trade on their acquaintances to get on. I'm sure you knew that a word with our Graham and I would have found you a place in the business here. But you made your own way. I like that."

Mr Murray's voice fell away as his attention moved to a large map spread out on the mahogany table that stood between them.

"Brady speaks very highly of you and he wants to take you as mate on the *Swan's* next trip," Mr Murray suddenly announced, raising his eyes from the map and giving Mungo a quizzical look.

"I would be deeply grateful for the chance, Mr Murray," Mungo said, barely able to contain his enthusiasm.

"But I have other plans that may suit you better," Mr Murray smiled. "You see this map?" he said, turning it towards Mungo. "It's Blairadam estate and it shows all our mines, farms and the other businesses. The trouble is things have moved so fast in the past few years that the accounts and records are in a bit of a fankle. I had no way of knowing about Cross's thieving although he had been at it for the best part of two years. I need somebody with your sharp mind to help me sort things out. I'm sure it's a job that would suit you very well."

Mungo peered at the map, studying it intently, trying to buy time before answering Mr Murray.

"Surely it's a steward or a factor you would need for such a task. Anyway I would not mislead you, sir. My main aim is to get back to sea."

"I thought you might say that," rejoined Mr Murray with no hint of disappointment. "My problem is time. I haven't the time to sort things out myself and anyway I've little talent and less patience with account books. A manager would only get in the road. I expect Graham will manage the businesses one day. Anyway I couldn't abide somebody, like that coof Scott that old Crawford has at Langmuir."

Mungo was a bit nonplussed by Mr Murray's direct and disparaging reference to Factor Scott. He thought it strange how folk see one another; Murray saw a fool and Scott saw an ogre yet Mungo thought both were decent men.

"I'll tell you what I'll do," Mr Murray continued. "If you'll help me for half a year I'll give you a mate's place on one of our ships." He paused then said, "and a year after that, if you do well, I'll find you a master's post."

Mungo quickly caught the drift; Mr Murray's latest offer was his last.

"Of course I'll come and work for you. The chance of my own ship in two years is more than I could ever have wished." Murray's reputation as a hard taskmaster hardly even crossed Mungo's mind.

"I'm sure you'll do very well, son," Mr Murray assured him. "Here's how we'll arrange things. You'll have heard that the *Heron* got stranded, so it'll be a while before she's refloated and repaired. I've dismissed the captain, of course, but I'll send the mate to Brady to replace that crook Cross. You'll be master's mate on the *Heron* when she's recommissioned. I've already told Brady what I have in mind."

He soon found the truth of Mr Murray's reputation for boundless energy and unrelenting stamina. They had no sooner shaken hands on Mungo's new job than they were off on a tour of the policies and the many businesses that Tom Murray had built up over the years. In the space of two hours they visited three mines, two farms and a sawmill. Going by Mr Murray's staccato commentary they had not seen the half of it. When eventually they found their way back to the big house Mr Murray turned his attention to Mungo's working arrangements.

"You'll bide with us at Blairadam," he said. There was no scope for discussion. "Move your gear in on Sunday and you can meet the family at suppertime. I expect Graham will be home this weekend so you'll have company. We work from first light to suppertime every day except the Sabbath and you'll only be needed for the forenoon on Saturdays." With that he shook Mungo's hand again. This time his manner gave the distinct impression that he had other things to attend to and Mungo was dismissed.

As Mungo walked back towards the harbour he tried to come to terms with his new situation. It had all happened so suddenly, but he knew at least one person that would be pleased with this turn of events. His mother had never made any secret of her ambition to see Mungo in a professional job and making his way in society. Of course, for his own part he might finally meet the elusive Margaret Murray. He had first to collect his gear from the *Swan* before going home with the glad tidings.

As he approached the harbour he still had some doubts. He wasn't sure his book keeping was good enough for the scale and complexity of Mr Murray's businesses. Still, by his own account, Mr Murray knew much less about accounts than he did. When he saw the tall masts in the harbour he knew he had done the right thing. No matter what tasks Mr

Murray put on him he would be a sea captain by the time he was twenty.

"Well, Mungo, you've been an excellent shipmate in every way," said Captain Brady as he helped Mungo on to the wharf with his gear. "Be sure to keep a good word for us with the owner." Then he lowered his voice and leaned close to Mungo placing a sack of coins inside his shirt. "Never a word about 'special cargoes' when you're at the big house, mind."

He was only a mile into his journey home to the Shaw when it came on to rain heavens hard. By the time he arrived at the farm he was like a 'drookit craw', as his grandfather would have said.

"For goodness sake come in out of that storm," his mother shrieked as she opened the door to him. "You'll catch your death in those soaking clothes."

Mungo grinned through his chattering teeth at his mother's alarm. If only she had seen him when he was fishing on the *Venus;* he went weeks on end with barely a dry stitch to his back.

As he undressed by the roaring fire his mother waited to carry away his wet clothes. In his haste to remove his shirt he forgot the money bag. It fell to the floor and burst open.

"What on earth...?" Jean was struck speechless by the sight of so many gold coins scattered about the rug and glinting in the firelight.

"Back money," Mungo spluttered. "It's been a while since I was paid."

Jean had a rare ability to frown and smile at the same time. It was a look Mungo knew and it told him she did not believe a word of his explanation. His mother always suspected that at least some of his earnings were ill-gotten but comforted herself that the share he gave to her would be honestly come by.

Chapter Ten

"You're a very quick worker," Mr Murray said to Mungo with an air of surprised satisfaction. "I had no idea that you would get on so fast."

Every waking hour for the last six weeks Mungo had wrestled order out of the chaos that was the Blairadam accounts and record books. He too was surprised at his progress even if a small but irritating pile of unallocated notes sat stubbornly alongside the shrinking mountain of paper. Mr Murray offered no explanation for the origin or purpose of these documents although the sums involved were quite large.

"Just you put them in a drawer and we'll come back at them later," he told Mungo. "No need to slow the herd for a few stragglers!"

Was he talking about cattle driving or rustling? Mungo wondered.

"Now that you've broken the back of that great pile of paper I want you to take an hour or two each day to teach our Margaret the basics of book keeping." It was not a request. Mr Murray did not make requests. Still there was a kind of awkwardness in the way he conveyed the instruction. Mungo was pleased that Mr Murray wanted Margaret to spend time with him if only to share the tedium of the estate accounts. In fact Mr Murray's proposal was not unexpected. Margaret had raised the prospect herself the previous week.

"Well, Mungo Shaw, is this where they've hidden you," the soft voice intoned from over his left shoulder, followed immediately by a waft of a sweet but strong scent. "Mother says I should take up an interest and I think book keeping would be suitable for a modern lady." She had drifted, floated maybe, to the front of Mungo's table and was now staring down at him in the most disturbing way.

Whatever was on her mind Mungo did not believe it had much to do with bookkeeping. He had noticed this look before, more than once, when he ate supper with the family in the small dining room. Usually he excused himself as soon as supper was over and went back to his books in the counting house. When Graham was in for supper, however, he would stay on and gossip about their mutual friends – and enemies – from school. Margaret would stay on too. After a short while Mr Murray would say to his wife, "Come away Lucinda and leave the young folk to their talk."

As soon as they were gone Margaret would move her chair very close to Mungo's. Much as he might have wished to return her advances he daren't risk so much as an encouraging smile. Graham's presence in the room was an obstacle, of course, but far more importantly he knew he had to be very careful of his position with Mr Murray. Anything that might look like familiarity with the daughter of the house could be easily misunderstood.

All of this was in his mind when she had been in the counting house the week before.

"I would be happy to tell you what little I know about keeping account books, but as you can see I have a year's work ahead of me and your father wants it all in six months." He threw his arms wide with a self-pitying shrug to demonstrate the enormity of his task, but he could see she was unimpressed by his pleadings.

"Oh, Graham says you are clever enough to have it all done in a month!" she protested with a hurt look. "Anyway I'll discuss it with daddy. We'll see if he believes you or Graham," she said defiantly and left as silently as she had come.

He knew at the time she would get her way and now, here was her hard-driving flinty-faced father doing her bidding with a plea dressed up as an order.

"I am sure an hour or two will not hinder the work over much, sir," Mungo tried to sound formal. "It would be a pleasure to pass on what modest knowledge I have to Miss

Margaret." It would not do if Mr Murray was to have even an inkling of what was in his mind or indeed in Margaret's.

"That's settled then," said Mr Murray resuming his masterly voice. "You speak directly to Margaret and arrange a time for her instruction."

That evening Margaret did not appear for supper. Mr Murray could see Mungo was wondering where his pupil might be.

"Mistress Murray and Margaret are away to a musical evening at the Provost's House," he announced, rather curtly, "so its gentlemen only for supper."

They had a roast duck each. Mrs Murray did not care for game and would have cared even less for their rather coarse conversation at supper. Mungo found it all very good natured and amusing. Since Mr Murray had to travel to Glasgow the following morning he made an early night of it and he left Mungo and Graham talking by the drawing room fire.

"I didn't know that your mother was on good terms with the Provost's family," Mungo said. "After our troubles with Charles Wallace at school you might have thought that the Murray name would be in poor odour at the Provost's house."

"It's a complicated tale. Margaret had a notion of Charles Wallace, which suited our mother. She is keen to see that Margaret is associated with the *right* family. Father on the other hand can't stand the Provost since he refuses to let our ships load on the north side of the harbour. As you know the coal carts have to come over the auld brig at a great cost in time and money."

"I wondered about that," said Mungo. "I suppose the Burgh would lose the large sum your father pays in harbour dues if he was loading on the Newton side."

"That's not the worst of it," said Graham. "The Provost has the law on his side. All foreign-going cargoes –

including Dublin – have to clear through a Royal Burgh. The whole thing drives father mad."

"Maybe it would suit your father's interests, long term, if he was to try to get on the right side of the Town Council."

"My mother has told him that a hundred times," said Graham wearily. "But it's personal between him and the Provost. You know when father heard about our fight with Charles Wallace he roared with laughter, saying he would have liked fine to heave the Provost into the river after his son."

"That was quite a day. Wallace near did for me with that pointed stick," Mungo smiled but the memory was not at all funny.

"You know for a long time after that Father would not allow the Provost or his family to be mentioned in Blairadam. Lately though my mother and Mrs Wallace have become friendly through good works at the Kirk."

Graham's description of the family feud with the Wallace's only increased Mungo's estimation of Mr Murray. When Mr Murray had announced that mother and daughter were out at the Provost's house Mungo wondered why he had not gone with them. He now realised that Mr Murray had much the same opinion of the Provost as Mungo had of the Provost's son.

"And what about the evil Charles," Mungo asked, "is he still chasing Margaret?"

"Well she's always said she doesn't care for him but that's not the way it looked to me the day I caught them in the summerhouse. You remember; that's what the fight was all about," Graham chuckled.

"That was all a long time ago, but what is the current position between Margaret and the awful Wallace?"

"Now don't you be getting too interested in our Margaret," Graham cautioned with a knowing smile. "She's a wilful minx but she's also the apple of father's eye. You could easy fall out with both of them if you're not careful."

"I assure you that my interest in your dear sister is no more than curiosity and of course an enduring hatred of the loathsome Wallace."

Mungo did not sleep well that night. Did he really have romantic notions for Margaret or was she just a convenient way of continuing his vendetta against Charles Wallace? He even began to wonder why he still had this fixation with Wallace. He was a bully of course but perhaps their original confrontation had been rather childish.

At the time he knew nothing of Wallace's reputation as a bully. By standing up to him Mungo had won cheers and even some applause. He realised now that it must have been a great humiliation for Wallace but as he rolled over and tried to sleep he was sure that in the same situation he would still do the same. Surely, he reasoned, Margaret could have no time for such a lout.

The next morning he took his porridge in the servants' hall and afterwards went straight to the counting house. He had started work by half past six. At nine o'clock the door swung open and in swept Margaret. She was demurely dressed with her auburn hair brushed back in a severely formal style. She carried a small silver inkwell and two freshly sharpened quills.

"This must be the school room," she smiled. "Where would you like me to sit?"

Margaret's very presence in the room both delighted and unnerved Mungo. He rose from his place and taking a gentle hold of her elbow steered her to a seat beside his own. He had given careful thought to how he would arrange things but the touch of her arm and the smell of her scent confused him utterly. His well rehearsed opening speech deserted him and he just sat and stared at her.

After a while Margaret broke the spell.

"Is this time inconvenient? I can come back later."

"Dear me no, Miss Murray you are more than welcome, any time."

"I think I prefer to be called Margaret," she said but retained her formal and rather haughty air.

"Just as you please, Margaret," Mungo said. He had now regained his composure and indeed he was beginning to feel just a little resentful of Margaret's superior attitude. "Perhaps you would like to begin by sorting those papers into their date order."

Without flinching she started straight away to make separate piles of the great mass of assorted notes, dockets and vouchers. Mungo looked on and after a few minutes she looked up at him and smiled. They were going to get on just fine.

Chapter Eleven

"I won't have him in the house any longer," Mrs Murray said in a quiet, cold voice.

"I can't see what you have against the lad," protested Mr Murray, "Mungo's been a great help to me. For the first time in years I know exactly where we stand financially and he has taught our Margaret to be a fine bookkeeper, as well."

"That's not all he's taught her! Have you seen that moonstruck look on her face every time she catches sight him? He's no better, strutting about the house like a dog with two tails. They're far too close to one another for my liking." Mrs Murray's voice had become louder, disturbing the late evening calm of Blairadam.

"Well she could do a lot worse," Mr Murray retorted.

"And she could do a lot better. My daughter should be keeping the company of a young gentleman; not this coarse sailor fellow. His people are Jacobites you know," Mrs Murray spat back, her anger bringing a flush to her cheeks.

"Oh so that's what this is about. Mungo is not good enough for us. Is that it?" Mr Murray was sneering now. "It's just as well your boozy old father forgot his sense of class in time or the whole lot of you would have finished up in the poorhouse."

Mrs Murray did not like to be reminded that Tom Murray – farmer's boy and horny handed coal miner – had rescued her clan from penury. If he had not bought their indebted estate old man Aird would have drank and gambled away what little they had left in a few months.

"We must not fall out about this. I only want what's best for Margaret," Mrs Murray took on a conciliatory air, trying to calm matters now that the argument had begun to run away from her. "I'm sure that Mungo has been a great help and Graham gets on well with him. But Margaret's too young to be getting involved in that way."

"I think she is much the same age as you were when we were first together," Mr Murray chuckled and put a consoling arm around his wife's shoulder. "You needn't worry anyway. Mungo is going back to sea next week. Mr Weston, the *Heron's* new captain arrived in Ayr last night. He means to refloat the *Heron* a fortnight tomorrow. Since Mungo is to be the master's mate he'll have to be fully involved in all the preparations."

* * *

Later that night as Mungo lay awake in the old governess's room at the top of the house he waited for the door to swing open as it had done nearly every night for the past three months. As he waited he reflected on his life, luck and happiness. These hours spent with Margaret were heavenly. It was even better than with Bridget. If this was what the Reverend Maclintock called fornication then Mungo could not see the sin of it. His earlier experiences with the farm girls in the stack-yard at harvest time were sinful, of course, and that's what made them exciting and enjoyable. But with Margaret it was true love and the deep passion between them was only partly due to the danger of being together under her father's roof and under her mother's nose.

He had been musing like this for maybe an hour when he was suddenly struck by a fear that maybe Margaret wasn't coming. After two hours he was sure of it. As the anguish in him grew he began to turn over, in his mind, the events of recent days. On Friday night she had stayed only a few minutes and made the excuse that it was nearly her time of the month. When he was at home at the Shaw on Saturday night both his mother and Factor Scott had asked him repeatedly if he was alright. His mother had said he seemed preoccupied although he had not been aware of any particular worries at the time. After the kirk that morning both Margaret and Mrs Murray seemed in a hurry to be away and hardly gave Mungo and his mother the time of day.

He had a long talk with Mr Murray, though, about refloating the *Heron* and the arrival of her new captain the day before. Perhaps that was why he had not been fully aware of Margaret's luke-warm reception for him. His mother noticed it though. She made some oblique remark at the time which Mungo could not now remember. All the same it slowly dawned on him that something had been amiss for maybe a week and he was angry at himself for missing the signals.

On the morning after a sleepless night he was in the counting house early but there was no sign of Margaret. At nine o'clock his heart leapt as the door swung open but it was Mr Murray.

"Good day to you Mungo. I'm hoping you can finish off the books this week," he said in his usual direct manner. "You and I will meet Captain Weston this afternoon. He's anxious to start preparations to get the *Heron* off that bank."

"That's good news, sir. It'll be good to get back to sea," Mungo said, but without his usual enthusiasm. "I should be able to tie off all the loose ends by next Friday or Saturday at the latest. There is still the matter of the unallocated notes. Is there something you would like done with them?"

"Aye, these notes... I'm not sure what to do with them."

Mungo had never heard Mr Murray sound so cagey. He even felt embarrassed for bringing the matter up.

"Are they perhaps investments, sir?" Mungo enquired with deadpan formality. "You would need to record enough information for you or your successors to realise the capital when the time comes."

"I don't know as you'd call them investments," Mr Murray struggled, looking heaven-wards. "Maybe more in the nature of loans."

Mungo's training prompted further questions, which he stopped himself from asking because he judged that Mr

Murray had already said more than he intended. Yet the silence hung in the air. He had an idea of how to resolve the awkward silence if not the mystery of the documents.

"I haven't mentioned these papers to Margaret but maybe I should discuss them with her?" Mungo suggested. "I take it that she'll be looking after things when I leave. I'll show her where we stowed the papers."

"Aye you do that son. Give Margaret the key to the drawer," Mr Murray agreed, relieved to settle the matter.

"Will Margaret be coming in today?" he asked Mr Murray while he riffled through some papers in a distracted way. "It would be fine to start handing the books over before too long if I have to be away by the end of the week."

Maybe Mr Murray knew that Mungo was searching for a way to find out how matters stood with Margaret but he also knew that Mrs Murray had forbidden Margaret to see Mungo again. For only the second time in Mungo's experience Mr Murray seemed genuinely stuck for words.

"Well you see that might be difficult. She and her mother have gone out for the day and we must away to meet Captain Weston." Mr Murray had said the minimum, buying the time to work out a more complete answer to the tangle of romantic and business problems that now beset the Master of Blairadam.

* * *

To Mungo's surprise Margaret and her mother were seated in their usual places when he came into the dining room that evening.

"I'm sorry to be late," Mungo said with a self assurance that seemed to clash oddly with the atmosphere in the room. Although no one had spoken, a sense of evasion and embarrassment pervaded the room. "I had to check some figures."

Mr Murray grunted in acknowledgement but neither Margaret nor Mrs Murray raised their heads from an intense study of the table linen.

"How did your meeting go with Captain Weston?" Graham asked in the hope of preventing supper from becoming a wake. "He seems to have accomplished so much at so early an age."

Henry Weston was only seven years older than Mungo but he had been to sea since he was twelve. The *Heron* was to be his first command though he had already made a dozen trips to the Indies, four as mate, apparently.

"I am sure we will get along very well," Mungo asserted, still buoyed up with his discussions with Mr Murray and Captain Weston that afternoon. It was also important that Margaret should understand that he was not completely distraught by her coldness towards him. He was moving on to better things and she should know it. "I am sure he will teach me a great deal and I hope he will be able to make some use of my experience of the Irish trade."

"Surely you are selling yourself short, Mungo," said Mr Murray. "The captain will rely on you completely to get the *Heron* off that bank. He fairly cheered up when you told us how the Maclure boys got the *Venus* off the Carrick shore."

"I am not sure that the *Venus* float-out will help us too much," Mungo said carefully; he did not want Mr Murray to think he was contradicting him. "There's a big difference between being stranded on the shore and being fast on a bank in the channel."

"How will you get her off the bank, then?" Graham asked his friend. It was not a well-judged gambit, for Mungo then proceeded to rehearse his plan, in great detail, for the second time that day. Graham's valiant attempt to lift the funereal gloom from the supper table was now in danger of descending into a seminar from Mungo on the finer points of seamanship.

Aware that the ladies were being excluded Mr Murray rejoined the discussion just as soon as Mungo paused for breath.

"What did you ladies get up to today?" he addressed his wife in a jovial but nervous tone.

"You know very well that we went to take tea with Mrs Muir," was the curt reply. The coal miner in him realised at once that this promising seam of conversation was worked out before it had even been opened.

The rest of the meal passed with occasional remarks from the men; mostly to each other and only about business. Graham had only returned from Edinburgh the day before. Usually his mother and sister were agog for news of the capital but not this time. It was all very strange and so awkward that barely had the last mouthful of food been eaten but Mr Murray withdrew, almost towing his wife behind him.

After they had gone the same painful silence returned to the room. Margaret did not follow her usual practice of moving over beside Mungo. She stayed rooted to her seat. Indeed it seemed that she had resumed her earlier study of the tablecloth, with even greater intensity. Mungo looked to the ceiling and whistled noiselessly. Poor Graham was caught in the middle of this glacial impasse and, for a while, he seemed at a loss for something to say. Then suddenly he breezed into life.

"I don't understand you folk any more. For months the two of you are thick as thieves then for no obvious reason you seem to have taken a vow of silence. For goodness sake at least be civil to one another!"

No response; the silence descended again. Then, Margaret's head nodded and her shoulders gave a shudder; she was sobbing. Before either of the boys could react she had pushed back her chair and was heading for the door with her face buried in a napkin. Mungo jumped up from his place and flew after her. He caught her in the hallway outside the dining room and put his arms about her shoulders, which were quaking now as her sobs gave way to a melancholic wailing. But still she said nothing.

There was a small sitting room on the other side of the hallway just a few paces from the dining room door. Mungo steered the tearful Margaret into this sanctuary and by the light of the single lamp which burned in the window recess he guided her towards a large couch set before the fire.

After a few moments Graham's head came round the door. He wasn't sure what was going on but quickly concluded he should have no part of it. With a slight bow of his head he withdrew, closing the door behind him.

Mungo had no idea what was going on either but he was more than content to hold Margaret close as they both sat silently staring into the fire. After what seemed an eternity Margaret pulled herself together, dabbing her eyes with the napkin she was still holding. Then she looked full in Mungo's face and said, "We have to end it. It will never work."

In the deeper recesses of his mind Mungo had probably expected the ending of the affair yet the directness of her words and the finality of her tone was deeply shocking to him. For a split second he wished he had ended it himself but he was heartbroken just the same.

"But why must it end? We are so good for each other. I have never been happier in all my life than when I'm close to you," Mungo pleaded.

Margaret was quiet again then slowly and unsteadily but with deep feeling she said, "You are married to the sea and there is no room in your life for me."

Mungo would not let it lie there.

"I would leave the sea in a minute if we could be together."

Margaret gave him a watery smile. "You are a fine man Mungo Shaw but you would never settle to life ashore and I couldn't settle to you always being away; a life forever looking out to sea watching for your return." Her voice was affectionate but full of sadness.

"You can't mean it. Your mother put this nonsense in your head." It was Mungo's rather desperate final fling but to his surprise it provoked a swift and unexpected reaction from Margaret. Her body stiffened in his embrace and she pushed his arm aside.

"I have agonised over how to tell you for days. Yes my mother doesn't think that you are suitable for me but she has only tried to support me and stop me making a fool of myself. Believe me; I came to this decision myself."

The two fell quiet again until Mungo broke the silence. The fire was flickering now and staring into the dying embers Mungo said, "I will leave at the end of the week and I'll be out of your life forever."

She took his shoulders in her hands and kissed him softly on the lips. "You'll be out of my life but never out of my thoughts."

As they left the little sitting room his arm was still around her shoulder. Once more they kissed then Margaret turned and walked away. He waited till she started to climb the grand staircase but there was never a backward glance. Mungo turned the other way towards the servants' staircase to his rooftop room.

Chapter Twelve

Like many another young sailor with three year's experience, there wasn't much they could teach Mungo, or so he thought. At first Captain Weston seemed to indulge his mate's self-regarding attitude. He even gave Mungo complete charge of refloating the *Heron,* though that was more a necessity due to his absence on business in Liverpool.

The *Heron* had been lying on a sand bank, off Irvine, for more than six months. Although she was still on a fairly even keel she looked a sorry sight; completely dismasted and a heavy coating of bright green weed along the waterline. Appearances could deceive, though, for Mungo noticed that she was full to the gunnels with water – at low tide. That was a good sign, he reasoned, for it meant that the hull was sound, otherwise the flooding would have drained on the ebb. She was also half full of limestone, so refloating was principally a matter of bailing her out and removing the stone. Of course Mungo did not share his analysis with anyone else. Suggesting that the task was straightforward would only make a rod for his own back. His time on the *Swan* had taught him to keep a margin in reserve to deal with inevitable problems, so he took the job at a steady pace and protested about every kind of difficulty, real and imagined. When she floated clear after only three weeks he was thought to be something of a genius.

After the *Heron* had been refloated she was brought into Mr Murray's shipyard at Newton to be repaired and refitted. During the refit he spent nearly all his waking hours in the company of Captain Weston. He came to realise that Henry Weston was like no one else he had so far met in seafaring circles. He was a young man – not quite twenty-five years old – of erect stature and handsome face. He was a very good seaman, a purposeful leader and above all else a strict disciplinarian.

His previous ships had been large oceangoing square riggers. Although his family home was in Whitehaven he knew next to nothing about the coasting trade. He had no direct experience, either, of the wherries, luggers and other small merchantmen that carried freight of all kinds between the large cities and the minor ports on the Narrow Sea. The barrage of questions which assailed Mungo every day made it clear that Mr Weston would not stay long in this state of ignorance.

For all his vigorous discussion of professional matters the Captain was otherwise a taciturn man. Sandy Maclure and Tom Brady may have lacked Mr Weston's professional attributes but they were always willing to pass the time of day with the men. Weston was a closed book and he gave every impression that he meant to keep it that way.

Mr Murray seemed to be the one person who could animate Captain Weston. He came often to the shipyard to discuss progress on the refit. On those occasions Mungo was more or less a bystander, a status he did not much enjoy.

Once, when all three men were poring over the plans for the vessel, Captain Weston stood upright and addressed himself to Mr Murray.

"Is there any reason why the ship should be rigged in this way?"

"Well it's the way she was when she was built and it's always suited well enough," Mr Murray responded, clearly taken unawares by the question. "Was there some change you had in mind?"

"If we step the mast two frames forward that would give us another six feet of canvas on the mainsail as well as easier working in the hold. With a topmast she could also carry a topsail," said Captain Weston, stating an obvious fact.

Mungo and Mr Murray were rather stuck for words as they tried to hoist in the captain's proposition. Mungo was about to ask about the effects on the ship's trim but the captain was ahead of him.

"If we fit a ten foot bowsprit as well, we can carry an extra jib."

"Well I'll give it some thought. What about you Mungo?" said Mr Murray.

Mungo vaguely remembered a drawing in his seamanship manual. It was an American ketch and it seemed like the rig the captain was describing. He thought that with all that canvas she might be knocked down in a gale but he had to get on with the captain if he was ever to get his own ship so he thought better of mentioning it.

"It seems like a good plan, if her old hull will carry that much sail," said Mungo, glad to be consulted for once. "The only drawback might be that she would make a lot of leeway sailing close hauled."

"That's a fair point, but the extra speed would more than compensate, don't you agree?" But before Mungo could respond Weston added, "You said yourself that the hull was sound. Strong as the Auld Brig you said."

Mr Murray disliked indecision so he was never slow to make up his own mind.

"Very well," he said. "Get the shipwright in and get on with it."

Reflecting on it later Mungo could hardly believe what had happened. Whilst others hesitated to ask Mr Murray about even minor matters Weston had got him to agree to completely redesign the *Heron* in a matter of minutes. Their acquaintance seemed to go beyond the master servant relationship. It was as though Mr Murray knew him of old, not personally but by reputation and in that reputation something demanded respect.

Thomson the shipwright was delighted by the chance to try something new and worked long hours under the personal supervision of Captain Weston. Mungo on the other hand had less and less to do and spent more time than was wise at Simpsons.

Every Sunday he went back to the Shaw. His mother was still recovering from his severance from Margaret and was finding it difficult to accept that he was not going to become a merchant gentleman immediately. Although she must have known that the whole episode had been very painful for him she would insist on raising the subject from time to time. This usually resulted in Mungo marching out of the house in high dudgeon, but his anger never lasted long. He was too fond of his food and anyway he was consoled by the knowledge he would soon be back at sea. Gradually his mother became content with Mungo's new station as master's mate.

A week before the *Heron* was due to leave the dockyard Mr Murray came on board to inspect the improvements. Like everyone else he was well pleased by the shipwright's work.

"It seems a pity to fill her up with coal," Mr Murray said, "so I've managed to get a cargo of barley to go to Wales and there's a back load of Welsh Oak for the yard here. I'm so pleased with the *Heron* that I mean to build a completely new boat to the same design."

Suddenly Mr Murray was full of surprises. Mungo would not miss the coal run but he had hoped to return to Dublin so that he might see Bridget again. It also occurred to him that loading casks of rum and brandy into a hold full of oak planks might be difficult. Then he remembered. He had not broached the question of contraband with Captain Weston and, somehow, he was not sure that he should.

"We'll manage the coal trade with the other three ships, now that we can be sure the full consignment will reach the buyer," Mr Murray said, smiling to Mungo.

* * *

The re-designed *Heron* sailed like a dream. Her speed to windward was a good three knots faster than the old *Swan* ever achieved. Running before the wind with two jibs and a topsail she was so fast that even hardened sailors were fearful the mast would split or the rigging tear.

For all that she was not yet a happy ship. Her new crew saw in their captain a dour man who was distant from them. He would appear on deck, unexpectedly, at any hour of the day or night. On those occasions he seemed always to be in a foul mood. He would go amongst the hands with words of criticism and even blazing rebukes for no obvious reason. He rarely had any praise for the men and certainly never asked after their welfare.

Alf Garvie, the third hand, was around the same age as the captain. He had a droll sense of humour and the men liked him. He was always ready to reassure any of the crew who had felt the rough edge of the captain's tongue without due cause and he did his best to engender a sense of comradeship amongst the men. This left Mungo in an odd position. As second in command he could never be openly critical of the captain, but he also found it awkward to raise his doubts and disagreements in private. Weston had a withering stare and conversation with him was a series of disjointed silences. He only spoke fluently when expounding his own ideas or giving instructions. Mungo had heard the phrase 'a difficult man' but this was the first time he had met one.

More and more Mungo confined himself to his principal harbour duty of loading cargo and dealing with the agents. At sea he kept his watches, supervised the navigation, and piloted the ship in and out of harbour. He even began to wonder if Cross had felt the same sense of exclusion. He reassured himself that the responsibility of the captain's post demanded a measure of distance from the men. Mr Weston's way of running the ship might seem harsh but he had to allow it was efficient. All the same, his own growing remoteness from the crew saddened him.

On their return from Wales Mr Murray met them at the yard. He was more than impressed that the voyage had taken a day and a half less than was estimated. He walked around the open hatch-cover inspecting the timber and seemed well pleased with the quality.

"Best of stuff," he asserted. "Mr Cunningham is already interested in the new boat and we haven't laid the keel yet." He chuckled for he was entitled to some self-congratulation. Cunningham owned a dozen mines around Saltcoats and was planning to build his own fleet of ships.

"So you may go into shipbuilding on a big scale?" Weston asked.

"Oh yes!" said Mr Murray. "There's plenty of ground here to lay out half a dozen hulls."

"I wonder why you don't build a wharf and coal yard here," the captain ventured. "It must be very costly having to haul everything over the Auld Brig and through the town."

"You tell him, Mungo," Mr Murray said, so exasperated with the Town Council that he could not even bring himself to discuss the matter.

Mungo explained the limitation on foreign cargoes having to clear through a Royal Burgh and that meant loading and unloading on the south side of the river.

"Nothing to stop you handling British cargo from this side though," said the captain, rubbing his chin.

"You're right," said Murray, "and who's to say where a load of coal for the Highlands might finish up." He chuckled again. "For now though we could build a trade in grain, timber and general cargo to mainland Britain."

He marched ashore with the captain and Mungo following him like two sheep dogs. He was soon stepping out to the open ground on the Newton shore of the river.

"We could have the slipways here and that would still leave plenty of room for a new wharf."

It seemed a pity to spoil the general enthusiasm so Mungo held his tongue. He knew that Mr Murray's restless pacing was on his neighbour's land. There was little Mungo did not know about Blairadam Estate following his six months rearranging Mr Murray's papers.

Before he left the ship that day, Mr Murray addressed himself to the more mundane matter of the *Heron's* employment for the coming months. There were to be two further trips to Wales followed by a cargo of corn and a backload of linen cloth through Dublin. Mungo was so cheered by this news that he did not notice Captain Weston's face. Weston swallowed hard on the word Dublin as though it were a draught of rancid beer.

Chapter Thirteen

The songs of the night's carousing swam in Mungo's head, occasionally bursting forth as tuneless snatches of unrecognisable Irish anthems. He made his erratic progress along the quay, oblivious to all the ills of life that afflicted lesser men. This sense of well being was founded entirely on the strength of that black beer the Irish call stout.

In the nine months since he joined the *Heron* he had gradually thawed towards Mr Weston though they were still a long way from anything approaching familiarity. He felt the captain was a good man but like everyone else he had his faults. He rarely went ashore and he prayed a lot. Mungo had nothing against a devout captain; he just did not choose to live that way himself. Captain Weston was a talented and experienced seaman and even if he was overly strict and lacked an inspiring manner, he did have an air of authority about him. To Mungo's thinking, though, his fatal flaw was that he had not the slightest inclination to run 'special' cargoes of any kind.

It had been a hard night's drinking and although Mungo hadn't quite lost the ability to walk he was not doing it very well. Being fearful of falling into the harbour, he sat down on a mooring bollard to regain his balance. Thus ensconced he looked down the river to where the *Heron* lay on the south side of the harbour. Another day's loading and she would be ready to sail. On this trip their cargoes of corn and bales of linen were far easier working than the usual traffic of coal out and limestone back. Hiding a few dozen casks of spirit amongst these bales of cloth would be no bother at all. Mr Murray paid a fair wage but a man came to look forward to a wee bit extra. He would raise the matter with the captain just as soon as he got back aboard.

Now that he felt more in harmony with his surroundings he made to rise from his temporary rest on the quayside. As he rose from the bollard down came the mist in his brain, and before he knew it he had resumed his cold iron seat with a thump. The shock of his landing caused Mungo to revise the advice he intended to give the captain. With outstretched arms and much dramatic irony he addressed his concerns directly to the River Liffey.

"Ah but our captain's a god-fearing man, you see. He'll not be tempted by the devil to run contraband on the Carrick Shore. That work's only fit for a sinner like Mungo Shaw!"

As he sat on his perch his brain raced and froze with an alarming rhythm but after a while a kind of calm returned and he dwelt on thoughts of his own sinful desires.

"Mistress Bridget O'Neill I love you," he called out to the murky black waters of the harbour. The belle of Malone's Tavern, once so accommodating, had rejected even his most earnest entreaties.

"*Not tonight my dear for old Declan is home from the sea.*" Mungo tried to sing in a tune borrowed from goodness knows where. Declan was the new man in Bridget's life – a seaman like himself but he made long deep-sea voyages to Virginia and the Carolinas. An acquaintance from the Inn had warned Mungo of Declan's murderous temper if anyone so much as looked at Bridget the wrong way. He had also told Mungo the name of Declan's ship. When the mighty three-master, the *Skibbereen,* edged into her berth downstream from the *Heron* that afternoon Mungo remembered he had always meant to try the taverns on the north side of the harbour. Brogan's, he had been told, was a fine lodge for good meat and strong drink as well as plenty of singing and dancing. Most of all it was a safe distance away from Malone's.

He felt the better of his rest and was about to take the road again when he heard a great riot of noise coming from the direction of the *Heron.* He got gingerly to his feet and swayed down to that point on the quay from where he might get a clear view of his ship. As he got closer the noise grew louder. He could see men struggling on the short deck in front of the wheel. Although his brain was still hazy and his focus indistinct he thought he could make out the captain and Alf, the third hand. They were being belaboured by three or four men armed with clubs. He was not sure what was happening but he knew it was not good. Instinctively he set off, upstream, towards the harbour bridge and the road back to the side of the river where the *Heron* was lying. As he approached the bridge his pace increased without any apparent effort on his part. In no time he was running at full tilt.

When he was halfway across the bridge he came to an abrupt halt with a jabbing pain in his side. As he bent over to clutch the source of this agony, with no warning whatsoever, he began to throw up the night's refreshments followed immediately by his supper. It was the best thing to happen for almost at once he began to feel somewhat restored, physically, although it would be a while before his brain could catch up.

By the time he reached the *Heron* the assailants had gone. Alf, badly beaten and bloodied, was draped over the guard-rail like a crumpled greatcoat. As Mungo clambered aboard Alf gasped:

"They took off along the wharf. You'd better see tae the captain. They gave him a terrible battering."

The sight that met Mungo in the deckhouse was gruesome and deeply shocking. The captain was sprawled over the mess table bleeding profusely from several wounds to the head and his face swollen almost beyond recognition. Worst of all his breathing was terribly laboured. Mungo hoped against hope that it was all a drunken dream but then he heard a horrible rattle coming from the captain's chest followed by a gurgling. Next a torrent of bloody foam issued from Mr Weston's mouth. He was seized with a panic that the captain would die there and then. He washed away the spume from his mouth and propped him up against the bulkhead and gradually his breathing resumed a calmer rhythm.

A sense of urgency now enlivened him, giving an illusory feeling of sobriety. The captain needed help straightaway. He rushed forward to the crew's quarters where he discovered that the two ships boys were, incredibly, in their bunks and fast asleep.

"Turn out, turn out," he roared at the terrified lads. "Billy, you go and get the rest of the crew. Just keep trying the taverns along the quay till you find them." He then turned to the older lad. "Peter, you go to the Watch Office along by the Bridge. The captain needs a surgeon. He's very badly injured. Now come on the two of you. There's not a minute to be lost."

He returned to the deckhouse where Alf had managed to stagger inboard. He had got as far as the stove and was trying to boil some water.

"I'll get that," Mungo said, easing the pot from Alf's grasp. "You just lie on the bunk there and try to get your strength up." In the ordinary way Alf would have been regarded as a serious casualty but compared to the captain he was no worse than walking wounded. Mungo would have to minister to both of them even though his head still throbbed from the night's excesses.

He split the hot water between two bowls. Alf would have to clean himself up as best he could whilst Mungo treated the captain's wounds. He staunched the blood from the open wounds and gradually got rid of the gore from the captain's face. Alf had made good progress with his own dressings. Mungo cagily asked him, "Who were the men that attacked you? Whatever did they want?" He thought he knew the answer to his own question.

"I think they got the wrong boat," Alf answered. "They just asked for the captain and when he came forward they set about him, shouting all kinds of abuse. They said they would teach him not to take what did nae belong tae him."

"You took some punishment yourself, though," Mungo observed as the lamplight caught a particularly deep gash on the third hand's temple. "Here," he said, breaking off washing the captain's head and laying his cloth on Alf's forehead. "Maybe it was you they were after."

"I never saw them in my life before," said Alf, shaking his head.

Maybe Mungo had boasted to the company in Malone's Tavern that he was now captain of the *Heron*. Either way, he thought it quite likely that it was Declan and his men who had mistaken Mr Weston for himself.

"How come they took off, anyway?" Mungo asked.

"Two Watch Officers doing their rounds heard the noise and ran over. When the gang saw them they bolted towards that big ship down the quay."

* * *

Billy was first to return from his mission driving the five other crewmen before him like a herd of recalcitrant bullocks. There was little sense to be had from these older hands for they had also taken far more than their share of black beer. Young Billy, though, was quite anxious to bring Mungo some news.

"Those men are coming back;" he said breathlessly. "The tapster at the Inn said something about them going to finish him off next time."

"Aye don't you worry about that," said Mungo. "Get that stove stoked up and put on the broth. It's going to be a long night."

By degrees he was starting to think more cleary. All he had was a shipload of drunks and walking wounded. There was no future in waiting round to take on a band of brigands. They would have to sail in the morning as soon as they loaded the last of the linen.

"Any sign of young Peter?" he called out to no one in particular.

Just then the deckhouse door opened. Peter had returned.

"The watch officer says there's no chance of seeing a surgeon till morning," he said despondently. "But apparently there is a physician somewhere in Temple Bar who'll come out if you pay enough," he added, hopefully.

"Did the Watch Officer say anything about the louts who were here earlier?" Mungo asked the lad.

"Oh aye," said the boy with some excitement. "They scattered in all directions. Three headed back towards the city and two ran off along the South Wall. There's no way through there unless they were making for one of the ships."

Mungo returned to his patient who was at last showing some signs of life although still far from being conscious. He was sure they had come from the *Skibbereen.* Two of them would be back there but what of the other three? Biding their time likely. As he carried on mopping the captain's brow Mungo mused on the similar effects of too much black beer and blows rained about the head with a cudgel. Then he reached a decision. He would have to sail that night. It would be another two hours till the ebb tide would be strong enough to carry them down the river to the open sea. That might be long enough to sober up the hands and it would bring up the first light of dawn but it was also more than enough time for Declan's brigands to return.

It was no easy matter trying to build a sailing crew from the debris of the night's festivities and hostilities and trying to bring the captain round from his trauma all at the same time. Still, everyone felt the better of a bowl of hot broth and plenty of that fine soda bread they always bought from the Dublin harbour baker. Over the next hour one or two groups of boisterous lads had come along the quay but none with murder on their minds.

Just when everything was about as ready as it would ever be he went out on deck for a breath of air. Almost at once he became aware of heavy footfalls ringing on the cobbled quay, though at first he could see nothing. Then from behind a nearby small building three burly fellows appeared. They were walking towards the ship and their bearing was hostile. Mungo could sense an imminent confrontation.

This was no time for talk or even argument. He picked up a heavy belaying pin. As they bore down on him fear started to clear his brain. The tallest came right up to the ship's side and made to climb on board. He started to say something but Mungo was for none of it. He brought the iron bar down on the big fellow's head. That single blow may even have killed him for with a roar he collapsed lifeless on to the quay. His companions also tried to board the ship but Mungo's boot came down on the knuckles of one and a wild swing of his pike in the face of the other was enough of a deterrent. The two then made to run off but after a hurried exchange of words they returned to recover their leader. They hoisted the deadweight between them and half carrying, half dragging him they returned from whence they came mouthing oaths and pledging to come back fully reinforced.

Even with all his hands on deck he doubted if his befuddled crew would be any match for these desperadoes. It was still half an hour till full ebb but Mungo decided to go anyway. After several minutes of barking orders till his head ached he managed to rouse the crew enough to cast off the moorings and bear the ship away from the pier. As they drifted down on the tide with only a headsail for steerage he wondered when, if ever, he would return to Dublin.

Chapter Fourteen

"Did you send that lad from the *Heron*? The one that was asking for Mr Quillan," enquired a grizzled retainer perched on a cask by the door of the warehouse. "I sent him away with a flea in his ear. The Master's a busy man don't you know."

When Peter had returned on board and reported this rebuff, Mungo had decided that he would go himself. Quillan was the agent at Peel for a firm of Douglas merchants called Black, Christian and Ross. Although they had a small store on the quay their main seat of business was a farm about a mile inland, an exhausting walk for a man in Mungo's condition.

"I'm acquainted with Mr Quillan," said Mungo in a tone befitting his new status as temporary master of the *Heron*, "and I'd be obliged if you would inform him that Mr Mungo Shaw sends his compliments and awaits the pleasure of an audience." It was a little speech he had heard a dozen times from self important visitors who came to call on Mr Murray at Blairadam. It did the trick and the old fellow scuttled off into a large warehouse.

Mungo had felt better. He was exhausted and fearful that he might not give a good account either of himself or the extraordinary circumstance that brought him to Peel. After a minute or two an ample figure filled the doorway. Mungo recognised Mr Quillan immediately. He had seen him once or twice before when the *Swan* was loading 'special cargoes' at Peel. There was very little trade, legal or otherwise, entering or leaving Man that did not pass through his firm.

"There's always a welcome here for young Mr Shaw," said the large man waving the retainer aside. Turning to Mungo he went on, "Your boy told Joshua here that your captain's wounded."

"Aye he's in a poor way of it," lamented Mungo. "I was hoping you might recommend us to a surgeon."

"Better than that," said Mr Quillan, grasping Mungo's hand. "I sent the surgeon down to the ship as soon as I heard. He should be there by now."

"I'm very grateful for your consideration sir," said Mungo in surprised delight. "We were making for home but an hour out of Dublin the captain took very bad. He was raving and his face was the colour of limestone. I feared he might die on us."

"Well don't you bother yourself any further; Mr Quirk is the best surgeon on the island," Quillan reassured Mungo. "But I don't think I know your captain. We did some business with the *Heron* under her old master but perhaps this Mr Weston is too cautious for the free trading. Where's he from, anyway?"

"He's from Whitehaven; still has family there. He was desperate for us to take him home but with the wind the way it is we would have struggled to weather the Mull of Galloway on the way back north. So we decided to put in here," Mungo explained.

"Very wise, very wise," said Mr Quillan, tapping his upper lip with his forefinger and looking distractedly into the middle distance. He remained quiet for the best part of a minute. Then his face suddenly lit up.

"Henry Weston you say – out of Whitehaven," Mr Quillan declared triumphantly, "I'm sure he was first mate to Captain Benson of the *Friendship*. The *Friendship's* owner got into financial difficulties about a year ago. She was sold in Liverpool and the crew were all put ashore."

Mungo wondered if the captain's fitful raving during their crossing to the Isle of Man was in some way connected to this shady passage in his mysterious past. In any case none of it made sense to him for he knew next to nothing about Mr Weston's old ships and there was nothing he wanted to know, either.

Fatigue had been coming over Mungo in waves all day and his head was still throbbing from the great quantity of

Irish stout he had taken the night before. He had not slept and the strain of his new responsibilities weighed more heavily than he realised. His haggard face must have made his nineteen years seem more like ninety. Mr Quillan could see he was out on his feet.

"You look drained. You should catch an hour or two's sleep," he said, pointing to the stair. "I'll send somebody to shake you when we hear from the surgeon, then we can talk some more."

As Mungo climbed the stair to the loft his mind continued to race. He fretted about staying away from the ship for too long yet could not imagine her coming to any harm. He was grateful to Mr Quillan of course, but his gratitude was tempered by the knowledge that men in Quillan's way of business do very little out of kindness.

* * *

Mungo was awakened by cooking smells, which became stronger as he stumbled his way down the stair. He was not yet properly awake and not entirely sure of where he was. Gradually his eyes became accustomed to the gloom and his mind regained some kind of focus. He made for the horse trough he remembered seeing in the yard. He found it by the pale gleam of a new-risen moon but it was not so light that he could read his watch. Going on the cast of the night sky he reckoned it was eight o'clock or maybe half past so he must have slept for about four hours.

He ducked his head into the trough. The shock of the cold water on his face brought him, abruptly, wide-awake. Although he was parched with thirst he could not bring himself to drink from the foul smelling water. Mungo quickly regained the scent of what he thought must be a fine mutton stew. He followed his nose to a second door on the large building. Inside was the source of the mouth-watering aroma.

"Come away in," Joshua greeted Mungo, "the master said I was to let you sleep but to see you got a good supper when you came to." This was a definite improvement on the hostility that marked his first encounter with Joshua.

"Is there any word from the surgeon?" Mungo asked.

"Well, the master said to tell you that your captain's been taken to the infirmary," Joshua replied. "He'll be back himself presently, but you eat up your supper for now," said Joshua, pushing a well-filled bowl in front of Mungo. "Will you take wine or ale with it?"

The very idea of strong drink caused an involuntary shiver to run up Mungo's back.

"I'll be right enough with a flagon of cold water, thank you."

In spite of his hunger Mungo ate slowly. He did not want Joshua thinking he was ill-bred. After he had taken about half the stew he casually addressed Joshua with some pleasantries. Had he been in Mr Quillan's service long? Had he always lived on the island? and so forth. Joshua answered each of his questions with no more than a couple of words. There seemed little prospect of conversation, so Mungo tried a new tack.

"Have you ever heard tell of a ship called the *Friendship?*" Mungo asked.

There was an instant reaction. A look of alarm stared out of Joshua's grey eyes yet he made no sound. As he made to draw away Mungo badgered him further.

"What about her first mate, Mr Henry Weston – ever heard of him?"

"These are not matters for me to talk about. You'll have to ask Mr Quillan."

Before he could press Joshua any further the sound of approaching horses distracted them both. Joshua rushed out of the door to help Mr Quillan down from his carriage. He was accompanied by another man, less well made than

Quillan and handsomely clad; every inch a gentleman. and to whom Quillan showed great deference.

"Well, Mungo, I can see you slept well. What did you think of Joshua's stew? He's the best cook on this side of the Island, you know." Mr Quillan's jovial manner reassured Mungo but it was also meant to impress on his companion that he knew Mungo better than he did. "This is Mr Christian, the principal of our company," he said, presenting the gentleman with due formality.

"And you must be Mr Shaw," said Christian. "Mr Quillan speaks very highly of you."

Quillan nodded his assent and went on.

"The surgeon has patched up Mr Weston but he'll not be fit to work for three months at least so you'll have to take the *Heron* back to Ayr without him." As Quillan spoke Mr Christian stood apart, eyeing Mungo in an unsettling way. "I'll get him a passage back to his own folk in Whitehaven in a week or two; when he's got his strength back. It's better that he doesn't tarry here too long," Quillan concluded in somewhat breathless haste.

Mungo did not enquire further about Mr Weston. There was surely some deeper story but Mungo did not want to know. After all he had come out of it very well. The cruel beating that Weston had suffered might have been Mungo's fate. No matter, he was now the temporary captain of the *Heron* and that was just fine.

"The *Heron's* a well-found ship, Mungo. I hear you have cargo of linen cloth on board. I didn't know Mr Murray had branched out from the coal trade," said Mr Christian. Mungo was surprised that he knew Mr Murray. He then sat down opposite Mungo and started sipping from the jug of claret wine that Joshua had brought him. "Would you care for a drop of this? Joshua, fetch another jug."

"Thank you, sir," said Mungo, though he was not at all sure that wine was a good idea. Still, he had to be sociable and it might be thought a sign of weakness if a man could not take a drink. In fact the wine was like nothing he had ever tasted before; smooth and mellow and not at all like the sour liquor the taverns passed off as claret.

"This is very fine wine, sir," Mungo enthused. "Mr Quillan has indeed been most kind to me. I don't know how we could have managed without his help," Mungo said with heart-felt gratitude.

"Think nothing of it," said the gentleman. "It would be an awful world if we could not do one another a good turn here and there."

They chatted on for a while but around ten o'clock Mungo announced he would have to go.

"Gentlemen, thank you both for all your help and kind hospitality but I must take my leave. If we are to get the best of the tide we'll have to sail about five tomorrow morning."

"Before you go," said Mr Christian; his tone was now quite formal, "There is a service you might do for us. There's a merchant in Galloway who's waiting for some tobacco and tea maybe forty casks; not more. I would be obliged if you could carry it to Port Castle on the Solway."

Mungo knew that some return favour would be asked but this was a surprise. Surely Quillan could have arranged some recompense without the head of the House to hold his hand. It was, in any case, such an odd proposal. Careful planning was needed for running contraband. A ship did not just arrive, unannounced, and start unloading casks onto the beach.

Mr Christian read the puzzlement on Mungo's face and turned to Quillan. "You must give Mungo the details," he ordered.

"I had arranged another vessel for this service, sir, but he is unavoidably detained. I am sure Mr Shaw will look after it very well," he explained, a little abashed. "The merchant's men will be on the shore in two days time just after eight at night."

It dawned on Mungo that Quillan had already committed him to this assignment.

"Of course, I am more than willing to help," he conceded with a bow of his head. "When can I expect to load the cargo and receive precise details of the landing?"

"The cargo is already on the way to the wharf on four wagons. It should be there by the time you get back. I left the chart for the landing with your third hand." Quillan's voice was no longer jovial. These were orders.

The presumption underlying the whole arrangement bothered Mungo. He knew the landing places around Burrow Point but he had not been in to Port Castle before.

"I trust the usual fee will be acceptable to you and your men," Mr Christian ventured in a tone that left no scope for bargaining.

The fee would indeed be acceptable – in fact it might be necessary to secure the compliance of the crew. It had always bought Mungo's silence. Mr Quillan handed Mungo a bag of coins. He didn't count them and put the bag inside his shirt.

"That will be fine," he said, taking Mr Christian's outstretched hand.

"Good luck and good sailing," said Mr Christian, his grasp almost crushing Mungo's hand; not at all what he expected from so refined a gentleman.

Quillan and Mr Christian called forward a carriage for Mungo. As they made their farewells they resumed the jocund and friendly manner of their talk at the table. Mungo could not make head or tail of it all. Whatever was going on, Christian and Quillan had told him less than the full story. He could not get it out of his mind that Captain Weston was connected with it all in some way. Why had the other ship pulled out of the assignment? It was nerve wracking and, somehow, being captain made the dilemma worse.

As he drove back to the ship Mungo reflected on the happenings of the past two days in the hope of making sense of his predicament. He had avoided Declan's wrath but maybe the captain had paid a heavy price in his place. Could Christian and Quillan be relied on to look after the captain? Even now his recovery was far from certain. For the time being, though, Mr Christian's cargo was foremost in his mind. He had run contraband many times on the Solway in the old *Swan*. The hazardous rocks, shifting sand banks and the fast running tides were the least of his worries for lately he had heard the government was making great efforts to stamp out the Solway Trade. It was common knowledge that the Galloway shore was overrun with excisemen and a Navy Brig patrolled the coastal waters. Capture was a fearful risk for it could mean confiscation of the ship. Explaining Captain Weston's fate to Mr Murray would be difficult enough but the loss of the ship did not bear thinking about. So much uncertainty – his every instinct was to sail without Mr Christian's cargo.

When the carriage eventually turned on to the harbour road a moonlit scene of bustling activity greeted Mungo. The *Heron* was going like a fair. Quillan's men were manhandling casks off their wagons. Alf and the two boys were swinging them inboard with the derrick and two deckhands were stowing them in the hold. Mungo was dumbstruck. There was no going back now. He could only marvel at Christian's effrontery. He had taken over the ship and, for the time being at least, Mungo's life as well. Maybe it took this kind of gall to be successful – and rich.

"Where the hell hae ye been," Alf shouted as Mungo climbed aboard. "First aff a surgeon billy cam' and took awa the captain. Then a big gentleman came wi' a muckle packet; only to be gie'n into yer ain haunds, he said. Noo we hae these lads tellin' us tae load this extra cargo oan your orders. Whit in the name o' blazes, is gawn' oan, Mungo?"

"Never fear, Alf; it's just some rum and tobacco to be delivered up the coast. There'll be a pickle o'siller in it for us all," Mungo replied with a knowing wink.

"I hae nae trouble wi' smuggling as long as I ken the risks," Alf said, "but I've only ever worked the Solway yince or twice."

"Well you'll be right enough then," he assured Alf. "I'll give you a hand with the last of these casks. It must have been heavy going with two men short."

Chapter Fifteen

There was no need to catch the early tide as Mungo had planned. The *Heron* would be in port for another day and a half. Everyone was the better of a night's sleep and a hearty breakfast of bread, eggs, fried herrings and tuppenny ale. After they had taken their fill Mungo addressed his ship's company.

"It's been a rough few days and you have all done very well to handle the ordeals that fortune put on us. I'm obliged for your hard work and loyalty." He was now, every inch, the captain of the *Heron*.

"Captain Weston is so badly injured that he'll be laid up for weeks to come. He's in the infirmary here in Peel and I'll visit him later this morning." His concerned tone came quite naturally. Although there was no bond of friendship between them he was beginning to wonder what might become of Captain Weston. "At all events I will be in command for the trip home." At this announcement there was a noticeable lightening of spirit in the company. Whether it was relief at seeing the back of Mr Weston or enthusiasm for his own captaincy, Mungo could not tell. "I have to tell you that further trials are ahead of us. In consideration of the help given to Captain Weston, in his hour of need, I have agreed to do a service for Mr Christian, a local merchant." Alf let out a gasp and Mungo wondered why Alf, no stranger to the Manx free trade, should be so affected by the mention of Christian's name.

"The cargo we loaded last night is to be landed on the shore near Burrow Point some 50 miles north of here. It is possible that some excisemen, or maybe the navy will be in the area so we must keep our wits about us. There will be extra pay for this service but it must be kept secret. In the meantime be about your duties."

* * *

Later that morning Mungo went ashore to find the infirmary. He felt he had a duty to visit his injured captain, of course, but he was also wanted to discover what episode in his past had caused the horror-struck reaction in old Joshua at the mention of the name, Henry Weston. He went first to Quillan's store but the boy there said he did not know where the infirmary was. Further along the quay he asked another man where Mr Quirk, the surgeon lived.

"In Douglas, I suppose," the man answered with a shrug. Just then the boy from Quillan's place appeared at his elbow.

"Mr Quillan said I've to take you to Captain Weston," said the boy.

After a short walk Mungo and his escort arrived in front of a well kept town house. Quillan had clearly been a little inventive describing it as an infirmary. The mystery deepened.

Captain Weston was in a room by himself. He was propped up in bed.

"Oh but you're looking a whole lot better," Mungo said. It was an honest observation. Although Mr Weston still looked very unwell he was better than the last time Mungo saw him. "I hope you are feeling the good of your rest."

"Thank you very much, Mr Shaw. I'll be mended soon enough." His words were punctuated by a dreadful rattle in his chest.

"I'm sure you will be fine," said Mungo. "All the same, the surgeon tells me you'll be laid up for a while, maybe three months; he says you've cracked four ribs.   I've arranged for you to be carried back to Whitehaven as soon as you're fit to travel. Mr Quillan has all the details in hand."

This news did not bring any sign of comfort or even relief from Weston.   Mungo turned to the boy who had escorted him.

"Maybe you could wait outside. The captain and I have things to discuss."

The boy went, but with an ill grace. No sooner had he gone than he reappeared by the window; no doubt intent on eaves-dropping their conversation.

"Be sure to tell Mr Murray that this affair was none of my doing. I'll be back at my post as soon as I'm able," protested Mr Weston.

"Don't you worry on that score, sir; he'll only hear good reports from me." He gave the captain news of the ship and her company but he did not mention Christian's cargo. Sick though he was, the captain started to give Mungo instructions on the course he should take back to Ayr. After a few minutes his energy seemed to flag. His condition and the hovering listener persuaded Mungo to conclude the conversation.

"You'll need a sleep now," said Mungo, rising to leave, but he was still concerned that something was not right and he was no nearer to finding out what it was about Mr Weston that so disturbed the Manxmen.

* * *

Mungo was glad to be back at sea though the responsibility of captaincy began to weigh heavily on his young shoulders. Before sailing he had a lengthy discussion with Alf on the best passage to the landing area. Surprisingly, it had turned into a rather heated argument. Mungo favoured a westerly tack all the way back to the Irish coast followed by a nor-easterly run along the main trade route towards the Solway ports. Alf was insistent that the more direct route due north then northeast from Peel carried less risk. Mungo stuck to his original idea. Although it more than doubled the distance they would have to run, he reckoned the *Heron* would attract less attention if she appeared inbound from Ireland rather than the Isle of Man. Alf took the huff at the rejection of his advice.

"We're about a mile off Ardglass now, so make ready to bring her about," Mungo ordered the helmsman. "Steering north of east should give us a good breeze on the starboard quarter all the way to Burrow Point."

With the freshening breeze the *Heron* made swift progress on her new course. After an hour Mungo fixed the ship's position and he began to worry that they might arrive at their landing place hours early. While Mungo was recalculating their arrival time Alf, who had gone down aft to fix a canvas dodger over the ship's name, suddenly cried out, "We've got company!" Pointing over the stern he shouted, "looks like the Navy Brig."

Mungo moved to the port side and fixed his glass on the silhouette of the ship rounding the Mull of Galloway.

"Too soon to know if he's trying to close on us," Mungo called back to Alf. "We'll hold this course for a while and see what he does. Keep her steady, helmsman," he ordered. "Call me at once if the navy man alters."

Mungo went into the deckhouse and began to study the sailing directions. They were exceedingly thorough. The charts, in particular, were completely up to date and very accurately drawn on the finest parchment. He was poring over the chart for Burrow Point when Alf came through the door.

"He's definitely following us."

"Well, what do you think?" Mungo asked. "At least we have an hour or two in hand if we need to make a diversion."

"Aye but there's nae muckle room tae manoeuvre," said Alf. "Maybe we can just heave to in Luce Bay and hope he goes by."

By Mungo's way of thinking this was no answer to anything.

"Stopped in Luce Bay with a hold full of rum and tobacco, we would be done for if the Navy decided to board us," said Mungo, thinking aloud. After a long moment's silence he continued, "Suppose we just carry on into

116

Whithorn harbour and tie up alongside. They would hardly want to board a boat like the *Heron* at a general cargo berth in a legal port. I doubt they would even follow us in."

"Aye, but then we would still hae tae beat back twa miles to windward to make oor landin," said Alf, anxious to make his point but reluctant to lose another argument.

Back up on deck the two men watched the Navy Brig, which was still tracking their course about a mile astern.

"Whithorn it is then," said Mungo, giving Alf no hint of the acute anxiety raging in his mind.

When the *Heron* entered the narrow channel leading to Whithorn harbour Mungo ordered the mainsail to be brailed up. Although they still had half a mile to run they could make enough way with just the foresail and the mizzen. Such a casual approach he hoped would impress the Navy as to their lawful intentions.

As the *Heron* was approaching the wharf Mungo looked aft. To his horror he saw that the Brig was indeed following them in. He moved, unhurriedly, across to Alf who, as acting mate, was on the wheel for entering the harbour.

"The navy man is still following. Bear away from the berth," he ordered quietly but firmly, "and steer for the channel between the island and the shore."

"But there's nae channel there, man. It's a' choked wi' sand," Alf was visibly trembling. "It's mair than ten year since ony body sailed through there."

"Keep her head away from the rocks and hold her steady," Mungo's tone was calm but insistent.

After only two minutes on this new course – disaster. There was a lurch and an ominous grating sound. They were still making some headway but it was painfully slow. The grating was intermittent but enough to warn of an imminent stranding. All the while the Navy Brig was getting closer.

Mungo could see that the water was darker closer to the island.

"Put the wheel hard to starboard," Mungo told Alf. Then he called out, "Set the main and bear out the boom to starboard! The rest of you get below and move as much cargo as you can to the starboard side."

More time passed and by now the men on the focsle of the brig were clearly visible. As the *Heron* began to list to starboard the scraping stopped and after several, seemingly interminable, minutes she began to find her way again.

Mungo reckoned, from Quillan's chart, that there should have been two feet of water under the keel at four hours before high water. He began to wonder if he had allowed enough additional draught to compensate for the weight of the contraband. Of course he only had Quillan's word for the weight of the extra cargo. In any event it had been a nerve-wracking way to learn a hard lesson.

Still, they were at last working their way clear of Whithorn and the much larger and heavier Navy Brig would not dare to follow their course. It was not even clear that the Brig could get back the way she came. As Alf had pointed out earlier, she would be battling a contrary wind in a narrow channel. With any luck, thought Mungo, she would go fast aground on the bank that the *Heron* had just scraped over.

There was much cheering by the hands as they rounded the island on the far side from the harbour. Next they tacked about a mile south before setting a new course to get back to Burrow Point. It took less than two hours on this north westerly heading to reach the landing place at Port Castle. Even with their excursion to Whithorn they had still at least half an hour to spare.

The *Heron* hove to off Port Castle as night started to fall and before long Mungo picked out the pre-arranged lantern signals and started to edge inshore. With his heart still thumping from the Whithorn incident his only thought now was to land his cargo and set course for home. Even so he remained watchful and cautious.

An old jetty once used for transporting cattle on the north side of Port Castle Bay was to be their landing place. According to Quillan's directions it would be deep enough for the *Heron* two hours either side of high water.

"Prepare the kedge anchor," Mungo ordered, "and when we get alongside no body uses names; only rank or numbers!"

"Surely there's nae need tae anchor up, Captain," Alf asked with a new note of respect in his voice.

"Always have two means of escape, Mr Mate!" Mungo smiled at his colleague.

They drifted in, stern first, on the flood tide, surging the anchor cable as they went. Mungo began to make out the smugglers by the light of their leader's lantern. They were a fearsome looking bunch; most of them were armed with pistols and cutlasses. They had about twenty ponies, more than enough for the cargo. No one on board or ashore spoke a single word.

The landing itself was uneventful and proceeded quickly. Just as the *Heron's* crew had just lashed up the last six casks for swinging ashore, the sound of gunfire ripped through the eerie silence. It seemed to come from the high ground above the bay. Mungo immediately reckoned that the excisemen likely had a watch keeper on Burrow Point and picked them up on their new approach which would have looked as if they had come from Man. It was also possible that the Navy men could have put a landing party ashore. It was only three miles from Whithorn to Port Castle overland. Mungo's men crouched behind the deck cargo while some of the smugglers moved their ponies behind the nearby rocks, but their leader and two others with ponies stood fast.

"They're a fair way off, captain," the leader called out. "Plenty of time to get these last few casks off."

"Nae bother," replied Alf who was working the derrick.

"Six and seven prepare to heave in the kedge anchor!" Mungo now seemed much less relaxed about the situation than Alf.

There were only two casks left on board when suddenly a horseman brandishing a pistol emerged from the gloom, riding towards the ship at full tilt.

"Push these last two over the side," Mungo ordered, "It's time we were out of here."

Alf swung the casks over the side and cut the rope. They sank like stones. Mungo was too preoccupied with getting away from the shore to concern himself with the buoyancy of contraband. Still, the oddity of it stuck in his mind.

"Heave away on the kedge and back the foresail."

As soon as the wind filled the foresail the bows moved quickly away from the wharf but the same action moved the stern closer in.

The horseman, oblivious to any danger, seized his opportunity. He jumped down from his mount and leapt for the stern of the *Heron*. He managed to grab the quarter rail and started to hoist himself up to get on board. Just then the breeze filled the mizzen, blowing it outboard with some force. The boom hit the horseman full in the face and propelled him backwards into the inky water. Mungo cast a nervous backward glance around the stern but there was no sign of the horseman.

"Hoist the main," Mungo roared as the sound of gunfire came closer.

The mainsail took the wind so quickly that the ship overran its anchor.

"Cut the cable and crack on more canvas!"

The men on deck hacked away the cable and heaved with all their remaining strength to set a topsail and the second jib.

Soon the *Heron* was close-hauled, all canvas spread and homeward bound Mungo was too relieved to give much thought to the fate of the unfortunate horseman.

Chapter Sixteen

Simpson's Tavern was full to bursting by the time Mungo arrived. Indeed there were even a dozen souls in varied states of intoxication lying outside the doorway. Arthur Simpson was always careful to reserve the available space inside the house for those still sober enough to buy drink.

"An a'll tell ye anither thing," roared Alf from his table-top dais, "there's no a skipper on the coast could hae gotten us oot o' there."

As near as Mungo could judge Alf was regaling his excited audience with an account of how they had slipped the Navy Brig at Whithorn.

"Here's the brave captain himself," cried out Alf, when he saw Mungo elbowing his way through the crush. "A flagon for Mungo!"

The rafters of the old tavern rang to a chorus of, "Mungo! Mungo!"

This reception was the tonic Mungo needed, for his meeting with Mr Murray that evening had not gone well. They had been in harbour for over a week unloading the linen they brought up from Dublin and then taking on more corn for their next trip, yet the summons to the agent's office had only come late that afternoon. Even then he had been kept waiting for more than an hour before he was called in. His instinct had been to tell Mr Murray the whole story but the master's distant manner put Mungo on his guard.

"You're a fine seaman, Mungo Shaw, and I'm grateful that you brought the *Heron* and her cargo safely home," Mr Murray said in stern measured tones, "but you took an awful long time on the voyage." He paused and seemed to be weighing his words with great care. "I know you had to put Mr Weston ashore but your version of how he came by his injuries seems far-fetched to me." Mr Murray paused again, either for effect or to await a reply. Mungo said nothing. "It's difficult to think of a reason why anyone should want to give Mr Weston such savage a beating," Mr Murray continued. His tone was strange; as if he knew the reason but sought to feign ignorance.

"I can only say what I was able to make out from his raving when he was in the fever," said Mungo. "Folk that have been cheated are very quick to anger and can be murderous when settling their scores."

Mr Murray's face was a study in scepticism. He seemed to know that Mungo's story was moonshine, perhaps because he had his own ideas or different information.

"Anyway, according to the surgeon, Mr Weston should be fit again in a couple of months so we should find out more then," Mungo said, anxious to change the subject.

"How did you come to put in at Peel, anyway?" Mr Murray persisted.

"The wind was wrong to take Mr Weston home to Whitehaven, as he wished, and he would never have made it to Ayr alive."

"How did you come to know Mr Christian?"

"I never spoke to him before that day," was Mungo's truthful reply. "It was the watch officer at Peel harbour that directed me to Mr Christian's agent when I was looking for a surgeon to attend Captain Weston."

"I'm glad Mr Christian was able to help. I know him slightly. He has business interests here, in Ayr."

Mungo was puzzled by Mr Murray's familiar and uncritical remarks about Mr Christian. If Mr Murray knew Mr Christian then he must know of Christian's business. More worryingly, he must surely have assumed that Mungo knew the business too.

The interrogation continued for another half hour with Mr Murray rehearsing and probing all the inconsistencies in Mungo's report.

"I'm still not convinced that you've told me everything that went on during your passage home. Still, with the exception of poor Weston, no harm appears to be done. You will make the next trip as Master of the *Heron*. Alf Garvie will be your mate and you can hire your own third hand or rate up one of the crew."

It was Mr Murray's usual way of closing a discussion; clear instructions with no scope for question or argument.

Mr Murray's rebuke still rankled as Mungo made his way across the crowded tavern but the deafening clamour of a hundred well-wishers reassured him completely.   Even the reek of tobacco and the stench of stale sweat and rancid ale were oddly comforting. He had to tell Alf the good news of his promotion, of course, but more urgent was the need to tone down these lurid and overly detailed reports of their recent voyage. Clearly, Alf had not understood that his handsome extra payment had come with a vow of silence.

Alf was very, very drunk. The affray had left his eyes blackened and the stippling of scars and bruises about his face gave him the look of a man with plague.   Grasping Mungo's wrist, he held it aloft to renewed cheers from the crazed crowd.   The harbour billies loved a hero nearly as much as they loved strong drink. Since Mungo was the kind of hero who brought them more and cheaper drink he could do no wrong.

"For God's sake, Alf, hold yourself together, man!" Mungo spat out of the corner of his mouth. "You'll have us all in the Tolbooth. This place is full of spies from the Excise."

He should have saved his breath for Alf was completely carried away by the adulation of the crowd as they hung on his every word. He just went on ranting about the *Heron's* exploits as if reciting some fabulous legend. He never yet heard Mungo tell him of his promotion.

Mungo decided that he should not overstay his visit for no good could come of so much passion mixed with over-proof drink. His progress to the doorway was even slower than his triumphal entry; the hail of slaps on his back and grasps at his hands and arms was well meant but, after a while, it became quite painful. Then he spied Hughie Maclure just ahead of him. Hughie was well known for his open happy face but that night you could have seen his smile in the next county.

"Stay here ony longer and they'll mak you the Provost," Hughie chuckled, holding his friend's hand in both of his.

"Push on for the door," Hughie said. "I hae tae talk some business wi you. You can hardly hear yoursel think in this rammy."

After what seemed a long age and a hundred greetings the two friends finally fell out on to the roadway in front of the tavern.

"It's never easy to join in the revelries when everybody else is a half cask ahead of you," Mungo sighed to Hughie. "I suppose Alf was telling the company that we ran some rum and tobacco on this trip?"

"Ye widnae ken whit Alf was talking aboot in there," Hughie laughed. "But that wis some story about your skipper gettin' a kickin' fae they Irish brigands."

Mungo was not keen to dwell on the matter of Henry Weston's beating, for he felt it would do him no credit if the story of Declan ever came out.

"What was it you wanted to talk about, anyway?" he asked Hughie.

"The McCullochs telt us they hae patched up their differences wi their supplier in the Isle o'Man" Hughie said. "Sandy wiz wunnerin if ye could pick up their cargo on your next trip south."

"I'm sure that would be possible but only for transfer at sea," Mungo said. "I think I've had enough of landings for a while."

Hughie gave him all the details of the consignment and where to meet the *Venus* for the transfer. They even worked out the timings and the signals. For the first time Mungo really felt his power as a shipmaster. He thought it suited him very well.

With their business settled the two made their way back towards the harbour. As they walked they shared gossip about their mutual friends and what was going on in the village.

"How are things working out now your father's back aboard?" Mungo asked.

"It can be a bit of a struggle at times. Ye ken the ol' man; if the weather's poor or the fishin's bad he's like a bear wi a burnt erse." Hughie laughed, "but we hae some good news; Sandy's tae get his new boat in aboot a month. He's bocht it fae a heilan man. Its ca'd the *Glory*."

"That's great news! Will you be going to the new boat, or staying on with your father?" Mungo asked.

"It's no settled yet. Faither'll mak a decision when the sale's final."

Mindful of his awkward relationship with Mr Murray, Mungo said, "Tell Sandy to keep me in mind if he needs a mate for the *Glory*." Then he had an idea. "How would you like to come on the *Heron's* next trip; just to keep me right?" Mungo smiled at his friend. He needed to find a third hand.

"That wid be grand. Sandy's aye sayin' I need mair experience," Hughie replied with evident delight.

"Well you square it with Sandy and your father. I'm hoping to sail on Monday."

* * *

Mungo rose early the next morning, with a clear head. A quick look into the crew's quarters in the fore-end confirmed that Alf was not aboard. At best he had taken up with one of the harbour dames. The worst did not bear thinking about. Still, Mungo could not wait for him to appear; it was Sunday and his sacred duty was to accompany his mother to the Kirk.

"Well stranger – we're surely honoured to see you," said Jean mocking Mungo's prolonged absence. It had been the best part of two months since he was last at the Shaw. Despite her pretended coolness she could not resist her instinct to welcome him like the prodigal son.

"I'll make us some eggs and bread and maybe some tea if you would like it," she beamed at Mungo, "then you can tell me all about your travels."

"I would like that fine and maybe some of your best cheese to go with it."

With any luck, he thought, the cooking and eating would use all the time and he could avoid the adventure story – for a while anyway. On his way to the Shaw he had rehearsed a version of events in his mind. It would be best to tell Jean at least part of the story if only to forestall the excesses of the gossip mill. There was no saying what hares would be set running by Alf's lengthy saga at Simpson's. Mungo plunged straight in.

"I'm captain of the *Heron* now; well for a couple of months any way," he said in deliberately flat tones.

Jean stood agape. Then she exclaimed "What did you say?" though she had heard and understood every single syllable.

Mr Weston fell among thieves in Dublin and was badly beaten.   We took him to a surgeon on the Isle of Man who said he'd be unfit for sea for at least three months."

Jean was at the news of this dramatic happening. She briefly acknowledged her delight at Mungo's new position but her sympathy for Mr Weston was genuine so no scope was left for any other discussion of the voyage. That suited Mungo very well.

In all the circumstances the church service that day was rather ironic; a lengthy sermon from Reverend McLintock about the evils of smuggling. The stool of repentance was full to overflowing with miscreants who had profaned the Sabbath. At least two of the faces were the same ones that had adorned Simpson's doorway the night before.

Many of Mungo's more respectable friends were milling around the churchyard after the service. Mr Scott was at his mother's side. Mungo had become accustomed to their friendship. He liked to know that there was a man about the Shaw when he was away and any way he had become quite friendly with Mr Scott. The Murrays were there and he was delighted to have such a warm greeting from Margaret who seemed well up to date with his new status.

"Do I have to call you captain now or will you still answer to Mungo?" she teased with a playful smile.

Before Mungo could reply the Reverend McLintock intruded on their conversation.

"It is a pleasure to see you at divine service," the minister said to Mungo. "I hear we have to congratulate you; Mr Murray has told me your good news."

Just then Murray himself approached and steered Mungo off to one side.

"I've just heard word that your mate Alf Garvie is in the Tolbooth," he told Mungo in a fierce whisper. "A gang of them, mad with the drink, stoned Mr Gordon's house, you know, the Inspector of Customs. They smashed all his window glass and put the whole family in fear and alarm."

"That's very bad news sir. I'll attend to it as soon as I get back to the ship."

"You'll attend to it now Mr Shaw! You have to get him out and sail in the morning before the Sheriff gets his hands on him."

Mungo quickly took leave of his mother with some cursory remarks about the burdens of command. He also gave a polite bow to Margaret and her mother. Then he was gone.

At the Tolbooth, like everywhere else, nothing much happened on Sundays. Alf and four of his fellow revellers lay like burst sacks of corn on the putrid pile of straw that passed for bedding in their shared cell. Mungo had no success in his attempts to persuade the jailer to release his man. Pleas that, as a seaman, he should be released into the charge of his captain got nowhere; he must bide and be brought before the Sheriff the following day, the jailer insisted. Even the sight of five shining shilling pieces failed to excite the jailer's attention. The offer of a further two shillings for Gordon's windows was treated with the same disdain.

Losing the master's mate was not the best start to his command. Mr Murray would be white with rage when he found out that Alf was still in jail. It was not just a matter of getting Alf away from the sheriff; Mungo would have to make his escape from Mr Murray's wrath. At least he would have Hughie with him so sailing the ship would be no hardship. But Alf's loose tongue was the real worry.

Chapter Seventeen

The run up the Irish Sea from the Isle of Man was painfully slow going. The wind – what there was of it – was dead astern and the long lazy swell gave the ship a sickly feel. Every seventh or eighth wave lifted the stern clear of the water making it difficult to steer with any accuracy. Mungo's mind was moving much faster than the ship but making less progress and in no particular direction. He still could not come to terms with the death of Captain Weston.

Mr Quirk the surgeon had been very precise.

"His shortness of breath I took to be pain from the bruising and the cracked ribs. It often happens, though, that the ribs are actually fractured and the lung is impaled." He told Mungo this as if addressing one of his students. "Captain West was a strong man so he was able to contain the symptoms longer than most. After a week he started bringing up blood and his breathing difficulties became more acute. He went down very quickly after that."

The medical explanation was satisfactory but somehow unsatisfying. After loading the MacCulloch's cargo he went to see Mr Quillan. The administrative arrangements were quickly dealt with but to Quillan's annoyance Mungo stayed on at the warehouse. He wanted to know when the body was taken back to Whitehaven. What were the funeral arrangements? Had Quillan met the next of kin and what recompense was offered to the dependents? He knew that Mr Murray would want to know these details but Mungo had to know for himself. Less precise matters, instinctive feelings really, continued to gnaw at Mungo's mind. Old Joshua's horrified reaction when Mungo had mentioned Weston's name had never been explained. That uneasy feeling he had when he last saw the captain alive at the little infirmary house. It was as if no one wanted him to see Weston again.

Quillan's reaction only deepened the mystery. He was not usually an excitable man but that day he hardly seemed to listen to Mungo.

"Never you mind about the dead!" was his stock answer to all Mungo's questions. "That Scotch duke will be the ruination of Mr Christian. Think about putting bread in the mouths of living, young sir. When our enterprise here collapses there'll be poverty and starvation all around."

According to Quillan, Christian was in London to see what could be done to stop the Duke of Atholl selling out his taxation rights on the Isle of Man.

"There will be a ruinous tax on everything that moves in or out of Man if the duke sells out to the English."

Up to that moment Mungo had no idea who the Duke of Atholl was let alone that he owned the Isle of Man with absolute power over the Island's customs and excise. It was all very interesting and no doubt troubling and perplexing to the Manx and their freetrading merchants but Mungo's mind kept coming back to the demise of Captain Weston. Could more have been done to save him? Was he just left to die? Was there skulduggery? His questions must have been more irritating than he thought because Quillan, in some exasperation, finally snapped.

"There's things about Henry Weston that's best unsaid. Better you turn your mind to saving yourself. There's trouble coming all around young, sir." With that he marched off leaving Mungo to his thoughts.

He was full of remorse. He should have made more of an effort to befriend Captain Weston. Despite his suspicions he still could not get it out of his mind that Weston's beating was meant for him. At the least he should have refused Mr Christian's assignment and stayed on at Peel to see Weston safely back to Whitehaven.

"So whit will ye dae when we get tae Ayr?" he heard Hughie say.

"What do you mean?" he replied, distractedly.

"Ah kent ye wisnae listening," said Hughie, "ye've no heard a word ah've said in the last half oor."

"I'm sorry. My mind was elsewhere."

"Ah ken that fine bit ye'll hae tae gie it some thocht. If the pier's crawlin wi constables when we get in ye'll need some kind o' plan tae get yersel clear."

Hughie was on the wheel. He had been recounting, in great detail, the news he had picked up on a tour of the inns at Peel the night before. Mungo scarcely heard a word.

"In the name o' God, Mungo, Alf telt maist o'the story that nicht in Simpsons. A bit o' persuasion in the cells and sheriff's men wid surely hae gotten the hale story out o' him."

"I can see it looks bad but the court never seems to bother too much with smugglers," Mungo said, trying to calm Hughie's anxiety. "The worst that can happen is Alf will get thirty days in the Tolbooth and Murray will put me ashore."

"It's no the smugglin, Mungo. Ah heard it said half a dozen times in Peel that the exciseman that got knocked ower yer stern is deid. When he was washed up a week later they say his face was battered past recognising. The Sheriff o' the Stewartry has already sworn oot a warrant for the arrest of his murderer."

"They'll never get Alf for murder," Mungo interrupted, though the certainty had gone from his voice.

"It's no Alf I wiz thinking aboot," said Hughie. "The story goin roon is that the captain o' the smuggling ship smashed the lad's heid wi a bearing-out spar."

As the gravity of his position began to dawn on him, Mungo went very quiet. On top of his anxiety and sadness about the demise of Mr Weston, Hughie's tales were almost too much to cope with. He walked away to the stern of the ship and stood there staring out towards the Irish coast but seeing nothing. Even if he was named for the murder surely he would find a way of getting off. Mr Christian would use his influence, wouldn't he? Mr Murray was also a man of some standing. How could he allow such an accusation to fall on one of his captains? That was the rub, though. Mungo was the captain of his ship, no matter that his position was only temporary. He was responsible for everything that happened on board.

Of course the exciseman had met his end by pure mischance. No one could be responsible for a mizzen boom thrust outboard on a gust of wind. Yet that was no defence either. Before he could claim accidental death he would have to admit he was at Port Castle that night.

Mungo's thoughts then turned away from himself and towards those who knew, trusted and indeed loved him. Mr Murray would be angry but would calculate his own advantage and then apply his considerable mind and personality to seek a satisfactory outcome. Mungo prayed that Mr Murray's interest matched his own. The fishermen would stand by him. It was their way. His poor dear mother, though, would be shocked beyond consoling.

It took a sudden change in the weather to rouse Mungo from this bout of self-obsession. A sudden freshening of the wind and a heavy shower of rain heralded the kind of storm that often comes from nowhere at that time of year. Mungo was angry with himself for not reading the wind with his usual sharpness.

Running before a freshening wind was always a concern. Mr Weston's re-designed rig gave the *Heron* greater speed but less stability. There was a danger that some vital rigging line would part under the sheer weight of canvas the old ship now carried.

In an instant he was back at Hughie's shoulder issuing orders to shorten sail and making small adjustments to the course to offset the worst of the blow. As with most summer storms the wind abated after a couple of hours and the *Heron* was back on her course and sailing with a fresh breeze on her port quarter.

The charge of nervous energy generated by managing this minor crisis set his mind racing again. He was now fully focused on dealing his own predicament. The dark thoughts and the self pity were gone. A plan was taking shape.

For the next three hours the *Heron* ploughed on towards Ailsa Craig. With another hour before the transfer Mungo ordered the hands to an early supper.

"Hughie you'll have to take the derrick for swinging the cargo over. I'll put Peter on the wheel. He deserves the chance," Mungo said.

"Maybe better with you on the wheel; we could easy get another squall."

"As long as you take her alongside the *Venus,* Peter can hold her for the transfer. Your Sandy will know if word of the Port Castle business has reached Ayr," Mungo said to his friend. "If it's looking bad I'll stay on the *Venus* and you can take the *Heron* back to Ayr."

"Whit can ah tell the crew if you stop on board the *Venus*?"

"I'm thinking I might hurt myself during the transfer and I'll be unfit to return," Mungo replied with a resigned kind of grin.

The *Heron* was first to arrive at the appointed position. Mungo became agitated and began to wonder if something had gone astray with the well worked plans he had agreed with Hughie. After a two hour wait and increasing concern, *Venus* approached at speed from the windward side of the Craig. With Hughie steering the *Heron* and his brother Sandy at the helm of the *Venus* the laying alongside went as smooth as silk. Hughie then passed the helm to Peter and took up his post at the derrick. The transfer began without delay and the first 'cargo' across was Mungo. Old Rab made to help him over the rail but before he could reach him Mungo had crashed into the gunnel and staggered over to Sandy, holding his shoulder.

"Hiv ye been at the casks in the hold, Mungo," said Sandy steadying him up. "If ye've no had a dram maybe you should be takin yin. The sheriff has a hale company o' dragoons is waitin' fur you at Ayr harbour."

Sandy never took his eye off the course and the progress of the transfer but from the corner of his mouth told Mungo the whole depressing tale. It was as bad as it could be. Somebody, on that night ten days ago in Simpsons, had heard Alf's tale and carried it to Kirkudbright where the Chief of Excise had paid him well for his trouble. The Ayr Chief, Mr Gordon, was determined to avenge the attack on his home, and was raging mad when he heard Mungo had tried to bribe Alf out of the Tolbooth. Between facts, gossip and a fair few downright lies Mungo's story was rapidly becoming a legend. The excise officers all around the coast from Ayr to Kirkudbright carried their 'evidence' to the Sheriff who laid charges for the murder of their man. So it was that Mungo's name appeared on the Sheriff's warrant.

As the *Heron* continued on her way to Ayr, Mungo watched from the deck of the *Venus*. He felt pangs of guilt at abandoning his command but anger too about the terrible unfairness of the unjust accusation that hung over him. It was an emotional parting for he was now standing on the very deck where his seafaring career had begun. During the past three years much had happened. It seemed like a whole lifetime and yet here he was, back at the beginning and scared to death about how matters might develop. There was only one penalty for murder.

"It'll be ower risky to put you ashore wi' the cargo at Croy. The MacCullochs are fine lads but some o' their men would cut your throat for tuppence," said Sandy, breaking into Mungo's reverie. "We'll tak ye into Dunure after the landing."

Mungo took up his old place at the derrick for swinging out the cargo. There was a pale moon but nowhere near enough light for him to be recognised by any of MacCulloch's men in the skiffs taking off the casks at Croy.

He seemed to think more clearly when he was busy and he turned his mind to what he would do when he got ashore. After his work was done he went and stood in the stern. "Sandy," he said, "when are you due to pick up your new boat from Tarbert?"

"A fortnight come Friday. Are you looking for a berth wi' me?" Sandy chuckled.

"Well no exactly but it would be fine if you could take me to Argyll. I have relations there. Maybe I can lie low with them, for a while."

"Aye that might be a good plan but we cannae put you ashore in Tarbert. I expect Tommy Kirkwood will be there for the herring. He would nae miss the chance to get even for yon time at Greenock," Sandy said. "Maybe somewhere up the coast would be better? There's a place called Port Ann. It's quiet enough there and there's a wee stone pier. I plan to cross overnight on the Thursday so I can put you ashore at first light on Friday fortnight. Will that be alright?"

"I am deeply grateful and forever in your debt. I'll be aboard if it's the last thing I do."

Now that Mungo had a date and a destination he could turn his mind to a more detailed plan.

It was near midnight by the time Sandy rested the bow of the *Venus* on the stone jetty at Dunure. Though the village was quiet as the tomb they did not tarry over their farewells. Hardly had *Venus* touched the pier than she backed off again, leaving Mungo on the harbour wall to ponder his fate.

Chapter Eighteen

News of Mungo's impeachment spread like chaff on the wind. Through the villages, into the towns and around the county, his name was on everyone's lips. The dominant opinion was that murder, any murder, demanded the ultimate penalty. Even though there was public anger at high taxes on drink and widespread disaffection with excise men, murder was still murder; an offence against God.

On the lower slopes of the Carrick Hills Mungo's mother Jean sat in her front room at the Shaw. She was inconsolable. Only prayer seemed to give her any relief.

It was in this distraught state that her good friend and neighbour, Mary Lamont, found her.

"What ails you Jeannie?" she asked, wrapping a comforting arm about Jean's quaking shoulders, "You've surely had terrible news."

Jean tried with all her might to hold herself together. Then, after a long period of silence:

"It's Mungo," she spluttered and immediately broke down again; wailing, tearing at her hair and rocking back and forth in her chair. "He never harmed a soul in all his life," she breathed almost inaudibly.

"Aye but what's happened?" Mary whispered.

"They say he killed an excise man somewhere on the Solway Coast. He's wanted for murder!" she shrieked.

"Oh that cannot be," said Mary, visibly shocked. "He's a fine God-fearing young man."

Mary held her comforting embrace closer. Jean never told Mary how she came by the news of this appalling misfortune. Every time Mary enquired she just dissolved, once more, into tears. Even in all her misery Jean knew that she could not tell anyone that Mungo had been at the Shaw during the night.

It must have been three in the morning when she woke imagining that she heard the low whistle Mungo always gave when he was coming in from the fields at the end of the day. But there it was again. She rose and went to the window but there was nobody in the yard. She waited for several minutes and was on the point of deciding it was her imagination when Mungo's face, a ghostly pale in the moonlight, appeared at the window. Quickly recovering her composure she threw open the door.

"What on earth are you doing, skulking round here like a thief in the night? You frightened the life out of me."

Mungo came into the kitchen and slumped down in a chair before the remains of the fire. Even in the flickering candlelight Jean could tell something was badly amiss. Her boy seemed deeply troubled and his slouched shoulders gave him a beaten look.

"It's as bad as bad can be," Mungo said, staring straight into his mother's eyes. "There's a warrant for my arrest – on a charge of murder."

At first Jean just stood in shocked silence then she said, "Don't be ridiculous," though she feared it was otherwise for Mungo was deadly serious.

He told her the whole story. She seemed shocked to learn he was a smuggler but swallowed hard and accepted it. But Mungo's account of the events at Port Castle Bay on that fateful evening mystified her completely. He turned his back to her, trying to improve his view through the window, lest he was pursued. It was then that the full enormity of the situation hit her and she began to sob.

"It's alright mother," he tried to console her. "It was all a terrible accident.   You'll see; these charges will come to nothing."

Mungo's reassurance had more effect than he had any right to expect. Somehow Jean composed herself.

"But you'll have to get away from here. It's the first place they'll come looking when they discover you're not on board the *Heron.*"

"Aye you're right," Mungo replied, though he was so weary he could have fallen asleep there and then.

Jean was suddenly completely composed as she took charge of getting him provisions, clothes, a knife, a tinderbox and other essentials he would need for living rough.

Mungo went outside and took his money chest from the thatch. He emptied the chest on to the kitchen table and surprised himself by how much he had saved over the years. He took what he thought he would need and asked his mother to look after the rest. In the half light she could not see exactly how much was there but she knew it was a considerable sum.

"Where will you go?" Jean asked.

"I'll have to hide out for a week or two, and then the Maclures have agreed to take me to Argyll. I hope our relations over there will harbour me till I can work out a way of clearing my name."

Jean was thrown off balance by this announcement. It was a long time since she last discussed her late husband's people with Mungo. It was even longer since she had been in touch with them. After all these years it was still best to keep the Jacobite past well hidden. Anyway, after some thought, she agreed it was a good plan.

"I'm sure they'll make you very welcome," she said with a watery smile. "Tell me when you're landing and where. I'll send word to let them know."

"Better that you get uncle Davie or someone else to send the letter. I'm sure the sheriff's officers will be watching for any sign you might know where I am."

They were both being so methodical and matter-of-fact that Mungo felt the need to add more words of reassurance.

"It may take a while but, believe me, I'll prove my innocence."

She fussed about him for another few minutes, giving him all kinds of well-meant but needless advice. Then he was gone and the world collapsed around her.

As Mungo set off from the Shaw he could see the lights at the harbour in the distance. The fishermen would be landing their catch soon. What he wouldn't give to be back at the fishing.

* * *

Hughie Maclure had brought the *Heron* into port late the night before. As expected the dragoons were on the pier to meet them. They quickly closed off the pier where the *Heron* lay and swarmed aboard. They began by searching the crew's quarters and then they started picking their way through the bales of linen in the hold. After a while the soldiers lost interest. Their search of the vessel yielded no trace of their quarry and Hughie met their enquiries with a succession of uncomprehending questions of his own. All the same, their activity attracted quite a crowd on the quayside even at that late an hour. The soldiers were soon beset by the hostility of the crowd; redcoats were never a welcome sight around the town. After a while their captain marched them off. Then Hughie was assailed again, this time by the fishermen and the harbour billies. Everyone wanted news of Mungo. Hughie was evasive without being discouraging. He had never spoken in public before but his feelings were so obviously heartfelt that he achieved a kind of eloquence in his advocacy of Mungo's cause.

"There's nae evidence to put Mungo ony where near Port Castle that night," he told his attentive audience. "Whoever was responsible for that excise man's end it could no hae been the captain o' the *Heron*, for he wisnae there."

Hughie must have found at least a dozen ways of repeating his message - Mungo had not been at Port Castle that night. The seafaring folk listened to him and muttered their approval. Some were even moved to more direct words of support. These men needed little convincing that the loss of a customs officer hardly amounted to murder. An excise man was the worst kind of parasite so his loss merited nothing more than a few words of sympathy for his family.

Though Mungo's supporters were loud they were but a small band. The majority of the crowd shared an air of resignation and fatality. It was written on their weather-beaten faces. A man had died a violent death and someone would have to pay for it. It was just the way of things.

* * *

By daybreak Mungo was making his way along a well-hidden track on the south of the river. He was heading for Leglen wood. Five centuries before the great Scottish patriot, William Wallace, had hidden from the English Army in those woods. He kept his pursuers at bay for more than two years. Surely Mungo could manage two weeks.

Blairadam House, Mr Murray's great mansion, towered above the trees on the opposite bank of the river. Unbeknown to Mungo, Mr Murray was in the drawing room in earnest discussion with, of all people, Mr John Christian. Mungo would have been very surprised if he had seen them for he had assumed that the two were merely casual acquaintances.

"There seems to be no stopping him," Christian sighed. "The Duke is determined to take the queen's shilling or at any rate a great many of them. No less than 100,000 English pounds, is the sum I heard, if he'll give over his taxation powers to the crown."

"They're saying in the Glasgow tobacco market that he is to have the Earl of Perth's estate into the bargain; it was forfeited after the rebellion," Mr Murray explained, adding to the deepening gloom between the two men. "You can't just give up though; you must have another plan."

"Well it's hardly what you'd call a plan," grunted Christian. "I'll just have to expand the warehouses at Guernsey and Dunkirk."

"That's fine for the English trade but it'll be a long haul for the merchants at the Loans and the Solway. Are your ships suitable for such trade?"

"I'm thinking we may have to build more ships – larger and faster," Christian conceded. "I'm told you have a good going shipyard of your own, which could provide the right vessels."

"I could build them right enough but it'll take a while. Every berth is taken up with new ships for the Cunninghams' coal trade," he conceded ruefully, concerned that some valuable business might go by him.

"My first priority is to move as much stock as possible out of Man. If the English tax us on all we have I'll be ruined, and I'm not the only one," said Mr Christian. "I'm talking to a wild Ulsterman called Brackenridge who plans to turn a small island south of Kintyre into a heavily defended free port. It's called Sanda, I think. He plans to supply the Scottish trade from there. It's early days though and, in the meantime, we Manx merchants will continue to polish our offer to the duke. Maybe he'll bite yet."

"Any way it's a relief to know you'll carry on with the guinea trade," put in Mr Murray, anxious to take what solace he could from the desperate situation Christian had described. "There are a great many plantation owners hereabouts at me all the time to bring them more Negroes. Those guinea goods are what the African elders demand for their strongest young men and women."

"I'm afraid I have some bad news about that side of the business too. Captain Weston did not survive," said Mr Christian.

"Surely not; what a tragedy," said Mr Murray with reproach rather than regret in his voice. "Young Mr Shaw told me Weston was in a bad way but it was thought he would recover."

"The damage to the ribs ruptured his lung, by all accounts. It was not obvious to the surgeon at first. There was little he could have done about it, in any case. We took his remains back to Whitehaven and gave him a good send off."

"I know you would have looked after his dependents. I will also settle an appropriate sum on the family," Mr Murray promised.

"I suppose it was all for the best in a way. The poor chap was never going to be free of those rascals from the *Friendship.* When the navy recovered the ship Captain Benson claimed the mutiny was due Weston's intemperate use of the lash. We'll never know the truth of it now though," Mr Christian added solemnly.

"I've heard these stories too but I can hardly believe them. He came to me with the highest recommendation and he did not disappoint. I suppose our new ship for the Indies will not be ready for a few months so we'll have time to find a new captain. Now that Mr Shaw is out of the picture for the foreseeable future I'll need a new master for the *Heron* too," Mr Murray said. He had been reluctant to raise the subject until then for he was uncertain how much Mr Christian knew of the circumstances leading to Mungo's impeachment. "He let me down very badly, you know." Mr Murray seemed to have no inkling of Christian's involvement with Mungo's ill-fated voyage to Port Castle Bay.

"It can do your own position nothing but harm to have one of your brightest young captains arraigned for murder," Mr Christian suggested. "No saying what might come out if he stands trial. I understand a lad called Garvie is still in the Tolbooth with promise of a pardon if he testifies against Mungo. We must find a way to shut up master Garvie," asserted Mr Christian. "Otherwise we can only hope Mungo Shaw stays on the run for a very long time to come."

"He might, at that. Mungo can look after himself. He could play tig with a fox and never be caught," Mr Murray countered with a grim smile.

Chapter Nineteen

Over the next two weeks there were frequent sightings of Mungo all over the county. One day he would be seen at Troon. Later the same day he was said to be in Girvan and at the very same time several seemingly sober farmers saw him in the mart at Kilmarnock. Most of the early sightings were doubtless reported in good faith but as time went on mischief became a significant motive. The various search parties that had been set up to pursue and arrest Mungo were running from one false sighting to another. The Sheriff's men were held up to ridicule and their energies were thus diverted from the all-important task of apprehending a dangerous felon.

The sea-faring fraternity was quick to realise that these diversions could be helpful to their friend. Some of these men had reason to know that Mungo was hiding close at hand, though none knew precisely where. Accordingly it was not long before sightings were reported in Dumfries, Glasgow, and even Edinburgh. No doubt Mungo's pursuers knew they were being led a dance but the hunt had to go on. Murder was the most serious of crimes and Mungo was also a known smuggler, a pernicious activity that the king, no less, had pledged to root out; Mungo must be caught.

In his wooded sanctuary Mungo knew nothing of the huge force of men pursuing him. Of course he reasoned that some kind of hunt must be underway and he took every kind of precaution to conceal his whereabouts and cover his tracks.

He had established a strict routine. He avoided all movements during daylight hours except when absolutely necessary. He set his snares as night was falling and cleared them before daybreak. When he was lucky enough to get a rabbit he would gut and skin it where he knew the buzzards would pick the area clean within the hour. If he had no luck with the rabbits he would go to the simple fish trap he had built in the river from boulders and gravel. In the shallow lagoon behind its small dam there would usually be a few decent trout which could be had by the ages-old practice of 'guddling'. His grandfather had taught him how to tickle a fish. He had never been much good at it but after a few days practice, spurred on by an insistent appetite, flicking his breakfast from the pool became second nature.

He could not risk lighting a fire near his hideout for fear of giving himself away by the smoke. At the edge of the wood, however, there was a tinkers' camp and they kept their fires going day and night. By setting his own fire a discreet distance downwind of the tinkers' fires his smoke was mingled with theirs. Once or twice his presence had roused the camp dogs but the tinkers paid him no heed believing him to be no more than the tramp he had become.

By an hour after dawn each day he was fed, watered and safely ensconced in the beech tree that had become his home. He had built a crude platform high in the boughs where he had a good view of all approaches and his scent could not be picked up by dogs on the ground. Two small tributaries of the river ran nearby. Though they presented no obstacle to man or beast they would further confuse any tracking dogs for he always waded along them to reach his tree.

Outside of hunting, cooking, eating and sleeping he had time to think. Indeed he had too much time to think. When he considered his situation in any detail he was often thrown into bouts of dark depression. He was arrogant enough to be sure that he would evade capture but what then? What kind of future could he have? Hiding away in the Highlands had seemed a good idea when he discussed it with his mother but now he was not so sure. The Highlanders had different food and clothes from other folk in Scotland. He could not speak even a word of the Gaelic tongue. He would surely stand out. He had no notion of how he would be received by the clansmen. Worst of all he had no idea of how to earn his keep. The prospects seemed bleak.

He knew that many Highlanders had been reduced to penury since the Rebellion; would someone discover his past and sell him out to the authorities? Even the money in his belt might seem like a fortune to such desperate men.

He also thought of more immediate matters. How would he get from the Leglen Wood to the harbour to take his passage to Argyll on the *Venus*? The only way was through the town. What if the *Venus* was delayed by contrary winds or adverse tides? He would surely be caught if he had to spend time without cover at the harbour.

He tried to lighten these woes by daydreaming of happier times. From time to time he thought of Margaret Murray. Did she still have any thoughts of him? She was surely the most beautiful girl he had ever known. As he indulged in these musings he began to think how wonderful it would be to see her again. He could meet her – deliberately by accident – for he knew that she rode out around the estate most mornings. The track she followed was around a mile downstream on the opposite bank of the river. Her route was always the same; from the big house to the home farm then along the mill lade, past the old cot-house and back to the stables. The more he thought of this scheme the more determined he became to give it a try.

He decided he would way-lay her by the old cot-house the day before he was due to join the *Venus* for his passage to Argyll. He knew the scheme was fraught with danger. He would be breaking his cover with very few options for escape if he should be seen by any of his pursuers. Even so, his planned excursion did not present any new hazard for he would have to pass through the Blairadam lands to get back to the harbour anyway. Making the journey in daylight was a huge risk, though.

The idea of meeting Margaret again stirred up long dormant romantic thoughts but the scheme had practical merit too. He had not spoken to a living soul for a fortnight. Margaret would surely have news of what was happening around the town and county. The sheriff's officers would have been to Blairadam to see her father, as Mungo's employer, so she would know how the hunt was progressing. She might even be able to help him slip though the town to reach the *Venus.*

The night before his planned tryst with Margaret he sat by his fire gnawing at the carcase of a big buck rabbit and drank the last of the tea he had brought with him from the Shaw. He became really quite excited about the prospect of seeing her again. He began to fantasise that all the old feelings might be rekindled and they would run off together, to Argyll. With his head full of these happy thoughts he did not return to the tree house that night but drifted off to sleep on the mossy bank beside his fire.

About an hour before dawn he was rudely awakened by the snarling of a tinker's dog. It was a fearsome brute but Mungo had the presence of mind to throw the hound the remains of last night's dinner before taking off along the track to the ford where he could cross into the Blairadam estate.

He had barely gone a hundred yards when he heard an unnatural sound in the predawn stillness. Maybe the same distant dull rhythmic beat had roused the tinkers' dog. He stopped stock still and strained his hearing. He heard a higher note; the barely audible whinny of a horse. He could not be sure but neither could he take a chance. It was the sound of marching men and riders and it put Mungo in a state of alarm for such a band could have only one object at this pre-dawn hour.

As he turned and raced back up-stream he cursed his casual attitude to the tinkers. There was bound to be a reward for his capture and the tinkers would be eager to have a share of it. If the lone tramp they had seen near their camp was the wanted man they would want for nothing next winter. Why should the tinkers care if the wretch was hounded by the soldiers?

The urgent need for self-preservation soon took over Mungo's mind. He was almost back to the tree house when he stopped for breath. He listened intently but heard nothing. He guessed that he had simply run out of earshot and that his pursuers would still be marching remorselessly towards him. He had to think fast.

They were bound to have tracking dogs so the river was his only hope. Further upstream, near his fish trap, there was a deep bend with high cliffs on the Blairadam side. Two or three days before he had noticed that a large tree, still in full leaf, that had been washed down from the upper reaches of the river. It was lodged in some rocks at the foot of the cliff. If he could get to that tree he had an even chance.

Mungo walked deliberately to the foot of his beech tree house. He then exactly retraced his steps to the path. He listened again and he thought he heard the dull cadence of the marchers. Then he jumped from the path into the river with a single leap.

He began to wade upstream. Although the margin of the river was fairly shallow, not much above the knee, the current was deceptively strong but not too cold. It took around quarter of an hour to get to the tree but the water there was much too deep for him to wade across. By now he thought his pursuers must be getting close. He could hear the horse again. They were not more than a half hour away.

The natural flow of the river was round the bend and close in by the cliff. If he could find a place to cross upstream he could then wade back downstream and hide himself in the boughs of the wind-blown tree below the cliff.

He continued wading up the shallow side of the river for another hundred yards when another problem became evident. The first pink streaks of dawn were becoming etched in the dark grey sky. Still the improving light was a help too; he could see that the river upstream from the cliff was running in broken rapids unlike the deep dark pools further down. It was not ideal but he would have to wade across. He took up a stout staff and struck out by what he took to be the shallowest route across. The crossing was arduous and slow going. Under the water there were large boulders surrounded by deep runnels. His pursuers were very close now. He could hear the whining of the dogs and the men crashing about in the undergrowth. He reckoned they had picked up his false trail and would soon find the tree house. That would hold them up for a while.

He was nearly two thirds across when he lost his footing. In fact his leg had been struck by a free floating tree trunk maybe two feet diameter and eight feet long. Instinctively he grabbed at the trunk and found himself in mid-stream drifting back, it seemed, into the very arms of the hunting party. He could see the danger but could do nothing to avoid it. He had to hang onto the trunk or he would surely be overwhelmed by the current and drowned in the deep water.

He clung to the old tree for dear life and in no time at all he was level with the fish trap where the current swept him close under the cliff. The water was colder here and he became strangely calm. He could make out the grey shapes of the men at the water's edge about fifty yards away. In his mind he was resigned to capture for there was nothing he could do except drift on the current. Suddenly there was a cry from deep in the wood and the figures who were close turned and ran up the bank into the wood. They had found Mungo's hideout. But the man himself was drifting by them.

Chapter Twenty

"You say the Sheriff's men found Mungo?" Margaret asked her brother. "I can hardly believe that. Father said they would sooner find the Holy Grail."

The two were taking tea in the morning room at Blairadam.

"They found where he's been hiding these last weeks but of the man himself, not a trace," said Graham. They both laughed in relief as much as amusement.

"But what if he was to come here," Margaret shrieked in mock alarm, though in truth she found the thought rather exciting.

"Maybe he's here now," Graham teased, "lurking in the court yard or hiding in an outhouse."

Graham was home from Edinburgh for the summer break between law terms. It was certainly no holiday, for his father regarded all Graham's home leave as 'serving his time' on the family estate.

"Do you believe he killed that man?" Margaret asked Graham directly. "I know he's strong enough but, even when he was very angry, he never had the kind of temper to lash out at some one. He would sooner try to reason or march off in the huff."

"Well you are the one to know," said Graham, "after all you did a fair bit of wrestling with him when he was here!"

At this remark Margaret threw a cushion at her brother, narrowly missing the small table where the delicate china cups were precariously perched.

"That's enough of that talk," she snapped. "You know I'm promised in marriage to Mr Charles Wallace." How Mungo would have hated to hear that. She gazed distractedly across the lawns towards the river, wondering at the strange turn of fate that had made Charles Wallace an exciseman. Her betrothed hunting her first love; it was agonising.

"If Mungo came here would you take him in and harbour him from the law?" she asked her brother as though thinking aloud.

"In a minute," Graham replied. "He was always a trusty friend to me. If he did crack that excise man's skull, then I'm sure the rascal deserved it."

Margaret sighed with relief and pleasure at her brother's loyalty but fretted about her own dilemma. She understood Charles's duty but no one would ever know of the smouldering affection she still felt for Mungo.

The two sat in silence for a while. Between them was an unspoken communion, praying for Mungo's preservation and redemption.

Graham broke the silence at last and rose from his chair.

"I only wish he was here now. I have to organise a cargo of coal for the *Swan.* The overseer's sick and I hardly know where to start. It's the kind of thing Mungo could do with his eyes closed," he sighed. "At least father won't be there – watching my every move!"

"When are father and mother due back?" Margaret asked Graham.

"Who can say?" Graham shrugged. "They always enjoy their visits to the capital. He did say he would try to call on Lord Dundas, though."

"Oh," said Margaret. "Is he checking on our golden boy's legal studies?"

"I was worried about that," said Graham, "but he said he wants to discuss the charges against Mungo with the judge."

"That's surely very strange. Two weeks ago he had not a good word to say for Mungo. Now he's pleading his case with the highest judge in the land?"

"I don't think there'll be much pleading. I warned him that his lordship does not take kindly to people trying to influence the justices. I am sure the great man will simply advise him to retain a good advocate," Graham said in a rather formal tone. "Anyway, father likes Mungo. He was most impressed with all the work he did on the estate papers. He was very angry after hearing about all the shenanigans that led to Mr Weston's death. Even so, I'm sure he'll do his best for Mungo in his hour of need."

As Graham turned to leave the room Margaret gave him a wistful smile and then slumped back in her chair and returned to her pensive survey of the rolling lawns and the river margin.

* * *

Mungo was sitting under a big hawthorn bush beside the track that ran from Blairadam Mill to the old cot house. Missing Margaret had compounded his misery for he was soaked to the skin, dog tired, bruised and bloody. The cold water had deadened the pain of his collisions with the sharp boulders in the river but as the morning sun began to warm him so his wounds began to throb and sting.

He was still bemoaning his misfortune when a little cock chaffinch settled on the branch of the hawthorn a few feet from his face. The bird began to sing with great gusto and for some reason Mungo was reminded of his grandfather. The chaffinch was Da's favourite bird but there was more than that to Mungo's reminiscence. Chip! Chip! Chip! Shooee! Shooee! sang the little bird from his blue grey beak. His little pink cheeks were so puffed up they seemed almost to double the size of his head. The bird's song had something of Da's voice in it. He remembered the stern rebukes when he felt too tired to rise on winter's mornings. 'Up, up, up!' the old man used to say. The chaffinch seemed to be making a similar call but in a gentler tone. He found this recital cheering and quite amusing, so much so that he laughed aloud causing his little companion to take wing.

The chaffinch's song did not inspire Mungo to any immediate burst of energy but it did remind him that he was still a free man. He was lost in those thoughts when he fell asleep.

* * *

For the second time that day he was roused from his sleep by distant hoof beats. His first instinct was to run but he was not sure of his cover. He knew that sudden movement could easily give him away if dogs were afoot or if the rider was being especially vigilant. He stayed where he was. He could see the track through the branches of the bush but anyone mounted on a horse would be too high to see him.

After a minute or two a lone rider hove into view. It was Graham Murray. Mungo's heart began to race. With Graham's help all his immediate problems could be solved. Yet, could he take the chance of accosting his friend? Was it fair to involve Graham in his troubles? After all young master Murray was apprenticed to the Lord President himself. In any case the elder Murray would have given his family strict instructions about any future relations with Mungo. Thinking back to his last meeting with Mr Murray Mungo thought these instructions were unlikely to be cordial.

Maybe it was the chaffinch's influence but all these doubts fled from his mind just as the horseman drew level with his hiding place.

"Graham, it's Mungo," he called out. "If you want nothing to do with me ride on but I could really do with some help."

"Where the devil are you?" said Graham, turning his mount towards the sound of his friend's voice. "Are you all right?"

"I'm under the thorn bush twenty yards in front of you," Mungo replied with a nervous chuckle. He was so happy to see Graham that he dashed out from under the bush leaving much of what remained of his breeches on the thorns.

153

"Have you been fighting a war?" Graham laughed, surveying his friend's dishevelled state.

"I suppose you could say that but there's too much to tell," Mungo replied. "I just need somewhere to lie up till tomorrow. I'll be no trouble."

"I can't stop now I'm on my way to the mine to arrange a load of coal for your old ship. I'll come back in a couple of hours with dry clothes and some food," Graham said. "For the time being you'll be able to shelter in the old cot house." They both knew instinctively that it would be too risky to spend time together in the open so they went their separate ways without ceremony.

As Mungo approached the cot house he had an odd feeling that all was not well. The door gave way with the merest nudge from his shoulder but once inside his worries multiplied. There were signs that someone had been living there, recently. The ash in the fire place was stone cold yet the straw palliasse and the horse blanket in the bed recess were quite clean and neatly arranged. Clearly he could not stay in the house. The risk was too great that the squatter would return and discover him. He replaced the door as he had found it and withdrew to a safe distance and crawled into the undergrowth.

After a short while he found a vantage point that overlooked the track as well as the approach to the cot house. This time he did not sleep but remained extra vigilant. The state of the old house troubled him. It was much too tidy to be used by a tramp or tinkers.

After an hour or so his curiosity was satisfied – in part. Two men appeared from nowhere, approached the cot house door and went in. They were not rough sleepers, being tolerably well turned out. They were not estate workers, either, or they would have come along the track. Their approach had been silent and even inside the house they were very quiet. Mungo did not get much of a look at them, for the whole encounter took only a few seconds, but he thought that one had a military look about him.

As he waited and watched he judged that about half an hour went by. Graham might return at any moment. There was nothing for it. He would have to backtrack in the direction from which Graham would return so that he could warn him. He also had to keep well away from the track to get any worthwhile cover. As he inched his way through the scrub he had a terrible thought. These might be sheriff's men posted on the estate in case Mungo returned there. Did Mr Murray know they were there? Did Graham?

He had no time to speculate on his theories about the two men for almost at once he heard the sound of a horse on the track. It was Graham all right and he had what looked like a bed roll and two large saddle bags on his mount. Rather than make a sound Mungo stood up in the heath and waved to Graham. Fortunately Graham saw him and gathered that something was amiss. He reined in his horse and waited till Mungo reached him.

Speaking in hushed tones he reported the strange events at the cot house. Graham seemed genuinely amazed. His reaction greatly heartened Mungo, who had begun to wonder if some elaborate trap was being laid for him.

"We can't confront these strangers now," said Graham. "I have to think of another place for you to hide." He turned his horse away from the direction of the cot house and went towards the Mill. "I know," he said, "you can lie up in the stackyard steading. No one goes there at this time of year."

After a quarter hour walk they reached the steading and Graham rode his horse straight in through the wide doors. Soon the two friends were enjoying a hearty meal of game pies and fresh milk along with some fine cheese and oatcakes.

"That's your mother's cheese," Graham said. "Cook buys it every Saturday at the butter market."

Poor Mungo found this information so moving that he had to stifle a tear and it took him quite a while before he could speak. When he did find his tongue the whole story tumbled out in every small detail.

"So what is your plan now?" Graham asked when Mungo paused.

"I have to catch a ship at Ayr no later than four o'clock tomorrow afternoon." Mungo said. "It's better that you don't know where I'm bound. You'll hear from me soon enough, though. I'm determined to prove my innocence."

They discussed back and forward the best way of getting Mungo to the harbour. Getting over the old Brig and through the town would be the worst of it. Suddenly Graham clapped his hands.

"You'll come with me at first light tomorrow morning with a wagon load of coal for the *Swan.* No one will think it odd because every wagon has to carry a second man to barrow the coal into the ship."

"It's a good plan but what if I'm recognised by any of the *Swan's* crew?"

"That's not a difficulty," Graham reassured him. "Brady and his crew all transferred to the *Heron* the day after you – um – left. The *Swan* is now crewed by lads from the Isle of Man."

It was now Graham's turn to do the talking. He told Mungo all about the hunt for him including an account of the false trails his friends had left for the Sheriff's Officers.

"I can't understand how they fell for it. Not more than a hundred people in all Ayrshire know you to look at yet half the county was claiming to have seen you in every part of Scotland."

Mungo pondered this thought, stroking the unaccustomed growth of hair on his face. Now clad in Mr Murray's over-large breeches even his mother might walk by him in the High Street. He was now quite sure that Graham's plan would work.

The two friends chatted on for another half hour. Mungo was particularly cheered to hear that Margaret had been anxious for his safety but quietly horrified at the news she was back with Wallace. This chilling information had tumbled out when Graham had speculated on his sisters divided loyalties. Mungo's silent rage was taken to be fatigue by Graham.

All too soon Graham had to return to his duties at the mine. When he was gone Mungo removed himself from the steading along with the clothes and provisions that Graham had brought. He took them to the top of a corn stack.. He just could not be too careful.

PART THREE

Treasury House
Parliament Square
Edinburgh
14th day of June 1766

Sir

I write on the vexed question of Mungo Shaw.

It is vital that this brigand is brought to justice without further delay. I do not breach any confidence when I tell you that the highest in the land attach the greatest priority to the capture of Shaw.

The evil of smuggling must be eradicated and those involved in this vile practice must face the full majesty of the law. It should come as no surprise that those who engage in the running of contraband are desperate men who will stop at nothing, including murder.

In order that this matter may be expedited I am authorised to offer the sum of one thousand pounds Scots for the apprehension and conviction of Mungo Shaw. Accordingly I would be obliged if you will arrange to have this matter advertised in whatever journals you deem apt and that you will publish handbills setting out this offer for distribution in all public places.

I believe that criminals of his type have little loyalty to one another and I am confident that this reward will bring us a rapid outcome.

I am grateful for the diligent way you have pursued this matter to date and I trust you will continue your valiant efforts and that the money offered will prove decisive.

I have the honour to be, Sir
Craigie

Chairman of the Board of Excise
And
First Baron of Treasury

James Hunter esq
Sheriff of Ayr

Chapter Twenty One

The shore at Port Ann was indistinct through the constant drizzle of rain. Mungo's sight was further obscured by the residual coal dust that was the legacy of Graham's bold plan to get him into Ayr Harbour twenty four hours before. It had not occurred to him when the plan was being hatched that he would have to wheel all thirty barrow loads of coal up the steep gang plank and into the hold of the *Swan.* There had not been much sleep on the crossing for with the extra hands needed to sail the new boat bunk space was in short supply. Still, these discomforts were a small price to pay for the sanctuary of the Lachlan Clan Lands.

"This is as far as we go," said Sandy as he edged the *Venus* in shore towards the small stone jetty. "I'm sure we'll see you again before long. You've got plenty of important people to speak up for you. The authorities will soon see sense."

"Thank you for everything and most of all for your belief in me," he said shaking Sandy's big hand. "I'll soon and put this terrible business behind me. If you can find me a berth I'll be back for the herring next summer."

"You'll be back with us before the New Year. You wait and see," Sandy laughed.

Mungo did have some very influential acquaintances, but would they ever lift a hand to help him? Graham's news that Mr Murray was to raise his case in Edinburgh was very hopeful but what about Mr Scott the factor and the laird for that matter? Most of all Mungo wondered about Mr Christian. If anyone could get him off then John Christian's elegant manners and low cunning must be his best hope.

"I'll tell your mother we put you ashore safe and well," Hughie said as he helped him over the bow. "I don't know how the post is round here but if you need anything send a letter to me care of McCulloch's shop; they'll know how to get it to me." Hughie squeezed Mungo's shoulder. "The very best of good fortune to you, old friend."

"May good fortune go with you too – you'll make a grand skipper before long."

As Mungo walked up the jetty he looked back at the boat receding into the mist. Wet and miserable as the day was, it gave him a warm feeling to think on what good friends he had in the Maclures.

Sandy had brought him a fair distance north of Tarbert so Kilmichael was only a dozen miles to the northwest. About a hundred yards above the beach he reached a rough track. He knew he must turn right from the shore but looking in that direction he saw two tracks. He worried that the unfamiliar surroundings and the half light of the dawn sky might have upset his sense of direction so he stood for a while pondering which road to take when he heard a soft voice coming from behind him.

"Are you Mungo Shaw?"

Mungo spun round to see a young girl wrapped up in a heavy shawl against the weather.

"Supposing I am?" rasped Mungo, confronting the girl with an aggressive stance.

"Your mother sent word that you would be landing this morning. I am to bring you to my father's house," she smiled. "My name is Catriona Stuart."

"I thought you were all called Lachlan hereabouts," said Mungo, still suspicious of this unexpected reception.

"That's quite true but my father is a Stuart of Appin. He's the Chief's Tacksman; he manages the clan lands."

"So your father's an important man in the clan, then, even though he's not a clansman?" said Mungo, sounding as knowledgeable as he could though he knew next to nothing about the clan system. He supposed that the tacksman must be like the factor at home.

"Well you could say that," she replied, still smiling.

160

Catriona led the way and after a few minutes the frostiness of their first encounter began to thaw. Mungo told her a bit about himself, but of the reason for his journey to Argyll he said not a word. He thanked her too for meeting him at such an unearthly hour in such foul weather. He was well aware that without her he could have been a long time trying to find his way.

"How far is it to Kilmichael?" he asked.

"It's half a day's walk," Catriona replied, "but we'll stop a while at our house to get you some breakfast. We should be there in an hour."

After they had been going about half an hour the weather eased and Catriona threw back her shawl. Mungo was very taken by her fair hair and big blue eyes.

"I never knew highland lasses were so good looking," he said, smiling at Catriona.

Catriona smiled back but kept her gaze firmly fixed on the road ahead.

Catriona's house was larger than the rather miserable looking croft houses they had passed on the way. It was of stone and about the same size as his own house, at the Shaw. Her mother met them at the door. She smiled at Mungo and nodded but said nothing. She had plenty to say to Catriona, though, but all in the Gaelic language. Mungo supposed she could not speak Scots.

The breakfast was simple but very welcome: porridge with cream, fried herring, bannocks and some kind of un-pressed cheese that Mungo had not seen before.

Catriona could see he was unfamiliar with the cheese.

"It's crowdie," she said, "Mother made it specially this morning."

Mungo took up a portion of the crowdie on his knife. He found it too soft and bland for his usual taste but to a hungry traveller it was more than passable.

"It's truly the best crowdie I ever tasted," he said, nodding to Mrs Stewart as he spoke. The mother seemed very pleased with his reaction, but Catriona who understood the joke just grinned and shook her head.

They set off on the next part of their journey about the middle of the morning. Mungo was now getting along famously with Catriona and he was tempted to think that his interest was being returned. He asked her a great deal about the clan and the district.

"Folk seem to be having a hard time of it in those wee farms," he said. "The bairns are none too well clad and they're surely all very thin. Yet they seem happy and content."

"It's not so strange. If the way of life is the same for everyone then the hardship seems normal and no one complains. My mother is a Lachlan," she said. "A cousin of your father's in fact. That's why I was asked to meet you." Mungo was slightly disappointed to discover that he was related to Catriona but he supposed there would be no sin in taking up with a second cousin.

* * *

By one o'clock they had stopped again at the house of another relative. Angus Lachlan was maybe ten years older than Mungo and he spoke the Scots tongue – after a fashion. He was a crofter like everyone else but he was also in a prosperous way of business as a cattle dealer and drover.

They were given a warm welcome but this time it was whisky rather than milk that slaked his thirst. It was very strong so Mungo drank slowly taking only a little at a time.

"Have you ever worked with cattle, Mungo?" Angus asked him.

"We always kept about a dozen milkers and a score or two of black cattle," he replied. "That's how my mother and father first met. Ian was my father and he and his father used to bring my grandfather highland beasts for fattening for the local market. Of course that was long before I was born."

"Your father was my uncle Ian," said Angus. "I was about eleven years old when he went away to the war."

"How many cattle do you have, yourself, Angus?" he asked.

"Well you see that would depend on the time of year," Angus replied. "I only rear about two hundred of my own but I buy in maybe ten times as many for the drove to the Crieff Tryst at the back end."

"That's an awful lot of cows! How long does the drove take? I'm thinking they'll not walk that fast."

"Ten mile a day is far enough but seven is ideal. It wouldn't do for them to be down to skin and bone by the time we got to the Tryst," he replied. "We start buying on Islay and it takes the best part of a fortnight to get them here. There's maybe another week for the Tryst at Kilmichael where we buy beasts from Kintyre and mid Argyll.   After that maybe another three or four weeks on the road before we would get to Crieff.   You never can tell though, what with poor weather, finding stances and grazing and of course there are always brigands on the road."

Mungo continued to ask questions and offer opinions about rearing cattle. It was a good way of keeping the conversation away from his own situation, but he found it interesting too. Angus clearly enjoyed his work and was, for his part, more than happy to discuss the trade in the greatest detail.

"You're surely very interested in the droving," Angus said, sensing a kindred spirit in Mungo.

"We always had beasts about the place," he said. "It's an interest that never leaves you." Then on an impulse he said to Angus, "I would like fine to come on a drove, one day."

"Oh I don't know about that; it's a very hard life on the road. Anyway it'll be another six weeks before we go to Islay to buy the first lot of beasts. Maybe something else will take your interest before then," he said, smiling at Catriona.

163

* * *

The chief of the Clan Lachlan was about the age of Mungo's late grandfather. He was a tall, rangy man. His hair had long since receded from his noble brow but his eyes were clear and sharp. His nose put Mungo in mind of a hawk's beak and together with his high cheek bones and square jaw he was the very image of the warrior chiefs Mungo remembered from drawings in his school books. Mungo and Catriona had arrived at his small castle about six o'clock. Like everyone else he had met that day the Chief was most welcoming and very hospitable.

"So you've come on a pilgrimage to your father's land. I'm afraid you may find us less prosperous than folk in Ayrshire but I hope we can make up for that with our welcome."

"Even in the few hours I have been in your land, sir, everyone has been most kind and made me feel at home."

"I was at your home once. My son Ian and I sold fifty beasts to your grandfather. We had a fine two or three days spending the luckspenny. I suppose that would have been the first time Ian met your mother," he said with a sad smile. "It's a terrible thing, war. Even though the cause was just, no good ever came of it."

They took a dram together and by now Mungo thought he had the measure of the 'uisgebah' as the chief called it. Two more mouths full, though, and he was not quite so sure. Luckily he did not have to test his drinking capacity any further for the Chief led the way through to a large barn-like room where maybe three dozen clansmen were seated at a long table. He had met four or five of them at various houses along the way. Angus the drover greeted him and sat with him at the Chief's high table.

Mungo was overwhelmed by the reception but he was struggling with the language. Still, those who spoke Scots kept him in touch with what was being said. For the most part only Gaelic was spoken but the night was full of lively talk and great goodwill towards the Chief's young guest. The sheer quantity of fish and game which loaded the table was more than a match for the fancy food at Blairadam and the copious quantities of drink – not just whisky but wine and brandy too – soon rubbed any rough edges off the quality of the cooking.

As the night wore on Mungo came to believe he could speak Gaelic and any number of other languages as well. As he listened to the clansmen's stories he was reminded of Bridget's mother and her stories of Connemara. The stories were different of course but told in the same lyrical style with plenty of raucous humour. Towards the end of the feast, allegiances were pledged, bed and board was promised, and employment was offered. He never knew a night like it and never once did he think of Port Castle or his pursuers. Though through the haze he wondered more than once where Catriona would be spending the night.

* * *

The morning after was a sorry affair. Catriona found him at eight o'clock fast asleep on a wooden settle in a corner of the chief's parlour. No harm was done though for the chief was still abed. After she had found him a bowl to wash his face and a cup of strong black tea she marched him off again to meet more relations.

They had been walking about half an hour before he regained the power of speech.

"I wonder if we should maybe wait a day or two before meeting the rest of the clan," he said, more in the nature of a plea rather than as a considered suggestion.

"Father gave me a list," she retorted. "I would not like him to think I was defying his orders," she smiled, rather enjoying the evident agony that the night's feasting was wreaking on Mungo's brain.

"Maybe we should go and meet your father," Mungo suggested, for he knew from the talk the night before that the Tacksman was away at Inverary and would not be back till later that night.

"We can do that tomorrow," she said, "but first we must find you a bed for tonight so you may be in some fit state to meet him."

Mungo fell asleep that night a contented man. Even the ache in his brain left by a night's carousing could not obscure his belief that he had now found sanctuary and his pursuers would never find him amongst the Lachlan Clan.

Chapter Twenty Two

To Mungo's relief, Catriona's father, the Tacksman, took him on as general assistant and dogsbody. Mr Stuart had asked him, outright, how long he meant to stay in Argyll when Catriona first introduced them. Although he had rehearsed all kinds of situations in his mind they related only to his reasons for being there. He had not thought much about how long he meant to stay. A year seemed about right; indeed he could think of nothing else at the time. When pressed further by Mr Stuart he explained the arrangement for him to take over the tenancy of the Shaw on his twenty-first birthday. He planned to stay in Argyll till then. Mr Stuart seemed more than satisfied by Mungo's explanation but he made it clear, just the same, that he could only keep him on for the busy period over the summer. He would have to find something more settled before the back end and in the meantime his only pay would be his board and lodgings.

Each day Mr Stuart would issue him with a list of tasks. At first he was hay-making and later on he would be expected to help with the harvest. Although he was mainly employed at the home farm he had also to help out crofters who were short handed or had fallen behind due to the weather. It was not at all like the drudgery of working with his grandfather at the Shaw. Every day, or perhaps every few days, there was a different challenge. He began to remember all the skills and knowledge he had learned from his grandfather and was surprised how quickly he slipped back into his old farming routines.

The crofters were interested in his way of working and amongst those who could speak Scots he discussed the different ways of raising beasts and crops. He told them about the light plough they had at the Shaw and how it could be worked with only a pair of horses. The Crofters listened politely enough but their disbelief was plain for they were still yoked to the old heavy wooden Scotch plough which needed eight or ten oxen. He didn't dare mention the seed drill. It had split the whole county in Ayrshire between those wedded to the broadcast method and the 'improvers,' like grandfather, who used the drill. Mungo had no wish to cause ill feeling amongst his own clansmen as he now thought of them. After all, the chief was his other grandfather.

For the most part Mungo was well received around the clan lands but here and there some of the crofters took against him. He was seen by that minority as the Tacksman's agent rather than his assistant. Where a crofter was in arrears with his rent, Mungo's arrival was treated with much suspicion. The younger men resented Mungo's privileged position. His relationship to the chief and his good living at the Tacksman's house was an irritant to those struggling to get even the barest subsistence from the unyielding soil. But other than these few malcontents, he was everywhere treated with the respect befitting his kinship with the Clan Chief.

On the days when the weather was poor and there was nothing to do out on the crofts, Mr Stuart found him small jobs maintaining the steadings at his own farm. He always preferred to be out of doors with the crofters for he was desperately trying to learn some Gaelic. But he could learn Gaelic, also, when working at the home farm; Catriona was an accomplished teacher, especially away from the watchful eyes of her parents.

She brought him scones and milk at the break time in the afternoon.

"Do you really have your own farm in Ayrshire?" she asked him on one of these visits. No doubt she had overheard her parents discussing him.

"Well, I don't own the farm but I am to have the tenancy next year," he conceded. He was not sure where her conversation was leading and was ever anxious that some damning detail might slip out.

"Surely you should be at your own place helping your mother and planning how you will run the farm for the future?" She asked in genuine puzzlement.

Her beautiful eyes bewitched Mungo and for a moment he was seized by a mad notion that he should tell her the whole story.

"It's not that easy," he said, desperately trying to recover himself. Maybe he should tell her about his mother and the factor. "My mother has her own cows and a dairy but the farm itself is managed by the estate factor for the time being. I just had the feeling I was getting in the way so I came away here for a month or two."

He must have looked rather pathetic for she leaned over and kissed his forehead. Perhaps Mungo misread the situation for he tried to return the endearment with a kiss on the lips. She pushed him away. Though he thought the shove was half hearted, he was anxious to avoid upsetting their friendship by overreaching himself too soon.

"You never know," he said. "I might stay on here. I have a little money put away so maybe I could buy a croft."

"Don't be so daft. You can't buy crofts," she stared at him in amazement. "The crofters just rent their ground. It used to be owned by the clan but it was taken away by the government after the war. My father answers to the Duke of Argyll now but his real loyalty is still with the Chief."

"All right then, I'll rent a croft."

"You'll have to wait a long time. When land becomes available it's given out according to strict rules of precedence and inheritance."

He had no intention of becoming a crofter but he thought Catriona might have been more impressed by his evident wish to be near her.

"There must be some other way a man can make a living in Argyll," he said. "Your father thinks I should look for something for the winter."

"There's only crofting and fishing and the herring season will be over in another month," she said with a disappointed shrug.

Their attempts to find employment for Mungo petered out and he went back to rebuilding the stone dyke he had been working on. Catriona stayed for a while asking questions about Ayrshire and generally hindering his work. Eventually she tired of this one-sided conversation and, gathering up the milk jug and basket, made to return to the house. She had only gone half a dozen steps when she turned back towards Mungo.

"You could always try the Iron Works," she said.

"Iron works!" said Mungo in disbelief.

"Yes, about half way between here and Inverary there's a company from Furness in Cumbria that has a great big forge there. There's all kinds of work – mining limestone, burning charcoal and working in the forge itself. Maybe that would suit you."

He had heard about the great iron works around Glasgow but surely they did not have that kind of industry here in Argyll. At supper that night he asked Mr Stuart about the iron works and he confirmed what Catriona had told him. Mungo said he would like to see the Iron Works and they agreed between them he could take a couple of days off before the harvest started.

In the two weeks before he set off to visit the Iron Works the indifferent weather meant he spent more and more time with Catriona. There was no doubting their affection for one another but Catriona was a virtuous young woman who imposed very strict boundaries on the expression of their shared fondness.

* * *

Mungo's trip to Furnace, as the village of Inverleacainn had become known, was fascinating. It was the first time he had seen a manufactory close at hand. He spoke with the overseer who said that he would be able to take him on coppicing the young oak saplings for making the charcoal. It was agreed that Mungo would return after the harvest was over.

He was well pleased with his visit but before taking the road back for Kilmichael he could not resist a visit to the little harbour. The ships brought in ore and general supplies before carrying away the finished iron. As he walked along the jetty he noticed that a young sailor was watching him from the deck of one of the ships.

He recognised the fellow but could not place him. What was worse, the sailor clearly recognised him. His every instinct was to flee but he knew that would only advertise the fact that he was a fugitive. He simply strolled on his way and as he got closer he noticed the ship was registered at Barrow. In his time aboard the *Swan* and the *Heron* he had known dozens of lads from the Cumbrian ports but this face was more familiar than these casual acquaintances. The young sailor's features became clearer. Now, he remembered; it was Jamie who had been a ship's boy on the *Swan*. In the past two years he had grown into a young man and Mungo yearned to shake his old shipmate's hand and share a glass in remembrance of times past. But he knew he must not give even a flicker of recognition. He just marched steadily onwards not looking to the left or the right.

He must have been ten paces beyond where the sailor was standing when the voice rang out:

"Mister Shaw!"

Now he was in a tight fix. It was not enough to pretend he had not heard young Jamie. Should he turn back, share greetings and swear him to silence? That would not do at all. Somehow he must convince his friend that he had been mistaken. He turned on his heel, looked straight in Jamie's face and began to spew out every word of Gaelic he knew in one meaningless but continuous stream. He kept up his

171

uncomprehending and incomprehensible diatribe for at least two minutes. In the end he threw his arms wide as if to say, 'I've no idea what you're talking about!' The ruse worked for Jamie became very confused and apologetic.

"I'm sorry, sir, I thought you were someone else."

All the way back along the road Mungo's mind was in turmoil. He could easily imagine Jamie relating the encounter to mutual acquaintances, 'I tell you it was Mungo Shaw as I live and breathe! And speaking the Gaelic like a native.' Of course few would believe him but if the reward for his capture was enough to tempt just one man to follow up the story… He shuddered at the prospect. One thing was for certain; he could not even consider taking employment at the iron works. As he made his way back along the loch shore towards Kilmichael, his brain kept turning over in time with the cadence of his march. As always the questions came quicker than the answers.

Gradually he began to reach some conclusions. He could not stay much longer at Kilmichael. It was not that Jamie would set the Sheriff's men after him. It seemed to him though, that he would always be at risk of a chance encounter or an unguarded remark. His mind kept coming back to Angus and the drovers. They were a secretive society within the Highland community. More important they were always on the move. It was staying in one place that threatened to expose him. More worrying still was the closeness of the crofting community. Everyone knew everyone else and their business too. Anyone out of place was totally conspicuous and a constant challenge to the curious and the inquisitive. He mused that he would be much better hidden in a big city like Dublin, say. By the time he reached the Tacksman's house his mind was quite clear.

"Oh I had a fine time at the iron works," he enthused. "You never saw such a place. The great fires in the forge were like you might imagine hell."

"Do you think you might want to work there?" Catriona asked.

"Well there's certainly a possibility but they're not putting anyone on until November."

"You'll have to get something before then; you remember our agreement?" said the Tacksman.

"I wanted your advice about that. I was thinking I might ask Angus if I could join the drove to the Crieff Tryst."

For their separate reasons both the Tacksman and Catriona were silent for a while, and then Mr Stuart spoke up.

"The drovers are wild men you know. Forever drinking and fighting."

"It would be an experience, though?"

"Surely you could keep him on here, father," said Catriona.

Mungo was flattered at her plea on his behalf.

"I would not hear of it, sir," Mungo protested. "You've been kindness itself to me and now I must make my own way."

"But you'll at least stay till the harvest's home," Catriona sighed.

"I'll be pleased to do that and anything else I can do to repay your hospitality. I am forever in your debt," he remarked with as much solemnity as he could muster. "I hope I'll be welcome to call again when I get back from droving."

Before her father could answer Catriona said through a watery smile, "You'll always be welcome here, Mungo Lachlan."

As he drifted off to sleep that night he had the same clear vision as when he stepped ashore at Dunure. He had a destination and a plan for how to get there. He would be sorry to leave Catriona but he would see her again after the drove. The one disappointment was that he had to deny his friendship with Jamie. He felt hellish about that.

Chapter Twenty Three

In all his time growing up on the farm Mungo had never taken too much to do with the cattle. The dairy was really his mother's domain and she called her beasts to milking twice a day with no help from her son. The fat cattle on the hill looked after themselves. He never imagined that he would end up driving cattle through highland glens and, even now, he couldn't quite believe it.

The snail's pace of the drove irritated the hard-driving seaman in him. Even after Kilmichael there would still be another three or four weeks on the road before the big Tryst at Crieff. He found the grinding tedium of it all nearly unbearable but it was a living. By all accounts prices at Crieff would be good and the pay was likely to be handsome. More importantly he felt safe amongst the drovers and their herds. No one would look for him amongst these men in these hills.

They had been stuck two days at Lagg by bad weather. The boatman had resolutely refused to brave the storm and take them across the Sound of Jura. Still, the Inn at Lagg was a hospitable place and was a welcome respite from the gale. The drovers took extra comfort from the endless drams that seemed to flow from a large whisky barrel in the corner of the Inn's front room. After the second day of hard drinking – and free spending – the drovers began to wonder if the boatman's refusal to sail was part of some commercial arrangement he had with the innkeeper.

By eleven o'clock on the third day the men were all gathered in the front room with throbbing heads and turbulent guts for the Inn's whisky was not the finest. Despite their poor disposition almost everyone had slept out in the foul weather making sure their beasts came to no harm in the night. Now, as they stood debating whether to have the first drink of the day, a man standing by the window spoke up.

174

"Who is yon fellow coming off the hill in the post-cart," he said. "He's not from round here, anyway, with his cocked hat and fine Ulster coat."

Mungo's first thought was that he might be a sheriff's officer or some official from the excise so he shrank back into the darkest recess of the overcrowded room.

"A foul day to be sure but I've seen worse," announced the new arrival as the drovers drew back to allow him into the middle of the room. "What time will the ferry sail?"

"I'm thinking he'll be going nowhere today," the Innkeeper replied. "He's stayed at the pier these past two days and now the wind's stronger than ever."

"Oh he'll sail today, alright, for I must be in Edinburgh the day after tomorrow," asserted the newcomer.

"And what business might take you there, good sir?" enquired the Innkeeper, the room having fallen silent as the drovers strained to understand the visitor through their uncertain grasp of the Scots tongue.

"I have lately become laird of Ardfin and I'm bidden to see my nephew wed in the old kirk of St Giles."

All this information was simultaneously translated, more or less, into Gaelic and, within a few minutes, the hubbub was deafening.

"Aye he'll have to get across," said one.

"Don't be too sure," said another.

"The boatman will surely oblige such an important gentleman," said a third.

Mungo was just mightily relieved that this fine gentleman had no connection with the Board of Excise.

Before long the whisky barrel was again running free as the drovers debated the arrangements for the crossing. Indeed after less than an hour they had planned the passage in the smallest detail even though no word of their propositions had yet been put to the boatman.

When the ferryman did arrive he was more than reluctant to make the crossing.

"I understand the urgency of your business, sir," he told the young laird, "but there is every chance the boat would founder in such a blow. You wait till the morn's morn. It'll be fine then. You'll see."

Despite the boatman's wheedling tone the laird was not convinced.

"If it's just a matter of money you can name your price," the laird challenged.

"No sir!" came the Ferryman's curt response. "Money is the last thing on my mind in weather like this – how much did you have in mind?"

The debate between the two men continued back and forth but was getting nowhere when Mungo's cousin Angus intervened.

"Supposing you were to take the gentleman across along with, say, a score of cows to give the boat some ballast," he ventured, "surely that would be worth a try?"

"Well it's a big risk but maybe it could be done," the ferryman pondered aloud, "but one of your men would have to come as well. If the cows get loose when we're out in the Sound it'll be the end of us all."

A murmur of approval and some words of praise greeted Angus's plan. Still the general tone of enthusiasm amongst the drovers stopped short of producing any volunteers to accompany the cattle.

"Well, that's the bargain," said the ferryman, "twenty cattle and a drover or we wait till tomorrow."

At this new impasse a more subdued rumble of conversation went round the room. Everyone knew of someone else who would be ideal to look after the live cargo. As the discussion ebbed and flowed Angus took Mungo aside.

"What do you think of the plan?" he asked.

Mungo looked out through the window at the far end of the room. The boat seemed well-found; broad beamed with a half deck at the fore end. Yet the wind was blowing against

176

the tide and he could see why the ferryman was worried. He looked back at his cousin.

"It would be safer to go in two or three hours," he said. "It should be slack water by then; not so much danger of broaching to in the wind."

"You seem to know a bit about sailing, Mungo."

"Oh I've picked up a thing or two, here and there," Mungo smiled.

"Would you cross with the cows?" Angus asked, outright.

"What's the rush? The ferryman's right. This wind will die back in the night."

"You can't be sure of that. Anyway it seems that boatman will use any excuse to keep us all here. Now if you could get across with the gentleman then he'd be obliged to take the rest of us."

Mungo stood silent for the best part of a minute though his mind was already made up.

"Yes I'll do it, but not before three o'clock."

Even in these grim conditions Mungo readily chose the seagoing risk over the tedium of being ashore.

By three o'clock all the beasts were aboard and tied by rope halters to iron rings along the gunnels. The beasts had less faith in the venture than Mungo. From the moment they were driven up the gangplank they kept up a terrified chorus of roaring and wailing. The laird and Mungo stood amidships on either side of Mungo's pony, its reins made fast round the mainmast. The boat had a crew of four including the ferryman himself. As they left the pier the boat began to roll. Mungo cast a glance at the laird. He looked very apprehensive. Cold though the day was, beads of sweat stood out on his forehead.

Within a few minutes of casting off they were in mid Channel. Now they felt the full force of the weather. The boat was driven forward at a dizzying speed before a fierce westerly gale. There was less rolling in the open water but still the beasts roared and tugged forcefully at their shackles. The laird seemed a little calmer now but he continued to cling to the pony's stirrup. Of those onboard the pony was the most anxious, tossing his head and stamping his hooves. Mungo thought the animal's fear was well justified. The ferocity of the following wind was driving the bows in far too deep and there was a real danger that they could be swamped.

The ferryman must have been aware of the risk for he tried to edge away from his course and put the wind on the quarter. Mungo shuddered when he realised what was happening; a quarter-sea in this gale was surely a lethal combination. Within a few seconds of altering course a huge sea hoisted the stern clear of the water and almost submerged the bows. Mungo held his breath. Slowly the bows re-emerged from the swell sending a small tidal wave over the foredeck. The cattle were now completely crazed and the laird clung to the pony's neck, his face whiter than the blown spume around him.

The next wave pooped the stern causing the ferryman to lose both his footing and his grip on the tiller. He was driven, with great force, against a rigging bollard. As the stern rose up again Mungo could see that the boatman was either stunned or dead for he lay quite motionless below the wandering tiller.

Mungo needed no second bidding. He made straight for the stern and, wrapping his arms around the tiller, tried to bring the boat round head to wind. It was a mad manoeuvre at the best of times but Mungo judged it was the only option; otherwise capsize and total loss seemed inevitable. As the boat started to turn he ordered the crewmen to ease off on the sheets. It mattered little that the crew could not understand Mungo's Scots tongue because the roaring of the cattle and the howling of the wind drowned out all but the highest pitched sounds. But Mungo had learned, long ago, that sailing orders had to be seen as well as heard.

The boat now pitched and rolled violently. Stability was not improved by the panic-stricken cattle striving to break free of their fetters and crashing into one another. The laird had forsaken his grip on the pony's harness and was now embracing the mast with vice-like intensity. Every second or third wave broke over the foredeck deluging crew, cows and passengers in an icy green brine. Mungo had to get steerage-way on the craft. He signalled and barked at the crewmen to shorten sail and then, by degrees, he managed to settle the boat on an easier course.

More by luck than judgement he passed north of the Dubh Sgeir reef only to be confronted with the long promontory that guards Kiells bay. He had no idea how deep the water was off the headland so he gave it a wide margin. As the point came up abeam the crewmen moved towards the cattle and motioned to Mungo that they should be put over the side. At first he was puzzled by this gesture but he remembered they had swum the cattle for the last few yards of the crossing from Islay. This must mean, he thought, that the crew knew he was in safe water, so he signalled his assent. The hinged traps in the gunnels were dropped and the halters cut. The laird completely misunderstood the loosing of the animals and feared that the vessel was lost. He grabbed hold of the saddle, hoping the pony might swim ashore and carry him to safety.

Although he had taken a heavy blow to his head the boatman had come to his senses by the time Mungo eased the boat into the small harbour at Kiells.

"You are a fine seaman," the boatman gasped taking hold of Mungo's hand, "you saved our lives and that's the truth of it."

Almost as soon as his foot touched solid ground the laird too regained his composure.

"We owe you our lives," he said. He then handed Mungo the agreed fee almost causing the injured boatman to suffer a relapse. "I trust you will soon find your cows and make a good price for them."

The laird walked off, rather uncertainly, towards his carriage which was waiting outside the Inn. He pulled his crumpled hat from inside his coat and jammed it onto his head. As he turned to board the carriage he gave an imperious wave and called out:

"Good luck to you, Mungo and may God be with you always, as He surely was this day!"

All of Mungo's cows made it to shore. A village boy found them grazing above the beach, about half a mile from the village. Before he set off to catch up with his cows he went in to the little tavern at Kiells to take a dram with the boatman. He gave the basic fare for the crossing to the Ferryman but kept back the laird's 'sweetener'.

"Well it's not been such a bad day for you," the boatman groused, accepting the reduced fee with as much good grace as he could muster. "You'll be the hero of the hour and you'll claim the best stance at the Tryst." His humour was soon improved by the whisky and the sheer relief of their safe landing, and all their anxieties were transformed into good natured banter.

When he judged that his pony might also be in a better humour, Mungo left the Inn, turned his back to the wind and rode off after his cattle. He knew that reports of the crossing would spread faster than the wind. The anonymity he sought amongst the drovers was gone. He wasn't sure why but most of all he worried about the laird repeating his name so emphatically; almost as though he had been determined to remember it.

Chapter Twenty Four

It was as much an entertainment as an education to watch Angus buying cattle. He first shoved his way amongst the beasts, and then chose a less than average specimen. He looked at the eyes and pulled open the mouth. Next he kneaded the flesh on the rump, the fore-quarters and around the ribs before standing back to study the animal's general stature and confirmation. Finally, and most important, he examined the feet, very carefully. These hooves would have to walk to Crieff for the Big Sale and many miles thereafter to their new owners' homes – some as far away as the middle of England.

With the inspection over it was time for the deal. Although the whole transaction was conducted in Gaelic, Mungo could catch the gist by watching the mannerisms and gestures. Angus was no doubt telling the seller that his animals were in poor condition. The other disagreed to the point of outrage. When a price was mentioned the same impassioned argument was repeated. This aggressive dialogue continued back and forth until, quite suddenly, a slap of hands concluded the deal. At that point the lifelong friendship of the two antagonists was revealed and reinforced by much backslapping jollity.

Mungo had not seen this many people in the same place since his grandfather's funeral but the atmosphere on this September day was boisterous and festive compared with that rueful, gloomy November gathering at Langmuir nearly four years since. Yet he felt his grandfather's presence amongst all these farming folk and he recalled the chieftain's story of how they had brought some of their cows all the way to Langmuir in the old days. Maybe it was this inherited memory that drew him as close to the drovers as he felt amongst the folk of Langmuir. For once he put the sea out of his mind and began to think seriously of life as a landsman.

Aside from the main business of trading cattle every kind of commerce was going on in the many stalls and improvised eating – and drinking – places which engulfed the village of Kilmichael Glassary for its annual Tryst.

"Aye you'll be Mungo, then," a farmer said, extending his hand.

"The very man that saved the ferry boat," announced another, sweeping off his bonnet with a most extravagant bow.

"Now, was your father Alistair or Ewan? Anyway you're a cousin of my own," said a sandy-haired giant grasping Mungo's shoulder.

So it went on as he made his way through the fair. Everyone knew each other and many of them were only too happy to parade their few words of English in praise of Mungo. For the first time since he waded ashore from the *Venus* he felt he was truly a part of the Clan Lachlan. He was completely secure within this vast family.

When he and Angus stopped to eat at the middle of the day they found the Village Inn packed to the door but Mungo's new fame found them a seat by the fire in no time at all.

"So, do you think you'll try the cattle dealing, Mungo?" Angus asked. "You've made a fair few friends here, this morning, and that's all there is to the dealing. You need an eye for a beast of course but knowing your man is the most important."

"Oh I think it'll be a long time before I can be upsides with you," Mungo replied with sincere modesty.

"Just the same, all the drovers that came up from Islay with us have been very taken with you. They've asked me to find out if you would be our topsman for the drove to Crieff," said Angus, with his head cocked to one side and his eyes wide with anticipation.

"I'm happy to take on any duty that will assist the company," said Mungo, "but I've no notion of what a topsman is or what he does."

"Well it's more or less what you did yesterday," Angus explained patiently. "You ride on ahead of the drove and find the best routes avoiding damaged roads, floods and other hindrances. You would have to find overnight stopping places with grazing for the beasts and shelter for the men, as well."

"I could do all that but I have no Gaelic and that would surely be a drawback."

"Not at all; you'll be dealing with estate factors and the like. They don't have much Gaelic, either!" Angus said with a hearty laugh. Then he turned more serious. "Some of the lairds try to charge a toll from us. If we don't pay they send us on long and difficult roads round their land." Looking straight into Mungo's eyes he continued, "We need a clever man who can get us the best deal. We have to keep the cows on the shortest road or they lose their condition. At the same time we can't pay too much in tolls, for that eats away at the final price," Angus went on. "Your sharp mind and easy way with the Scots tongue is just what we need."

Mungo was flattered by the offer. He was however more than a little nervous of the skills and knowledge required for a 'topsman.' It would be a heavy responsibility for the herd must now have grown to around 1500 after Angus's energetic dealing that morning.

Just as they were about to discuss the finer details of Mungo's new position an older man sat down beside them at the table. He introduced himself to Angus in Gaelic.

"This is Donald Baan," Angus said to Mungo, "he was at the battle of Prestonpans with your father."

"It's an honour to meet you, sir," said Mungo. He was always anxious to hear more of his dear departed father, especially since his mother always seemed reluctant to speak of her late husband.

'White' Donald was well named. A shock of pure white hair tumbled over his noble brow and seemed to exaggerate his handsome but heavily lined face. Although still under fifty he looked much older. On a nod from Angus, the innkeeper brought a jug of ale for Donald.

His story was delivered in a mixture of broken Scots and Gaelic. Donald's lively animation and deep feeling helped to carry the thread of the story where the language faltered. He held Mungo and Angus's undivided attention for the better part of half an hour. It was all new to Mungo though Angus had heard some of it before. The legend of how a spirited band of a few hundred highlanders had routed General Cope's army of near three thousand foot and cavalry was dramatic in every way. Towards the end of his tale Donald's excited recitation tailed off to a more measured pace and a sombre tone. Right at the end, very deliberately and in clear English, he said:

"It was a great victory but a terrible tragedy, just the same." Looking straight at Mungo, Donald shook his head slowly and went on. "The only man we lost at Prestonpans that day was your father. Cut down in the first blast from the English field guns."

All three men sat in silence for a while. Mungo was stunned by this last revelation.

"It was good of you to take the time to tell us all this," said Angus slowly in the older man's own language. He too had been deeply affected by Donald's story. He rose from the table and walked over to the tapster. Mungo just sat staring into the fire. After several long minutes he turned to Donald.

"You are quite sure it was my father who died at Prestonpans?" he asked in a distracted yet unbelieving voice. Mungo had always understood his father was lost at Culloden.

"No doubt about it," said Donald, giving another shake of his head as he rose to go. "I knew him all his life."

As the shocking detail of the story sank in Mungo was overtaken by a mixture of emotions. The warm feeling of belonging that was such a comfort a few minutes before started to drift away to be replaced with anxiety and uncertainty.

Donald Baan had gone by the time Angus returned with a tankard of beer for each of them.

"Well, will you be our topsman, then?" asked Angus, trying to bring Mungo back to reality.

"I'll be very pleased to do it," he agreed, though his mind was still on Donald's tale. How could the old man be wrong about such a thing?

The two men took their ale in silence. After draining his jug Angus rose to go.

"Maybe you should take the rest of the day to yourself," said Angus, showing a sensitive side Mungo had not seen before. "Mind and be at the stance by six tomorrow and we can discuss your duties then."

Mungo nodded and followed Angus to the door. As they parted Angus laid a reassuring arm on his shoulder. He knew this first-hand account of Ian's death would be upsetting to Mungo. Dear dead Ian was his uncle, too, after all.

Mungo wandered aimlessly through the bustling crowds. His mood swung from shock and sadness to self pity and then to a steely defensiveness. For no apparent reason his attitude to Kilmichael and its people began to change, too. The fugitive Mungo had re-entered his soul and, quite suddenly, he trusted no one.

He was still being greeted and hailed on every side. Yet this familiarity, so recently a source of joyful reassurance, now seemed dangerous, even sinister. His mind went back to that night in Simpson's Tavern when Alf was singing his praises to the drunken rabble. It was exhilarating at the time yet someone in that friendly, frenzied crowd must have betrayed him. This was just the same. Here he was in Kilmichael surrounded by a crowd of well wishers and he had an unreasonable fear that one of them would give him up to the authorities. It was only a matter of time, he thought. His worries began to fester into an irrational rage. He needed time to work out a new plan.

Lost in his thoughts, he wandered away from the crowd and out past the vast herds of beasts. To the west of the village was a prominent hill called Dunadd. At its top there were traces of an ancient fortress going back to the earliest times. After a while he found himself at this mystical place. He could see across all the surrounding land towards Port Ann where he had landed from the *Venus.* In the other direction he could see clear across the flat ground to Crinan Bay in the west. To the north lay the broad strath leading to Loch Awe. That would be the direction the drove would take in the morning.

The peace of the hilltop eased his mind and the high vantage point gave him a kind of security. Now he could think more clearly but in truth he had very few options.   He considered going south to Campbeltown. He knew Irish fishing boats came in there and he might get work at the fishing and get to Dublin that way. Still, the customs men at such a busy port would certainly know all about the warrant for his arrest. Maybe he could stick with the drove until Ardlui and take off for Glasgow. He had heard it was a busy place where a man could be lost in the crowd but he knew next to nothing about Glasgow. Maybe he could get to Greenock where he even thought of signing on as an indentured servant for a plantation in the Indies.

The more he considered these increasingly desperate options the more the job of topsman began to seem like a heaven-sent deliverance, or at least he thought he could make it so. As long as he was away from the herd and out on his own he would have early warning of any trouble that lay ahead for the drove, and for himself. If trouble loomed he could always avoid it; something he could not do if he was with the herd.

He must have sat at the hill-top for a long while for the warmth of the day had gone and the sun was slipping behind the Paps of Jura by the time he started to walk back to the village. He was settled in his decision to become the topsman for the drove but a much larger conundrum now haunted him.

The Battle of Prestonpans was fought on 16th September 1745. Mungo was born on 20th November 1746. If Iain Lachlan really was killed at Prestonpans then his mother's husband was not his father.

Chapter Twenty Five

The murder of Joseph Reid and the impeachment of Mungo Shaw had been a formal topic for discussion at the Michaelmas meeting of the Board of Excise in Edinburgh. The same subject dominated all the casual conversation amongst commissioners and inspectors. On the day following the completion of their deliberations the Inspectors were preparing to return home when the Chairman took William Baillie, Chief Inspector of Customs for Kirkudbright, off to one side. He sympathised with Baillie for the loss of Reid.

"It was a bad business," said Baillie. "I saw it all and was able to do nothing."

"Maybe there is some hope though," said the chairman. "My kinsman is the laird of Ardfin on the Isle of Jura," he confided. "I had dinner with him last evening. He told me a most singular tale of his crossing from Jura to the mainland a fortnight ago." He went on to explain that their boat had nearly foundered and that those on board were only saved by the skill of a young drover. The drover was a dark stocky fellow called Mungo who spoke little Gaelic."

It was not long before James Gordon from the Ayr Office was pulled in to the discussion. Since the wanted man also came from Ayr, surely Gordon could recognise him. In truth Gordon could not have picked him out from amongst the dozens of other young rogues who frequented Ayr harbour. Still, it would not do to admit this to the chairman; even after ten years in his present rank Gordon still entertained hopes of promotion.

"It cannot be assumed that the Mungo who saved your relation is also the wanted man," Gordon suggested to the chairman, somewhat tentatively. "Drovers come from all over Scotland, even from England."

"That's as maybe Mr Gordon but how many of them are skilled mariners?" said the chairman. "This sighting is the best prospect we've had since the dastardly deed was done."

Gordon pondered a while.

"In fact, sir, I have a young assistant who was in school with Shaw and would recognise him at once."

"Lose no time, then, in returning to Ayr and despatch your man forthwith to the town of Comrie in the county of Perth," the chairman ordered. "Mr Baillie, you'll go to the same place, straightaway. There you will make yourself known to a Mr Muir who will help you to form a plan to nab that rascal Shaw." Muir it seemed was a former drover who was now the herdsman on a nearby estate owned by another of the chairman's kinsmen.

* * *

It was the day after they met Muir at Comrie that the sheriff officers appeared. Presumably they had been alerted by some other member of the chairman's extensive family. The sheriff's men remained quite reticent about who they were and whence they came; they were rather a mysterious pair. But on the subject of how to trap the quarry they were very outspoken. Indeed one of the officers was a former military man and he took responsibility for working out where best to intercept the Kilmichael drovers.

Baillie, the Kirkcudbright Excise Chief, resented the military man's assumption of command.

"And how do you propose to catch this fellow," he asked, "if none of us knows what he looks like?"

"Were you not told? A man from Ayr, who knows Shaw, is coming to join us and we must wait here until he arrives," retorted the old soldier, further undermining Baillie's position.

* * *

Charles Wallace was a very unhappy man. Now an assistant to James Gordon, the Collector of Customs at Ayr, he was well used to chasing smugglers on the Troon shore. It was his job. He understood it and he enjoyed it. Yet for the past week he had been cooped up in a bothy overlooking the drove road at the head of Glen Ogle. This was as near to living hell as he could ever have imagined and it was certainly not why he had joined the Excise. Indeed, he began to wonder why he had joined the excise. He was only too well aware of Shaw's popularity in his home town and he had long suspected that his fiancée, Margaret Murray's regard for Shaw went beyond mere popularity.

Wallace along with William Baillie and the two sheriff's officers made an unlikely party of deer stalkers; their chosen alibi should anyone enquire as to their business in that remote place. One of the sheriff's men, the former soldier, prided himself on cooking up the coarsest of food. In the way of fighting men this fellow affected to enjoy their wretched subsistence in that stone cell. He seemed unmoved by the howling winds, relentless rain and a bitter cold that chilled the very marrow of their bones. All the same he was always careful to ensure that the ponies were sheltered and well fed.

"I think it's time to call a stop to this nonsense," Wallace said to Baillie, blatantly exceeding his rank. "As soon as that soldier fellow gets back we should find an Inn or something that passes for civilised lodgings in this god-forsaken country."

"We can hardly give up yet," Baillie protested, "the Kilmichael drove should be here any day now." Three droves had gone through earlier in the week but they were from the North Country; Breadalbane and Rannoch way. Wallace no longer believed in the existence of any Kilmichael drove.

"The whole thing is preposterous," Wallace grunted, pulling his plaid closer to his quivering shoulders.

Half an hour later the soldier was standing at the door though no one had seen or heard him ride up. He seemed oddly despondent.

"He's not with the Kilmichael men," said the soldier. "I shadowed them for a couple of hours this morning; no one looked anything like our man. They're all sandy haired."

"Maybe he left the drove somewhere along the road," Baillie suggested, rather limply.

"Well maybe so, but I spoke to their leader," the military man said, "and he was adamant that no one called Mungo was with them."

"Thank the Lord," said a much relieved Wallace. He had been dreading a meeting with Mungo, in any case. He had nothing but contempt for him of course. The hostility of their school days still rankled with him. But, worse than that were his fiancée's parting words: 'If you harm a hair of Mungo's head I will never speak to you again.'

"Now we can look for somewhere warm with some decent food. You two can hunt him to the ends of the earth for all I care," Wallace said, casting a derisive look towards the sheriff's men.

On the insistence of Wallace the 'hunting party' rode straight through Lochearnhead heading for Comrie and the Inn where they had stayed at the start of their fruitless hunt for Mungo.

"At least we know the place will be clean, dry and warm," Wallace asserted, "we had a fine supper there, too. Mind you anything would seem like a feast after the swill we've had to endure this past week."

The attitude of the others to Wallace's constant whingeing had varied from mild amusement to stony silence, but now it was beginning to wear very thin. They had been riding since nine and it was early afternoon when they reached St Fillans.

Everyone was hungry and Baillie decided they should try for a bite to eat at the Inn. This reasonable suggestion was met by a tirade of dissent from Wallace.

"We'll be chewing on some old bit of scrag end whilst all these drovers take the best rooms in Comrie," he moaned.

The sheriff's men dismounted outside the Inn and made to go inside.

"Where are you two going?" Wallace shouted in his usual arrogant tone.

The soldier looked at him with ill-disguised disdain and carried on into the Inn. Wallace continued to parade his irritation. It had not occurred to him that these men were not his employees. They could not be ordered around like servants.

"Well," said Wallace, trying to assert his imagined command of the situation, "we'll take half an hour, not more." By now he was talking to himself as Baillie had joined the sheriff's men by the fireside within.

"I have a feeling Mr Wallace's heart is not in this venture," said a rather disconsolate Baillie.

"It's as though he wishes to see the blackguard go free," added the soldier, looking straight at Wallace who was now coming through the door.

If Wallace was in any doubt that the others had taken against him then the coldness of his reception must have made the position clear. Still, he was not the kind of man to consider the feelings of others. He did wonder though if the soldier might not have read his mind. If Shaw was brought to book Wallace knew there would be trouble. Only two months before his master, Mr Gordon, had brought a charge against James Hay, a notorious smuggler from the Loans. The rogue had beaten one of Gordon's best men to within an inch of his life but when the sheriff came to hear the case neither the accused nor any witnesses could be produced. Maybe things were different in Kirkcudbright, but he doubted it.

The fare at the St Fillans inn was surprisingly good, consisting of a generous bowl of broth and some tender boiled mutton with potatoes. For a time at least, tempers were assuaged by full bellies. At around three o'clock the four took to the road again and reached Comrie at six.

At Comrie the earlier antagonisms resurfaced. The Coaching Inn was nearly full – as Wallace had said it would be – but two rooms were eventually procured. So rancorous was the atmosphere that none of the others would share so much as the air that Wallace breathed. So, in his misery, he had a room to himself.

"Supper is at seven – no later," said the innkeeper as the ill-tempered quartet wandered off to find their sleeping quarters.

* * *

Mungo had taken to the road before daylight, at least two hours before the herd set off. Angus had agreed that, on the next day, Mungo should set up the route all the way to Comrie with night stops at Lochearnhead, and St Fillans. He arrived at Lochearnhead just after the Rannoch drove had left. In the wet weather their herd had eaten or trampled all the grazing around the village. After consulting the Innkeeper, Mungo secured another field with plenty of grass and a dry steading for the men, all at a good price. He then took his breakfast of eggs, bannocks and ale and was back on the road by nine o'clock.

Less than a mile out of the village he caught up with the Rannoch drove. It was enormous; maybe three thousand head. They were making hard going of it and had turned the low lying track on the loch side into a complete quagmire. Mungo immediately decided he should try to find another route. He doubled back to the village and discussed his dilemma with the Innkeeper.

"There's a good road on the south side of the loch," the innkeeper suggested, "but it's scarcely used by the drovers because the estate charges a toll."

"We'll have to give it a try," Mungo decided. "The main road's hopeless."

In fact no drovers at all had used the southern route that season so Mungo managed to make a deal with the factor for half the usual rate to include a grazing stance at St Fillans. He was feeling quite pleased with himself as he rode along the near perfect track on the south shore. He was sheltered from the wind by the birch wood on the lower slopes of Ben Vorlich and the rain had stopped. As long as there was enough grass at the St Fillans end of the road it would be a good morning's work.

The grazing, although close to St Fillans, was not ideal. Even so it was likely to be greatly superior to the trampled earth he expected the Rannoch drove to leave in that village as well. He was fortunate too in finding a ramshackle wooden shed close by the stance. It would at least break the wind and keep the worst of the weather off the men, but the crofter who owned it drove a hard bargain and that delayed him a while.

He had finished his business by early afternoon and thought of stopping at the St Fillans Inn for a bowl of soup and a bag of corn for his horse. However, when he saw four ponies tethered outside he decided to ride on by; ever anxious to avoid strange company. Though he had been riding all day his pony had rested at breakfast and had grazed well during the hour or so he was wrangling with the crofter over rent for the shed. He decided to push on to Comrie. With any luck uncle Davie would be ensconced somewhere in the little town. Davie had told him long ago that he used to come by way of Glen Artney when he was going to buy beasts at the Tryst. He always stopped at Comrie in preference to the crowded Inns at Crieff. It would be good to see him and he would bring word from home.

Mungo reached Comrie at about four o'clock but he still had work to do. Although the herd would not arrive for another two nights it was essential to find a reasonably dry place with a good cover of grass to rest for the night before the final drive to Crieff. Angus had been most insistent on this point. The last night on the road could make a huge difference to the condition of the beasts and therefore the price. Two hours and several unsuccessful calls later he found a suitable stance about a mile out of Comrie on the road to Crieff. It did not come cheap but it was good grass and a mile less for the beasts to walk on the final day.

With his work done Mungo went back into Comrie on the more pleasant task of finding his uncle. He first tried the two drovers' Inns. These were hardly Inns at all, being large croft houses offering rough spirit, two penny ale and pot luck. The first of the two was so full that he did not get beyond the door. The second was less overwhelmed but still very full. Sleeping was a dozen to a room – no bedding provided. Some of the patrons had already retired for the night, propped up around the corners of the front room, still clutching their ale jugs. There was a stench about the place too. The crofter's shed he had secured for his own men now seemed palatial by comparison. The only other place in town was the Coaching Inn. By country standards it was a grand place; plenty of chairs in the front room, a separate dining hall and no more than four beds to a room. Somehow he could not see his uncle stopping in such a place but then he remembered the alternatives. As he came through the door he caught the strong smell of beef stew and he could see that the dining room was already filling up. He looked in at the open doorway to see if his uncle might be at his supper. There was no sign of him but just then there was a shout from behind:

"Mungo my boy," cried the strong Ayrshire voice. "Just look at you with that black beard. You're every inch the wild Highlander. Whatever would your mother think?"

"You are a welcome sight yourself," Mungo laughed, clasping his uncle's hand in both of his.

At a table tucked away just through the dining room doorway four men sat in startled amazement. They could scarcely believe their luck.

Chapter Twenty Six

It was the clanking of gates and the rattling of keys that woke him. Despite the inky blackness he knew exactly where he was. The stench of piss and rotting straw was more pungent than the byre, at the Shaw, on the hottest summer day. That stink would stick in his mind for always, even though 'always' might not be all that long. Trial for murder in those parts rarely ended in acquittal, whatever the evidence. The very accusation of murdering a crown servant was more serious still; hanging was as certain as night followed day. The chief jailer had explained all this to him, in a smugly cheerful tone, as they marched him to his cell the previous afternoon.

He had slept fitfully in the long hours since he had landed in that awful place. During his rare lucid moments his forebodings of his fate seemed to eclipse almost every other thought. They say that impending death sharpens the mind. It was not Mungo's experience. The most he could manage was a towering red rage against the injustice of it all. The unfairness was compounded by how easily he was caught. He was still haunted by the sneering eyes of Charles Wallace. "That's our man," he had announced, his talon-finger not six inches from Mungo's face. When the sheriff's men first confronted him Wallace had slunk to one side, unwilling to look Mungo in the eye – what on earth could Margaret see in such an apology for a man? Even to the last moment he had hoped that Wallace would lose his nerve and say, 'It's not him,' or at least 'I don't know.' But in his heart he always knew that it was a forlorn hope. The enmity between them was too deep rooted.

The great studded cell door swung open and the guttering light from a lantern lit up the jailer's face. "You'd better have a wash and take some porridge," he ordered. "You have visitors; a titled gentleman and your mother." The jailer's assistant set out the wash-basin on the table and threw down a bundle of clothes. "They brought you these," the jailer announced, pointing at the bundle and passing Mungo a bowl of porridge with his free hand. It was the first he had eaten since noon on the day before in Castle Douglas. The wagon had stopped in the Town Square in pouring rain. Mungo was made to sit there, in his fetters, supping the rapidly cooling broth whilst the townsfolk looked on.

"Hurry yourself!" the jailer shouted. "Yon birkie's no of a mind to be kept waiting." The porridge was as good as he ever tasted but he could have done with maybe five times as much. After rinsing his face in the icy water he hurriedly put on the clean clothes. Now he felt fit to face his mother but he worried how she would receive him. How would he cope if she started weeping? He marvelled, too, that Sir Archie Crawford, the laird of Langmuir, the only titled gentleman he knew, had come all this way to see him.

As soon as the door opened his mother gave an anxious cry. "Mungo!" she called out and even before the jailers had got him through the door she rushed towards him. She hugged him, nervously; unsure of what was permitted. Stuck for something to say, she chuckled, "You look a fright with all that hair on your face."

The assistant jailer sat down on a chair at the door and his chief withdrew, locking the door behind him. They were in a large sparsely furnished room with bare stone walls and a rush-strewn floor. It was dominated by a barred window that looked out towards the sea and carried in a cold salty breeze. The bright sunshine highlighted the smiling faces of his mother and the laird, lifting Mungo's spirits as high as they had been in many months.

"How have they been treating you, Mungo? Are you getting enough to eat?" Sir Archie asked with a gentleness that struck Mungo as quite out of character for the laird. He knew him as a kind enough man but one who was invariably formal in his speech.

"I'm sure they treat me no better and no worse than all their prisoners."

"You are not a prisoner. You've been convicted of nothing," Sir Archie asserted. "You must be kept in clean, dry quarters and be well fed while you await trial." This was Sir Archie's view of how things should be, but it was far from the normal practice in Kirkcudbright Tolbooth.

"Well, I don't know about that. For the last day it's been one bowl of porridge in a stinking dungeon with only a basin of cold water for washing."

The old man's brows knitted. "Guard, call the jailer," he boomed with such force that everyone in the room fell silent. Mungo was amazed that an elderly man might be capable of such rage. The guard gingerly gave a tug on the bell-pull beside his chair.

Almost immediately the door flew open and there stood the jailer, looking less happy than before.

"What is your name sir?" the laird demanded. "I mean to report your treatment of this man to the Sheriff Principal."

"I am Edward Bell, sir. What seems to be the trouble?" the jailer asked. He appeared nervous, obviously alarmed by the laird's hostile outburst. Sir Archie then laid down the minimum treatment he expected for Mungo.

"Well it's not so easy, sir. My first duty is to keep this man securely locked up until the next sitting of the High Court."

"Do not lecture me about your duty, mister. Unless you can find a dry cell with clean bedding then you'll answer to the sheriff. Now, away with you and find Mr Shaw more suitable quarters."

As he watched the heavy door close on the jailer's back, this altercation aroused a strange feeling in Mungo. He was greatly heartened that Sir Archie spoke up for him with such vigour and to such obvious effect, but he was puzzled too. He knew all about the bonds going back to the Jacobite war and the strong friendship between the laird and his grandfather but his depth of feeling that day seemed more personal than these old loyalties. Surely Sir Archie wasn't mixed up with the smugglers? For a while he tried to make sense of it and then decided it was just the laird's compassion for a doomed man.

"How are you keeping your mind occupied?" his mother asked. "We must bring you books to read. I suppose they've given you a bible?"

"What?" Mungo muttered, his mother's words had been barely audible to him amidst his thoughts about the laird. "A bible? No, no bible."

"This is an outrage," the laird exploded, sending the guard's hand twitching in search of his bell pull.

"No need for that," he motioned towards the rope. "Just make sure he gets a bible," the guard nodded, cowering, as if Sir Archie had aimed a blow at his head.

After a few moments silence his mother observed, in a matter of fact sort of way, "The laird has sent Mr Scott, the factor, to Edinburgh to find an advocate to prepare your defence." Perhaps she thought an advocate was all that was needed to save his neck.

"The only advocate than can save me now is the Lord God Almighty," Mungo said in a mournful voice and both his visitors were depressed to see a beaten look come into his eyes.

"You keep your spirits up and say your prayers, young Mungo, and we'll see justice done. You're an innocent man and I'll make sure you walk free if it's the last thing I do."

His mind went back to the old drover who told him his mother's husband was killed at the battle of Prestonpans, fifteen months before he was born. Surely the laird could not be his father? He banished the notion from his mind as soon as he thought it but still he longed to know the truth. He gazed at his mother. She seemed somehow serene in this terrible place. How could he question his parentage to his own mother?

"I never heard of this man Joseph Reid," he suddenly roared out as if trying to relieve the turmoil in his own brain. "How can they say I killed him?"

"You keep your own counsel until your advocate comes. Many an innocent man has condemned himself by protesting too much," said Sir Archie.

Old Archie's words managed to avert the threatened emotional outburst and the danger of Mungo saying more than was wise in front of the guard. The three settled to a calmer discussion of family news and village gossip until after an hour the jailer returned.

"There's a Mr Graham Murray here asking to see Shaw," said the jailer, his eyes shifting nervously between his mother and the laird.

"Let him in," said Mungo, resolving the impasse and giving himself some sense of control over events.

There was an unsettling awkwardness between Sir Archie and Graham Murray. Of course they were perfectly civil to one another as might be expected of two well bred and well educated men. Graham was also suitably deferential to the elderly nobleman and Sir Archie, for his part, was generous if a little patronising towards Graham. But there was no warmth in their dialogue. The demeanour of both men was formal, even stiff. Neither of them seemed willing to look in the other's eye. Mungo remembered the factor telling him something about a boundary dispute between Graham's father and Sir Archie that ended up in the courts. He supposed that might be the cause of the distance between them. Mungo was discouraged that the only two men in the world who had come to his aid showed so little empathy for each other.

If Mungo's mother had sensed this lack of rapport she made no sign of noticing it.

"I think it's just magnificent that two of the finest families in Ayr should come to Mungo's defence in this way," she said, her face inclined towards Graham.

"The whole family wishes Mungo well," Graham said, "and my father is very willing to meet the cost of the finest advocate in Edinburgh and to give Mungo a new position as soon as he is free."

"Your good wishes and the offer of employment are both welcome, but your father's money is not needed," Archie put in before Jean could reply to Graham's handsome offer. The old man had taken full responsibility for Mungo's defence and he was not about to share it.

An awkward silence followed. Graham looked down at the floor, the laird looked at Jean, and Jean looked out of the window. Suddenly Jean became very anxious about Sir Archie's manner. She turned quickly and fairly glowered into the laird's eyes. Mungo could make nothing of what passed silently between his mother and the laird. His only concern was to rescue his friend from the laird's appalling snub. But before he could think what to say his mother stepped in:

"It is a great kindness of your father to make such an offer and I hope you will convey to him our heart-felt gratitude. As you will have gathered though, Sir Archie has already made arrangements to retain the services of an advocate."

"Just as you say," said Graham, but he still seemed rather crestfallen.

"Of course I am sure you could help us a great deal through your knowledge of the legal system," Mungo said, attempting to oil the troubled waters.

"Indeed," said Sir Archie, realising his over-protective instinct had been misunderstood. "If you can catch up with our factor, Mr Scott, in Edinburgh you could recommend a good man. I will write him a note so there are no misunderstandings." For the first time he smiled warmly at Graham.

"I will help as much as I can but I must be careful. Being a servant of the Lord President my relationship with the

Faculty of Advocates is governed by certain rules and conventions. Maybe the best way to proceed is through a Writer who will instruct an advocate for you," Graham explained. He was still smarting from the rejection of his father's largesse.

"I used an Edinburgh Writer once, a while ago. It cost me a lot of money and little ever came of it," groused the laird.

"I'll seek out Mr Scott when I return to Edinburgh in the morning," Graham finally assented but his hurt was not completely mended.

Mungo did not fully understand what had been agreed but he was more than content that the laird and his friend Graham had matters in hand.

Chapter Twenty Seven

Walking the few dozen yards from the Tolbooth to the Court House reminded him of carrying the coffin at his grandfather's funeral; the clear blue sky, the pristine white of the hoar frost on the ground and the legions of black-clad folk standing around, in silent groups, staring as he went by. He thought he should be scared but loneliness had numbed his feelings. So much had happened since Da took his final earthly journey. He had made so many friends, at school, at sea and as a drover. Where were they now? It was just him and Mr Cameron against the hangman.

There had been two consultations with Mr Cameron, his advocate. The first was all about the importance of saying nothing. It was for the Crown to prove guilt, not for him to demonstrate innocence. At the second encounter he had asked Mungo all about the important people in his life. Who did he like best? Had anyone inspired him? Who had stuck by him in difficult times? As Mungo spoke he wrote screeds in his big black book. He also gave a grim recitation of how he expected the Crown to make out its case. The prospects looked bleak, and yet Mr Cameron had an arrogant confidence about him. His attitude confused Mungo but it left him with just a glimmer of hope.

As the jailers marched him along menace seemed to stalk his every pace. Mostly the onlookers were silent and brooding though some muttered obscenities as he passed. As they steered him round the Mercat Cross the rusting gibbet was twisting slowly in the breeze. The sight of it left him fighting for breath.

At one point he was confronted by a bewildered looking wretch.

"Repent, sinner, before you meet your God!" he ranted over and over.

His shrieking voice moderated Mungo's fear with bemused irritation. The more the demented soul raved the closer Mungo clung to his memories. Four years had passed since grandfather's death. He missed the old man and remembered the happy times they had spent together. He thought, too, of his own more recent adventures. For the life of him he could not think of much reason for regret let alone repentance.

The crowd at the court house door had come too late to find a place on the public benches. They had the look of a defeated army. The resignation in their slumped shoulders and the fatalism in their hollow staring eyes caused a strange churning in the pit of Mungo's stomach. The sea of soulless faces seemed to engulf him. His spirit had no depth left to plumb.

Suddenly he caught sight of a familiar fresh-faced youth. He would be about fifteen, standing at the front of the crush, staff in hand and a collie at his heel. He looked Mungo straight in the eye and slowly his face broadened into a grin. The sight of the lad was thrilling; like seeing a shining pearl amongst so many pebbles. Almost at once confidence began to fight its way back into his brain. It was Peter, the ship's boy from the *Heron.* His smile meant more than the fine words of a thousand advocates. Peter's demeanour, indeed his very presence, was a guarantee that none of the *Heron's* crew would give evidence against him, Mungo was sure of it. He returned Peter's smile and with a nervous chuckle threw back his shoulders and stuck out his chest. Da had often told him that having 'a guid conceit of yersel',' was the most important thing for getting on in life. Maybe it was important, too, for hanging onto life.

As they came close to the Court House he could hear the hubbub within. It must be packed out, he thought – like that night in Simpson's Tavern when Alf Garvie had told the baying mob of the happenings at Port Castle. He tried not dwell on that painful reminiscence.

They entered the Court House by the prisoner's door and waited several long minutes in an outer lobby.

"Put up Mungo Shaw!" the Clerk of the Court's voice rang out. His escorts jostled him forward and up the half dozen steps into the narrow enclosure of the dock. Five lawyers in their black gowns and grey wigs sat with their backs to him. The polished table in front of them groaned with books and documents. Mr Cameron half turned in his place and gave Mungo a reassuring nod. Facing the lawyers from the other side of the wide table sat the clerk of the court and his minions. To the right and above the well of the court sat fifteen hard faced men. They would be the jury that Cameron had told him about. To his left was a small pulpit; the witness box. High above them all in a great chair fit for the king himself sat Lord Ochiltree. The scarlet crosses on his dazzling white robe matched the fat face framed within his full-bottomed wig. That sight might have seemed rather droll to some but it put the fear of God into Mungo.

The whole spectacle was awe-inspiring and it was a while before he was able to take it all in. Indeed it was many seconds before he was even aware of the rows of faces craning to look down at him. The gallery ran along both sides of the Court House and right round behind him. In the second row his mother was seated between Sir Archie and James Scott the factor. He nodded and gave the merest hint of a smile; Mr Cameron had been most insistent that he should not acknowledge anyone except the officers of the court. Elsewhere amongst the throng he picked out Graham Murray and his father.   Hughie Maclure was there too, along with old Rab. The sight of family and friends at once cheered his spirits and stiffened his resolve; he began to believe that he could survive this ordeal. He was still scanning the faces when his attention was arrested by a fine gentleman, his patrician features stood out beneath his pale periwig. He had only met John Christian once before but he would know him anywhere. What was he doing here?

"…and did beat him about the head to his grave injury and did murder him."

He was so distracted by Christian that he missed the start of the Clerk's recitation of the charge.

"To the charge of murder, how say you? Are you guilty or not guilty?"

"Not guilty, my lord," he spoke in a loud clear voice. It was to be the only public sound he would utter for the rest of the trial.

The trial proceeded exactly as Mr Cameron predicted. Mr Robb, the prosecutor, called a procession of witnesses – mainly excisemen – to describe the events of that fateful night. They told of the pitched battle between the excisemen and the smugglers and attested that Mungo Shaw had beaten Joseph Reid repeatedly with a spar and had killed him. Mr Robb had a rhetorical turn of phrase and was quite theatrical in his manner as he played on the obvious sympathies of the Jurymen who were all local worthies.

"Have a care, Mr Robb," Lord Ochiltree exclaimed in one of his many interventions. "The court is interested in what the witnesses have to say. Not what you might wish them to say."

Mr Cameron contested the testimony of the Crown's witnesses in an understated manner, relying on cold logic to make his points.

"Surely Mr Reid could have come by these fatal injuries in many ways? For example, he could have fallen from his horse and broken his head on the sharp rocks."

This question seemed only to encourage the witnesses to ever more gory details of Mr Reid's battered face.

"How could you be sure it was Mr Shaw you saw on the ship? Is it not quite dark by nine o'clock at the end of August?"

Mungo worried that Mr Cameron's relaxed style did not seem to trouble the witnesses and made no visible impression on the jurymen. Yet the advocate seemed content; as if biding his time.

Mr Cameron asked each witness in turn for their recollections of the precise appearance of the ship making the illegal landing the night Reid was killed. Again and again they all described the ordinary rig of a typical coasting wherry; almost as though they were reading from a prepared text.

The eighth prosecution witness was Mr Baillie the Chief Inspector of Customs and the man credited with Mungo's capture. He was a quiet, even timid, man. After a few preliminary questions about the apprehension of Mungo, Mr Robb asked about the band of smugglers on the shore that night; how many, how many ponies, how heavily armed. He also wanted to know the circumstances of Mr Reid's attempted boarding. In a series of thoughtful replies the inspector explained that the excisemen were beaten off by the heavily armed smugglers. The attempt to seize the runners' wherry had been his own idea.

When he rose, Mr Cameron rolled forward on the balls of his feet with his open palms pressing on the table. He missed out his usual preliminaries and seemed to ignore the witness altogether. Looking straight at the judge he said:

"You are quite sure, are you, that it was the *Heron* you saw that night?"

The witness was confused for he had made no direct reference to the ship or her name during his testimony. He seemed lost for words and just as he made to reply Mr Cameron carried on.

"In the failing light and being some distance from the landing it must have been difficult for you to see anything at all?"

Again the witness hesitated and Mr Cameron rounded on him like a stoat cornering a rabbit. Now his questions became relentless with barely a pause between them. The hapless witness was confined to occasional grunts and mumbles by way of response.

The learned judge was also rather taken aback by Mr Cameron's onslaught.

"This will not do at all, Mr Cameron. I will not have you badgering witnesses in my court. You must allow time for an answer."

"As your lordship pleases," Mr Cameron replied with a bow before pointedly resuming his seat.

For several seconds nothing happened. Then instead of asking for the questions to be repeated the Chief Inspector began making disjointed responses in no particular order and making less and less sense as he went on. Mungo became quite excited; at last Mr Cameron was making an impression.

The judge did not share Mungo's enthusiasm. His annoyance seemed to grow as the Inspector rambled on. Lord Ochiltree was about to intervene again when Mr Cameron rose. This time he looked straight at the witness.

"Of course you could see very little in that poor light. I put it to you that you saw neither Mr Shaw nor his ship that August night."

After a long dramatic pause the inspector was still visibly confused. Reluctantly, he acknowledged that the darkness had obscured his view of the vessel. It was the first crack, albeit a small one, in the prosecutor's meticulously presented case and Mungo noticed more than a flicker of interest amongst the jurors at the Inspector's faltering replies to Mr Cameron.

By the time that this phase of the prosecution case was complete it was late morning. While Mr Robb was rearranging his papers he was handed a note that seemed to worry him. Presently he approached the judge's bench. Mungo noticed that his flamboyant mannerisms and dramatic speech had given way to a bowed head and an almost penitent demeanour. The judge looked concerned and an uncomprehending grimace spread over the great man's face giving him an unaccustomed pallor. The knuckles of his clenched hands were as white as his robe and purple veins stood out on his forehead. Mungo could have sworn they throbbed. No doubt about it; Lord Ochiltree was an angry man.

He could hear very little of what passed between Mr Robb and the judge. Then Mr Cameron was called forward. All three men now buried their heads in animated discussion for two or three minutes. Finally his lordship raised his hand.

"I will now hear legal submissions," the judge announced with great solemnity. "The jury may stand down until half an hour past one o'clock."

As the jury was shuffling out Cameron came forward to the dock and whispered to Mungo:

"An important crown witness has failed to appear and Mr Robb has requested an adjournment so that they may trace him. I shall oppose any delay, of course."

Mungo wasn't sure what this meant but from the look on Cameron's face he thought it might be good.

The legal debate was hard to follow since much of it was in Latin. The arguments flowed back and forward for a good fifteen minutes until the judge called the two advocates to order. He had given the matter careful consideration, he said, but had decided, on balance, to dismiss Mr Robb's motion. He reasoned that the crown had more than two months to prepare their case and an adjournment at this late stage would impede the course of justice. Having delivered his decision the Court was called to order whilst his lordship rose like a ship in full sail and floated out through a side door.

After this grand exit Mungo was hobbled down the steep stair and confined in a small cell below the courtroom. The jailer brought him a bowl of rabbit stew and potatoes, which he devoured almost instantly. The apprehension of these last few days had robbed him of his appetite but now that battle had been joined he could have done with another bowl, or maybe two.

Just as he finished eating he heard the door being unlocked and Mr Cameron was shown in.

"Well Mr Shaw," he said, "how are you bearing up?"

"I'm all right," Mungo replied. "Just a bit puzzled by everything that's going on."

"The only thing you have to understand is that we now have a fighting chance

Chapter Twenty Eight

When the court reconvened that afternoon Mr Robb deployed his considerable powers of oratory as he examined a procession of witnesses called with the sole object of diminishing Mungo's character. 'Shaw was well known for his violent tendencies', seemed to be the burden of Mr Robb's case; 'just the sort of villain who would kill a man with no remorse or even a second thought.'

Mungo's every confrontation was rehearsed. His fight, as a schoolboy, with Charles Wallace was related by someone Mungo did not recognise. The stranger was well through his evidence when Mungo remembered him as the boy that arrived with Wallace but who ran off at the first sign of trouble.

The prosecution case began to sound rather desperate as it stuttered through an obvious parcel of lies from the appalling Kirkwood. He had tried to make the battle at Greenock sound like the slaughter of the innocents. Mr Cameron had little difficulty in exposing his half truths, evasions and falsehoods. He even wrung from Kirkwood a concession that the aggressors were mainly the Greenock small boat men.

Most ridiculous of all was a complete stranger who tried to give an account of the incident at Dublin when Captain Weston was so savagely beaten. His testimony was so obviously a fabrication that the judge reluctantly ruled it inadmissible hearsay.

Mr Cameron's expert dissection of the Crown's tainted character evidence contained much impressive logic, but Mungo was alarmed to note that the jurors seemed to prefer the lurid fictions uttered by the over-rehearsed Crown witnesses.

When Mr Robb announced the conclusion of the case for the Crown there was relief on all sides of the court. The evidence given by the last few witnesses was embarrassingly thin and a judge less inclined towards the Crown than Lord Ochiltree might have imposed sanctions for wasting the court's time.

Any respite was, however, short-lived. No sooner had Mr Robb resumed his seat than Mr Cameron approached the bench. The judge seemed to be waving him away but Mr Cameron persisted. After a few minutes, and with all the enthusiasm of an over-burdened mule, his lordship agreed that he would hear legal submissions for the defence. Mungo had no inkling of what was in Mr Cameron's mind but he certainly did not care for the judge's reaction. For the second time that day, the jury was stood down.

Mr Cameron argued that the prosecution had offered no credible evidence that placed the accused at the scene of Mr Reid's unfortunate demise and that there was therefore no case to answer. After a brief debate Lord Ochiltree addressed the court.

"What is alleged against Mungo Shaw is a crime of the ultimate gravity and I will not deny the jury the opportunity to determine the matter. The defendant's motion is refused." Mungo was surprised that Mr Cameron reacted so calmly to the judge's ruling but neither he nor Mr Cameron was prepared for what happened next.

"Due to the lateness of the hour," the judge announced wearily, "the court stands adjourned until ten o'clock tomorrow." It was only half past three and there was time enough for at least another two hours before the lamps were lit. The look of injured innocence on Mr Cameron's face seemed to suggest the curtailed session was some kind of gratuitous judicial rebuke. Mr Robb confirmed this interpretation when he turned to Mr Cameron.

"I'm obliged to you," he whispered, an ill concealed smirk playing on his lips. "Maybe half a day will be long enough to find my missing witness!"

Less than a mile out of the village he caught up with the Rannoch drove. It was enormous; maybe three thousand head. They were making hard going of it and had turned the low lying track on the loch side into a complete quagmire. Mungo immediately decided he should try to find another route. He doubled back to the village and discussed his dilemma with the Innkeeper.

Mungo was back in the Tolbooth by four that afternoon. His day in court had been like riding out a storm at sea; one minute high on the crest of a wave and the next cast down in a trough of despair. Just like being storm-driven, the experience was utterly exhausting. Yet he could not rest. His mind jumped from churning over the evidence to trying to anticipate the reaction of the jury and all the while wondering what went on behind Lord Ochiltree's beetling brows.

He took no supper but that was not for want of an appetite; the evil-smelling boiled meat was in no way redeemed by the thin gruel or the stale bread. Now his mind started running back to the puzzle of Mr Robb's mystery witness. Mr Cameron would have known his identity but he never said and Mungo never asked; he couldn't bring himself to believe that someone had betrayed him. It was some solace that the man had now thought better of his treachery but not knowing who he was started to eat into his imagination. Could it have been someone from the smugglers' band, on the shore that night? But they knew neither his face nor his name. It must be one of his own crew, he thought, but then none of them was capable of such a base act, he was sure of it. This conundrum denied him sleep for most of the night.

At about six o'clock he was roused from his fitful drowsing by the noise of the jailers changing watch. Suddenly he remembered; Alf was still in jail! The sheriff had given him and his drunken cronies six months for mobbing and rioting. Had the prosecutors threatened Alf – with transportation perhaps – unless he would turn King's Evidence. That must be it; Alf was always inclined to deal with the present danger and to trust the future to Providence.

Mungo was so hungry he bolted down his porridge and then managed to wheedle another helping from the chief jailer.

"You'll be better fed when you move to the condemned cell," sneered the jailer, handing him the refilled bowl. Mungo supposed that this kind of black humour was the jailer's stock-in-trade. Straight after he had eaten his fill the jailers took him down to the Court House. He was installed in his cramped cell below the dock long before any of the ghoulish spectators had assembled on the street. He was grateful for that small mercy.

Mungo was brought up to the dock about fifteen minutes past ten. Everyone looked exactly the same as the day before. The scene had the quality of some recurrent nightmare.

"Does Mr Robb have any further evidence to offer against the accused Mungo Shaw?" said the judge, addressing the court in general. "No further word of Garvie?" Although Mungo had deduced who the mystery man was, the mention of Alf's name still came as a shock.

"No my lord, he apparently went missing after a mass break out from Ayr Tolbooth." Mungo was as pleased for Alf as he was for himself. "There is no further evidence for the prosecution."

"Very well," said Lord Ochiltree. "You may proceed with the defence, Mr Cameron."

Mr Cameron's opening speech was alarmingly brief. He concentrated on the Crown's doubtful attempts to prove that any crime had been committed and the prosecutor's complete failure to place Mungo anywhere near the scene of Reid's death. As he listened Mungo thought Mr Cameron was taking a fearful risk. It seemed to him that his advocate was carrying a couple of the jurors with him, at most. Maybe he should have made a clean breast of it from the beginning. Surely a truthful plea of accidental death or at least self defence might have had some prospect of success. How he longed for just one witness who would swear that he had been elsewhere. He knew that no one could do that but, just the same, he looked up to Mr Christian's place in the gallery. His seat was empty, but maybe, just maybe… It was a daft thought but time was running out and desperation was again invading his mind.

In the event Mr Cameron called only five witnesses; two to establish matters of fact and three more to rebut the prosecution's attacks on Mungo's character.

He started by reading out letters to the court from the harbour masters from Peel and Ayr. These documents established the dates and times of the *Heron's* departure and arrival at each port. Mr Robb raised no objection to them being read into the evidence. Mr Cameron then called the Kirkcudbright harbour master to the witness box. He was a tall dark man, his hair greying at the temples. His soft brown eyes scanned the courtroom like a master mariner fixing his position. His great experience as a seaman was legendary all along the Solway Coast and indeed far beyond. Clearly he was well known and respected and maybe half a dozen of the jurors nodded appreciatively in his direction.

"Captain Paul," Mr Cameron began. "You have seen the letters from your colleagues at Peel and Ayr. Taken together they indicate that the *Heron* made her passage between these two ports in three and a half days."

"Yes, sir!"

"How long would the passage have taken had they gone first to Whithorn, and then laid over for a couple of hours at Port Castle before finally setting sail for Ayr?"

"It's not easy to say without knowing what the wind was doing."

"It is a matter of record that in the days before and after Mr Reid's unfortunate death there was between fifteen and twenty knots of wind from the south west."

"In those conditions you would struggle to do that trip in four days, maybe nearer five. Weathering' the Mull O' Galloway would be the worst o' it. I've seen boats out o' here take a full day just to get round the Mull in such a south west blow."

Mr Cameron continued to rehearse all possible combinations of the alleged route and Captain Paul confirmed it was not possible to make the trip in three and a half days. His evidence seemed to stun Mr Robb who sat staring blankly in the general direction of the judge.

"Well Mr Robb, do you have any questions for the witness?"

"No, my lord; nothing further." He had no wish to compound his misfortune.

Mungo was startled too. It was the first time he had seen any obvious doubt on the faces of the jurors. But they were not to know that Captain Weston's improved rig enabled the *Heron* to sail ten degrees closer to the wind and to make as much as three knots extra when running before the wind.

Mungo knew the next witness; he was Jack Thomson, the chief shipwright at Mr Murray's shipyard in Ayr and the man who had re-rigged the *Heron* to Captain Weston's specification.

"Can you tell the court about the modifications you made to the vessel called the *Heron*?" Mr Cameron asked.

The shipwright was proud of his trade and described the refit down to the smallest detail. Indeed he spoke at such length that Mr Cameron feared he might be boring the jury. Once or twice he made to hurry the shipwright along only to be waved away by the judge who was fascinated and appeared to be making a sketch from the shipwright's description. After he had concluded his peroration Mr Cameron asked:

"As a result of all this work was the vessel's appearance altered in any way?"

"Yes indeed, sir; she bore no resemblance to her former appearance as an ordinary cargo wherry. Although I say it myself she had more the look of a cutter."

"What would be the main differences?"

"Most obviously her main mast was further forward and rigged for a topsail. She could also carry two foresails on her extended bowsprit."

"Could she be mistaken for her former rig?"

"No sir."

"Could she be mistaken for any other cargo wherry working in these waters?"

"Definitely not, sir!"

The shipwright was not let off so lightly as Captain Paul. Mr Robb began his questions in a markedly respectful tone having noted, no doubt, the judge's rapt attention to the craftsman's evidence.

"The court is obliged to you for your expert explanation of the finer points of rigging a ship. You must have re-rigged a great many vessels in your time?"

"Certainly sir; more than a dozen."

"What would you say was the usual purpose of altering a vessel's rig?"

"There can be many reasons sir," but before he could launch into an exhaustive list, Mr Robb came back:

"What did Captain Weston hope to achieve with the *Heron*?"

"Well sir, she had been badly damaged during her grounding and the new rig was part and parcel of the repairs."

"We understand that but surely he sought some improvement, some advantage from these works?"

"Stepping the mast forward, certainly improved access to the hold, sir."

"Yes, yes but all these additions; larger mainsail, new topsail and an extra foresail. That must have given her more speed."

"Yes indeed but it had to be carefully used. Her old hull was not designed to carry so much canvas."

"Even so, how much faster would she be, two knots, maybe three?"

"That would depend on whether she was close hauled or running free. Only a master mariner could answer precisely."

"I put it to you that the *Heron* was very much faster than any other coasting wherry and could indeed have covered the whole trip from Peel to Ayr with a detour to Port Castle in three days."

"I honestly could not say, sir. I am but a humble shipwright."

Although the shipwright could not confirm Mr Robb's contention, his theory caused a stir in the jury. Captain Paul's evidence now looked much less conclusive.

Mr Cameron's final evidence was character testimony given by Dr Guthrie, his school master, the Reverend Maclintock and Mungo's employer Mr Murray.

Dr Guthrie was very precise and proper in making Mungo out to be an exceptional pupil with all the necessary attributes for University. His manner seemed to intimidate Mr Robb for he asked him no questions. Mr Maclintock was kept firmly to the point by Mr Cameron but his answers to Mr Robb were rambling and equivocal. Mungo began to fear the minister would give less than the hoped for testimonial. He must have realised it himself for he recovered enough to make clear his unshakeable belief in Mungo's good character and agreeable nature.

It was Mr Murray who carried the day, though. His wealth and his reputation for hard work and honest dealing were well known in Galloway. He declared that Mungo was the finest employee he ever had. He was a man of the highest principles and his skill as a seaman was equalled only by his fine head for business affairs. Mr Robb's attempts to diminish Mr Murray's testimony were swept aside with barely a moment's hesitation. Mungo worried that the jury might find him too good to be true. Far from it, he held their attention from beginning to end with many an approving nod.

The closing speeches by prosecution and defence were mainly a repeat of their opening statements and the whole matter was concluded by noon.

"The court will adjourn until two o'clock at which time I will charge the jury," Lord Ochiltree announced and the awfulness of his situation again gripped Mungo. Nothing more could be said or done to save him. Soon, too soon it would be over and his fate would be sealed, one way or another.

Chapter Twenty Nine

Locked away in his cell below the courtroom there was little to do but think. He tried very hard to decipher the true meaning of Lord Ochiltree's summing up or, at least, what effect it might have on the jury. Would the speech have any effect at all, he wondered. How could the jurors *'clear your minds of what you knew of the case before coming to court?'* These men were farmers and merchants from ten miles round and likely to have known all about Reid's death since the time the body was found. They would not be human if they had not formed their opinions at the same time. But then why should these Kirkcudbright men show any particular favour to an exciseman from Whithorn? As a breed 'the excise' had few friends anywhere. In his mind, he rehearsed these possibilities along with many other prospects and prejudices that he hoped might win him his freedom. He kept a surprisingly optimistic frame of mind. He had persuaded himself that there was still hope.

At six o'clock there was a rattling of keys. The door opened and the jailer showed Mr Cameron into the cramped space.

"The jury is split," he announced. "They are asking for further directions from the judge."

"Is that good?" Mungo asked.

"Maybe; it depends how many are on each side. His lordship's humour is a consideration, too. I know he had meant to be on the road back to Edinburgh tonight; not much chance of that now."

"The two big fellows at the end of the middle row seemed very impressed by Captain Paul," Mungo volunteered. "They also listened very closely to your final speech. It was a very fine speech, sir."

"Thank you, Mr Shaw but we should not get ahead of ourselves; we'll call it a fine speech when you're released.

Until then just concentrate on keeping your spirits up. I'll keep you informed about what's going on." Then he left.

This brief interlude introduced a new uncertainty into Mungo's mind. Now, he was not so positive. If it was only the two big fellows who were standing up for him then there must be a dozen who would sooner see him hang. Over and over he had told himself not to draw conclusions from his own imaginings. Then he thought, maybe there was a majority for acquitting him. Although this prospect was also in his imagination it restored his optimism, so he was content to hold on to it.

Slowly he managed to wrench his mind away from pointless speculation and he tried to make a balanced review of the trial. Mr Robb was a clever man and a persuasive speaker – Graham Murray had said he would be a judge before too long. Yet Mr Cameron was also intelligent but in a quieter, more calculating way. His closing speech had made it clear that although the prosecutor had suggested much he had proved little. The jury could not convict unless they were satisfied that Mr Robb had proved his case and in that matter at least, Lord Ochiltree's direction to the jury was clear and emphatic.

As he tried to imagine the debate going on amongst the jurors his mind wandered to the question of why he was in this dire situation at all. Certainly he had been running contraband on the Galloway coast that fateful night and he had been in command when Joseph Reid was swept off the stern by the mizzen boom. The hail of gunfire directed at the ship would have made any attempt to recover the man completely futile. He had no option but to make a run for it. Maybe he was guilty of something but certainly not murder.

He thought again about Mr Cameron's line of defence. His painstaking arguments about the precise identity of the *Heron* was surely asking too much of the jury's powers of concentration. In their minds the ship at Port Castle that night was the *Heron*. To entertain any other possibility was beyond their imagination. The shipwright's evidence was an education. Certainly it seemed to fascinate the judge, but did it interest the jury?

Mr Cameron had seemed to be on firmer ground by casting doubt on whether any ship could have made that passage in three and a half days. Even now Mungo could not quite believe it himself. He shuddered to think of the old ship creaking and straining with every scrap of canvas set and her head closer to the wind than ever seemed possible. The thrill of that mad dash to weather the Mull of Galloway still caused his heart to beat faster. Just like the old ship's rigging his heartstrings were tight as a drum and his pulse was pounding like her bows in that short, steep sea. Maybe Alf was right and he really was the best skipper on the coast. His seamanship could not save him but he still took much pride from his reputation as a deft and courageous mariner.

It was then he remembered that these same skills had set the sheriff's men on his trail. If the Laird of Ardfin had not sung his praises in the drawing rooms of the Edinburgh gentry he might have just disappeared back to the north with his band of highland drovers. Yet he knew the droving life was not for him. It would have destroyed his soul, sooner or later. Even so he was sad and even ashamed that he had letthe drovers down.

His mind strayed here and there following no particular pattern. He had heard it said that a dying man sees his life run forward before his eyes and he wondered if it was all up for him. Then out of nowhere anger replaced his morbid cast of mind. His thoughts went to Charles Wallace. It was bad enough that Margaret Murray was promised to Wallace but being arrested by him was almost too much to bear. As he brooded in his cell, hatred of Wallace gradually took over his whole mind and drove out his doom-laden thoughts. If he did nothing else for the rest of his life he would run Wallace to ground and send him to his maker. If he had stood charged with murdering Charles Wallace and not Joseph Reid he was sure he would face his fate with a calm mind.

He was still lost in planning how he would dispatch the loathsome Wallace when the door of his cell opened and the jailer announced:

"The jury's back."

It was all so sudden. Mungo was in a state of shock as he stumbled up the short stair to the dock. The courtroom was nearly empty and eerily quiet. A lantern burned above the judge's chair but there was no sign of the great man. The lawyers and the Clerk of the Court sat at the great table – in silence. The jurymen were in their box. They made no sound either but it seemed to Mungo that they looked strained and haggard. It was so quiet that for the first time he could hear the ominous tick of the clock on the wall above the jury. It showed half past one. He had no idea it was so late.

After a minute or two a few bleary-eyed men staggered into their places in the gallery. There were no more than a dozen in all and Mungo did not recognise any of them.

"All rise," the court officer announced in a subdued voice as if fearful that he would wake someone. A second or two later Lord Ochiltree made his way, unsteadily, to his chair. Mungo wondered if he had been roused from his sleep to reconvene the court.

The judge's arrival provoked whispered conversations between the court officers and the lawyers that seemed to go on forever. Mungo found the wait so excruciating that he thought his heart might stop at any moment, saving the hangman the trouble.

"Carry on," barked the judge.

"The foreman of the jury will rise," ordered the Clerk of the Court. The man who rose was one of the big men who had caught Mungo's attention earlier. Was this a good sign? He dared to hope.

"Have you reached a verdict?"

"Yes sir."

"And is it the verdict of you all?"

These questions only took but a few seconds but Mungo was so far gone with anxiety that they seemed to hang in the air for an eternity. He felt he might lose consciousness at any moment but somehow he hung on. Maybe it was just the need to know.

"Yes sir."

"On the charge of murder what is your verdict?"

There was a pause as if the foreman had misheard the question. Then in a loud clear voice he replied:

"Not proven, sir."

There was an audible sigh that went all around the echoing chamber. Mr Cameron turned and smiled broadly to Mungo whilst looks of puzzlement animated the faces of the sparse gathering of bemused onlookers in the gallery.

Mungo had expected to hear 'guilty' or 'not guilty.' He was not prepared for these new words and was unsure what to make of them. Suddenly he was seized with a fear that the whole trial was about to start over again, but his panic was almost immediately displaced by the Clerk's next instruction.

"The accused will rise."

He shot to his feet and, gripping the rail in front of him, staring towards the judge.

After another long pause Lord Ochiltree returned his stare.

"You are a very fortunate young man," the judge began. "The jury find that the prosecutor did not prove his case but they stopped short of finding you not guilty." The judge's words made little sense to Mungo. He just needed to know; was he free or not?

But Lord Ochiltree was in no mood for simplicity. He explained the unique refinement in the Law of Scotland that permits three verdicts in a criminal case. He then droned on about the significance of the court's finding and the shades of meaning that might be attached to it. He then launched into what he no doubt meant as a learned dissertation on the principle of the 'not proven' verdict but his speech had become slurred. Mungo wondered if he had been overwhelmed by fatigue; the judge was not a young man, after all. A few minutes into his tortured oration and Mr Cameron became restive and stood to raise a point but the judge waved him back to his place.

"Your skilful pleadings have won your man his freedom but his innocence is not absolute." Then turning to Mungo he said, "You are indebted to the skill and wisdom of Mr Cameron and to the friends who have spoken so eloquently on your behalf. I hope you will honour them all by being of good conduct for the rest of your days. Make no mistake, had the prosecutor been able to make the most of his case you would be facing a very different, and much shorter, future." Perhaps realising that he had said too much, he paused and looked down at his papers. Then quite suddenly he declaimed:

"You are free to go!"

Before these momentous words could fully register in Mungo's fevered brain the Court Officer called for order.

"All rise!"

The Officer then helped the judge from his chair and out of the side door.

Mr Cameron came straight over to Mungo.

"Well, Mr Shaw it was a near thing but we have carried the day."

"Thank you, sir," Mungo said with evident feeling as he grasped the advocate's hand. "I am forever in your debt."

Mr Robb also offered his hand to Mr Cameron but he said not a word. The judge's injunction on the prosecution case had clearly left its mark.

"It's such a pity my mother is not here," Mungo said to no one in particular. Just then the chief jailer came forward carrying a bag.

"These are your personal effects," he announced, tipping out some clothing, Mungo's money belt and his grandfather's watch. "Check all is in order and sign that you have received everything you are due."

At that point Mungo would have signed a pact with the devil to be free of the place that had so recently seemed like his tomb.

"I fear I cannot delay overlong," Mr Cameron said, interrupting Mungo's muster of his belongings. "I have an early start tomorrow and a mile to go to my lodgings."

"Thank you again," he said to the retreating figure of Mr Cameron. "Before you go, can you tell me what the judge meant at the last? I had difficulty making him out."

"I fear his lordship had dined well but not wisely. For all his maunderings, not proven has exactly the same effect as not guilty, but with a more subtle shade of meaning. Do not concern yourself any further. You are a free man."

The small gathering in the courthouse dispersed quickly and almost before he knew it Mungo found himself alone with his worldly goods on the steps of Kirkcudbright High Court, in the middle of the night. He had nowhere to sleep but that did not concern him. His elation would keep away the cold of the night. He was sad, though, that he had no one to share his good fortune. His mother, the Murrays and the laird all had rooms in the Selkirk Arms across the street, but the hotel was in complete darkness and his attempts at entry were frustrated by a stout lock.

He was wondering what to do when two familiar figures at the courthouse door were lit up by a shaft of pale moonlight. It was young Peter whose appearance in the crowd had so cheered him on the first day of the trial. He was accompanied by Hughie, his best friend in the whole world. They two had been sleeping in an outhouse at the back of the court and although they had been roused by the commotion they had arrived too late for the verdict.

"Ah aye kent ye wid get aff," roared Hughie, putting his arm around Mungo's neck. "Come away doon tae the boat and we'll see if we can get a dram."

Then it was Peter's turn to embrace his old friend and all three set off on the short walk to the harbour.

All was quiet on board the *Venus*.

"The old man is well asleep," said Hughie as he lit their way forward with a lantern. "I can offer you some of the finest French brandy or a flagon of black rum; we brocht it special – for this day."

"To be honest I could do with something to eat," said Mungo.

Hughie rummaged around in a locker by the flickering light of his lamp. "We don't hae that much aboard. We've been taking oor vittels in the town." Eventually he produced a large crust and handed it to Mungo.

"Thank you," he said. "Half a loaf is better than no bread – just like the verdict."

Chapter Thirty

Mungo and his mother walked briskly to fend off the creeping cold of the dying day. How many times had he passed these sentinel beech trees, guarding the broad approach to Langmuir House? They never seemed particularly threatening - nor welcoming, come to that. Today their frosted branches made a kind of ornate filigree that contrasted eerily with the blackening sky. The last of the crows flapped off lazily in search of a roost for the night and the smell of wood smoke drifted up from the village. Any warmth there may have been in the sun was gone but there was still enough light to pick out the haunts where he had spent so many hours of his boyhood. He had often met Sir Archie who always gave him a smile and passed the time of day. Yet as he grew up he learned of the Laird's reputation for being ill-tempered and impatient – 'Carnapcious Crawford' folk called him behind his back. He was often short with children but that had never been Mungo's experience.

The day had begun like all the others since the trial. He was restless; not knowing what to be at. He had been offered work by Mr Murray but not at the sea; he was a marked man to every exciseman in the country. Still, he was fortunate that he had the farm. Many a young man would have traded everything for a farm tenancy but to Mungo it was simply a last resort. That night he was bidden to the Laird's house for his supper; to sign the lease he supposed. He would do it, if only for his mother's sake.

The laird was every inch a gentleman and he had stood by him and his mother all through the recent ordeal. He even carried them home from Kirkcudbright in his own carriage. Yet he was also known to be shrewd in all his dealings so there would likely be some hard bargaining over the rent. The night before Mungo had tried to analyse the farm accounts but he could not concentrate and retired soon after nightfall. He slept till nearly eight o'clock. Instinctively ashamed of his idleness he started studying the accounts again in the morning. He was half way down his third column when his mother came in from the milking.

"How are you this fine morning," he greeted her with rather forced cheerfulness. She nodded but said nothing.

On the rare occasions when he was at home he used to have breakfast with him and they would always spend a happy half hour chatting about the farm and the village gossip. Since the trial, though, she was much changed; nervous, even frightened. It once crossed Mungo's mind that she might believe he was a murderer, after all. Of course he knew in his heart that she believed no such thing but her indulgent smile and her easy self-confidence were gone. For long periods she hardly said anything at all, lost in another world. He wondered if it was, perhaps, his own listless melancholy that made her so fearful. It was only six months since Andrew Maxwell took the depression and hanged himself.

She was more detached than ever that morning; her face as pale as whey and her hands shaking so much she could hardly hold her porridge spoon. Mungo could not bear to see her so anxious but what could he do? Even in the best of times she never spoke much about her own feelings and yet he had to find some way of reassuring her.

"M....," he began but pulled up short when he realised she was already speaking.

"I should have told you years ago, but first Father wouldn't let me then the time was never right," she drifted back into her dream-world again.

He knew it must be something very painful so he got up and went to the other side of the table. He cradled her head in his arm and looked steadily into her green eyes.

"What is it, mother?" he asked. She did not reply and after a few moments he tried to lighten the mood. "Have you seen a ghost?"

"Maybe I have at that," she stared at him through a watery smile for a long time then she blurted out. "Your real father is Archie Crawford," she paused, causing Mungo's face to take the colour of her own. "Young Archie, I mean, the Laird's first son."

In an instant, vivid thoughts crowded his mind; he remembered tales of the gallant captain's death in battle and of course she had always told him his father died at Culloden. Then there was the old drover's tale that his mother's husband died at Prestonpans. It was a kind of relief; unlocking so many mysteries. The Laird's unfailing kindness to the family when he was growing up; his support for Da's improvements to the farm; his payment of the school fees; his faithful visits to him jail and his constant attendance at the trial. He did not find the news at all shocking.

His mother looked at him with a kind of wistful agony, at once seeking forgiveness and offering reassurance. She willed him to say something.

"Is that a fact?" was the best Mungo's overworked brain could manage.

"You are the strangest boy!" she exclaimed in exasperation. Her face had taken on a more serene look as twenty years of half truths and evasions slipped from her shoulders. Then she rose and walked to the window. She stood looking out towards Langmuir House, her shoulders heaving as she began to sob. Then she turned to him. "I know you must be angry. It must be a terrible shock. Believe me; I have carried the penance of silent shame, all these years, only to protect you."

At first her revelation had resolved so many of the questions that had haunted him and had remained unspoken throughout his life. That relief was short-lived, though, and it now gave way to a more ambiguous state of mind. He felt both pity and resentment towards her. This distraught woman was his only flesh and blood and he loved her dearly, but how could she have denied him his birthright? He had a right to know who his father was. Being told her silence was for his own good only stirred a smouldering rage in him. But it was pity that prevailed as he steered her to a seat by the fire.

"I have to know, mother. Please tell me."

After a long and tearful pause she began.

"When the Prince's Army came back I went to Glasgow to meet Ewan but it was Archie that met me. He told me about Ewan being killed at Prestonpans. I was distraught but Archie looked after me. He was a great comfort. One thing just led to another. After a few weeks he marched off and I never saw him again. Every time I look at you, though I can still see his laughing eyes."

Mungo was horrified at the casualness of it all and his shock must have showed on his face for his mother quickly went on.

"It all went back to childhood; Archie and I had been close for almost all our lives. Ever since the war of 1715 my father had been on good terms with Sir Archie. They had been comrades in arms. We were often asked to Langmuir. Archie was ages with me, we used to play together. Later on we became sweethearts. It was not fitting of course," she paused, swallowed hard and then continued. "Lady Crawford was always polite enough but no son of hers was going to take up with the daughter of a tenant. Your grandfather was just as disapproving. He even said I was abusing the laird's hospitality. Between them they put an end to our 'dalliance' as they called it." The awful sadness in her face brought a tear to Mungo's eye.

"What age were you, then?"

"Fifteen, nearly sixteen; when it ended. It was the saddest day of my life. I remember it like today."

Mungo thought of his own star-crossed romance with Margaret Murray and his mother's anguish began to soften his ire. Yet his soul demanded to know more about Ewan

Lachlan. Until that morning he was the only one he had ever called father.

"Was it long after that you met Ewan?"

"Ewan's father used to bring us cattle for fattening every back-end, for as long as I can remember. I had just turned seventeen the first time Ewan came with him. I found him a bit awkward and he spoke very little Scots," she smiled, "yet, over the next year I found myself thinking about him, more and more often. By the time he was due to come back I was counting the days." There was another long pause though she was more composed now and she continued in an almost matter of fact tone.

"Anyway, a year later we were married. Six months after that he marched off and I never saw him again. We were too young, married too soon."

"What does the laird think of all this?" Mungo asked after a while.

"Oh he has known the story since the beginning. Archie wrote to him very often. He always wanted to acknowledge you as his own but neither his wife nor my father would ever hear of it. He might want to talk to you tonight."

She did not say she needed to tell her story first but Mungo knew that's what she meant.

* * *

Langmuir House was an ancient fortified tower, at least two hundred years old. The facing stone, although rough-hewn, had a warming richness to its dull golden colour. The windows to the front of the house were small, almost dainty, but it was no part of their duty to look pretty. The huge studded oak door was reached by a dozen or so narrow stone steps between chest high balustrades. The Crawfords had always been minor lairds compared to the mighty Earls of Cassilis and Stair on either side of them. Over the centuries these fortifications must have deterred many an unwelcome visitor.

Old George – or Dod to everyone except the laird – was the longest serving retainer at Langmuir House. He opened the door to them before they had even reached the first step on the stair.

"I saw you on the road," he said, addressing himself to Jean. "It's cauld tae be on the road the nicht," and looking over Jean's shoulder he asked, "and how are you faring, Mungo?"

"Never better," Mungo replied, "now I've seen the back of Kirkcudbright Tolbooth."

"The laird's no been great this last wee while but you'll fairly cheer him up. Cook is making some venison collops. That'll soon warm you up," Dod enthused, as he helped Jean up the last few steps.

The great hall of Langmuir House was at the back where the fortress stood on the edge of a small but very steep cliff. The hall had a high ceiling with three large windows looking out over the sea towards Arran.

"Mistress Shaw and master Mungo," Dod announced with practiced formality.

Sir Archie came forward and helped Jean onto a richly cushioned settle.

"You look tired lass," he wheezed, grasping Jean's hands.

"You look worn out, yourself. I heard you haven't been keeping too well these last days," Jean said.

"Oh, George fusses about nothing," said the laird, immediately denying his own words with a rasping cough.

He showed Mungo to an elegant brocaded stool.

"So this is you, Mungo," Sir Archie said with a twinkling smile. "A free man at last!" His voice was brimful of celebration and affection.

His greetings complete, the laird settled himself in a great wing-backed chair, its cracked leather seeming to mimic his own careworn face. The open fire that stretched across most of the gable wall was well ablaze with a mixture of peat and pine logs. A few moments of awkward silence followed. Sir Archie knew very well what was on Jean's mind but he was reluctant to confront it so he took another tack.

"I've always been fond of you Mungo, even as a wee lad; full of devilment and adventure." Then he turned back to Jean, "Supper's at seven and we'll be joined by Mr Scott and Macadam the lawyer. I'll ask George to bring some tea for now, if that would suit you?"

Jean nodded. "That will be fine."

When the tea came Dod placed it on the table by the window. He took up the silver tea kettle and expertly dispensed the dark brew into three elegant chinaware cups. On previous visits to the house Jean had seen some of the many beautiful artefacts the late Lady Crawford had collected but she had not seen this crockery before.

"What a bonny tea service," she said, her eyes shining in admiration.

"Lady Crawford had it put by as a wedding gift for our Archie," the laird sighed, "but we never saw him betrothed, never mind married." The laird was suddenly aware he had trespassed on their unspoken quandary. He paused, seeming to lose his thread, before continuing in a distracted voice. "He had a great notion of you but his mother was keen to see him wed to one of the Cassilis girls. She was always very class conscious, you know," he said through a forced grin.

Jean did not care for the laird's evasiveness but was reluctant to provoke any embarrassment.

"Mungo and I had a long talk this morning," she said. "It is important to put the frightening events of these last months behind us. For the future it is best we have no more secrets."

"I see," he said, pausing as if to gather his thoughts. "You are quite right. Let me speak plainly," he said turning his gaze to Mungo. "Even if the law does not allow it, you are my grandson. I meant to wait till Macadam and Mr Scott had arrived but what I have to say will come just as well among the three of us." At this he rose and ambled towards the window.

Jean was rather agitated. She had not intended anything dramatic but her anxious look seemed to accept she had put the laird in a corner.

"By all means let us wait for the others," she mumbled yet somehow accepting that this cat could not be put back in its bag.

Sir Archie more or less ignored Jean and, picking up a sheaf of papers from a side table, he said, "Macadam prepared this deed last week. It conveys the ownership of the Shaw to you, Mungo."

Mungo hoped his surprise and gratitude showed on his face, for he was struck completely dumb.

Chapter Thirty One

Mungo had rarely been at home for more than a week at a time in the past four years but now he had been at the Shaw for nearly three months. In the weeks before the momentous meeting with the laird, Mungo's moods had swung between elation and despair. He was so worried about how he could settle to life on the land. The public reaction to the court's inconclusive verdict also upset him. Old acquaintances seemed uneasy in his company and were always in a hurry to be off elsewhere. Those he knew only rarely returned his greetings and many ignored him completely.

Now that Sir Archie had settled the Shaw on him, his attitude changed completely. The farming life became an enthusiasm and was no longer a reluctant acceptance of the inevitable. Strangely enough, the distant demeanour of his neighbours and acquaintances seemed to deepen his resolve; the more society shunned him the closer he stuck to his land. Every dry day of the early spring he was busy extending the hedging and drainage improvements his grandfather had begun. He had quite forgotten how he used to berate the old man, under his breath, about the pointlessness of it all. When the weather was poor he threw himself into all kinds of repairs and alterations to the house and outbuildings.

His mother was heartened by his newfound industry and, of course, more than delighted with the impending change in his circumstances. Although she was irritated by the coolness of some of the townsfolk who came to her stall at the butter market it did not restrain her joy. Mungo and she would talk well into the small hours about what a great success they would make of their 'wee estate.' He was glad to see that she had put all the tribulations of the past months behind her. It still rankled that she had kept his father's identity from him for all these years although he knew that his birth out of wedlock was no small matter had it been widely known. At least now he understood what a crushing burden it had all been for her so he made nothing of it..

As time went on he began to notice that the folk of Langmuir had become friendlier. The self same people who so recently cut him dead now sought him out. They accosted him at the kirk, the mart and even when walking in the town. It was as if he had become a long-lost friend. He was not completely sure why the public mood had moved in his favour.. Lingering doubts about his innocence seemed to be receding along with the winter weather. All the same, he instinctively kept his distance from all but his closest friends and family. Although it was not in his nature, he became standoffish to the point that some thought him aloof. The strain of it all was just as bad to Mungo as being ostracised.

About a week before Easter he had a surprise visit from his old friend Hughie Maclure. His delight at the prospect of good fellowship and plain speaking must have shown on his face as he welcomed his visitor into the warmth of the kitchen. Hughie had been away at the sea, almost continuously, since they celebrated Mungo's freedom that night, aboard the *Venus* at Kirkcudbright.

"Weel I'm no rightly sure if I should bend the knee to oor new laird," Hughie roared with laughter, shaking Mungo's hand and wrapping his free arm around his shoulder.

It suddenly dawned on Mungo that the changing attitude of the local people had nothing to do with an improving view of his ordeal and trial. Yet how had it become known that he was to be a landowner; it was supposed to be a closely guarded secret amongst the few people who had been at Langmuir House that evening six weeks before. If Hughie knew then it must be common knowledge so there was no point in evasion.

"Steady, Hughie, I don't own anything yet," said Mungo in mild embarrassment. "The transfer doesn't take place till Martinmas – too many problems with taking over during the farming year – much tidier to wait till the harvest is in."

"Aye, well, when I landed this morning Ayr harbour wiz fair buzzing wi' the story; yin meenit yer fightin' tae save yer neck next yer a laird. Folk don't ken whit tae mak o' it," said Hughie shaking his head, "ony way ye deserve a bit o' luck!"

"Thank you kindly, my man," Mungo said in a tone of mock haughtiness, "but what about you; are you still sailing as mate with your father?"

"The old man's no been too great this last long while," Hughie sighed, "so ah've been skipper since Sandy went to the *Glory*."

"Good for you, Hughie," Mungo exclaimed in genuine tribute to his friend. "But I hope Rab will mend soon. Still, maybe it's time he took a rest from the hard graft, just the same."

"Right enough," Hughie nodded. "It's the chance of a skipper's berth ah wanted tae tell ye aboot; Billy Ferguson is building a new boat and he means tae sell the *Trojan* at the back end." He paused at Mungo's lack of reaction, "yon nicht in Kirkcudbright, mind, ye said ye had a notion o gaun' back tae the fishin." Seeing the lack of enthusiasm on Mungo's face he quickly added, "Maybe it was the rum talking!"

"I don't know," said Mungo. "I mean to get back to the sea one day; maybe on a square rigger in distant waters, but who knows? For now I have more than enough to keep me busy here, but a lot can happen before the back end."

"Whatever ye decide ye'll no be troubled by yon serpent, Wallace, ony mair. He's been drummed oot o' the excise."

"I never heard that," said Mungo. He was startled at the news but his face remained motionless.

"Seemingly he had been spending his time wi Bessie Hay from the Loans when he was meant to be keeping night watches for smugglers at Troon."

Mungo looked quizzical.

"Ye ken Bessie, Mad Tam's daughter."

"So old Gordon got rid of him," said Mungo in a matter of fact voice that did not quite conceal his glee.

"Aye but that's no the best o' it. When Tam heard aboot it he flew into a black rage. Wi' Tam oot to get his blood, Wallace had to make a peace offering. He gave Tam the key tae yon big barn where the excise men store the cargo they seize from the smugglers. Well, ye ken whit the Loans smugglers are like; they had cleaned the place out within the hour and word of Wallace's connivance wiz hame afore him."

The two friends laughed fit to burst. It was the best news Mungo heard since the judge told him he was free.

After they had run out of witty, and some very crude, rejoinders Mungo asked his friend, "I suppose Wallace's misdeeds did not go unnoticed at Blairadam. Mr Murray has never had much time for any of the Wallace tribe."

"Oh I thought your friend Graham might have mentioned; Margaret finished wi him just after you were nabbed. It seems Mr Murray accused him of being a Judas and threw him out of the house the next time he came to call on Margaret. The news could hardly get any better but it was no time to crow.

"Margaret is a wise woman," said Mungo. "Have you time for a dram?" he asked as he showed Hughie into the front room.

* * *

Easter day dawned cool but by mid morning the sun was well up and there was warmth in the air. The peewits wheeled above the new-ploughed ground and everywhere small birds chattered as they mated and carried twigs and straw to their new nests. The hedges at the Shaw were in bud now and from a distance the early blossom on the thorn bushes seemed like clouds of pale mist floating over the deeper green of the new pasture. Mungo had seen all this before but he never really paid it much heed. Now that he was to own the land every detail was important to him. As he and his mother walked together to the Kirk he had a powerful sense of well-being; this year the Festival of the Risen Christ was truly, a new beginning.

As they found their way to their usual pew James Scott was already seated there. Mungo was aware of how happy everyone looked. He put it down to the good weather but that hardly explained the warmth and generosity of the greetings that pressed in on them from every side. Even the Reverend Maclintock's sermon had a whiff of optimism and it was mercifully free of the usual forebodings of hellfire and damnation.

"Good day to you, Mistress Shaw," Mr Murray greeted his mother, "and how does it suit you to have Mungo at home?" Although they often spoke with the Murrays in passing, after divine service it was unusual for Mr Murray to seek them out in this way. Not only did they give a fulsome greeting, but Mrs Murray even forced a smile in Mungo's direction.

"He does well enough," his mother replied, "but I think the time hangs on his hands some days. It'll be different when he takes over the farm at Martinmas." Since there had always been an expectation that Mungo would inherit the lease, Jean's remarks gave nothing away. All the same Mrs Murray was not in the habit of befriending tenants. Mungo's interest was not straightforward either. Over his mother's shoulder he could see Margaret in conversation with another young lady but he judged it best to let her come to him; no point in seeming over anxious. In any case he had still to return Mr Murray's interest in his health and progress.

"You're looking very well," Margaret said softly with that demure smile he remembered from their first meeting. "I hear you are to settle to the farm after all."

"I could do a lot worse," he said with a kind of superficial smile.

They talked a while about mutual friends and recent news but Charles Wallace's name was not mentioned by either of them. By and by Mr Murray announced they would have to be on their way but oddly enough it was Mrs Murray who was most reluctant to break off the conversation.

"You must come and take tea with us one day," she said as they made ready to leave.

"I would like that very much," said Mungo.

On the road back to the Shaw Mungo's mind was buzzing with the possibilities of a new romance with Margaret. He was sure Mrs Murray knew that he was to become a landowner and if that's what it took to remove her objections he was content. It was Margaret's motives that required deeper thought. She had not quite set her cap at him but neither had she turned him away. He wanted to take his time but he hoped the summons to Blairadam would come sooner rather than later. Could it be that her mother was pushing her forward to cover the embarrassment of Charles Wallace? It was all very difficult. He was so deep in thought he did not notice that his mother and James Scott had fallen behind on the path and were chuckling to each other like a young courting couple.

Easter dinner at the Shaw was always special. Jean had spent most of the previous day roasting two ducks and poaching a salmon. Before going to church she had set a lamb to turn on the spit over some low embers. When they got into the house she sent James to fetch wood for the fire to finish the roast.

"It's all right, James, I'll go," said Mungo. There was a brief embarrassed silence which Jean broke.

"No, you go on James," she said quite firmly. "I have something else in mind for Mungo."

As James disappeared through the kitchen door she looked steadily at Mungo.

"James has asked me to marry him," she said, her sparkling eyes lighting up her broad smile.

Mungo had never seen her so happy. He remembered, as if by instinct, when James Scott had first come to the Shaw. Even then she had acted quite oddly as the tall man with his mop of jet black hair stood in the yard discussing farming matters with his grandfather. She had asked if she could get him something to drink but whether he had no thirst, or he was just put off by the scowl on old Shaw's face, he politely refused. Later that day there had been some altercation between his mother and his grandfather. There was nothing unusual in that but thinking back now he wondered if the old man had warned her off from the new factor. After the death of his grandfather Mr Scott had been often at the Shaw looking after the estate's interests. He had seen the way they looked at one another and had wondered when James Scott would make an honest woman of her.

"I hope you said yes," Mungo said, giving his mother a mighty hug.

Over dinner, which seemed to last most of the day, everyone was happy and agog with plans. The date was set for the end of July, at Lammas tide, a natural break between haymaking and harvest. After the wedding she would move to the factors house but keep her cows and the dairy business at the Shaw.

As the night wore on they were joined by some of their neighbours. A half case of Gascony wine was spent in celebration of Jean's news. By the time the conversation turned to Mungo's future they had graduated to the French brandy. James was full of bright suggestions for developing the Shaw but careful to give Mungo his place as the future laird. Like everyone else in Langmuir, Gregor Lamont knew all about what he called 'Mungo's promotion from tenant to landowner'. It seemed that word had got out from Writer Macadam's chambers; some gawky young clerk had failed to understand the confidential nature of the land transfer and blabbed the whole story to the patrons of a local Inn.

"Well Mungo, I hear that your old enemy has got his comeuppance," Mr Lamont ventured, his tongue well loosened by the fine brandy.

"What's all this?" his mother enquired looking at Mungo. There was a moments silence then Mungo began to roar with laughter. He told the story of Wallace's downfall, more or less as Hughie had told it to him but with only a few exaggerations for effect.

"Well, well," said Jean, remembering their encounter with the Murrays that morning. "Maybe the Reverend Macklintock will have a busier year than he planned."

Chapter Thirty Two

From the top of Brown Carrick there was a clear view all around the whole of South West Scotland. The alternate earthy and verdant hues of the small farms and woodland plantations gave the coastal plain the look of a patchwork rug as it stretched away to the Renfrew Hills. A Southern redoubt was formed by the majestic Galloway hills and in fine weather Ireland glanced out from her misty veil reminding her northern neighbour of her presence. To the East were the high moorlands bordering Lanark. All the while, in the restless firth, Arran slumbered, guarding the mystical islands that lay beyond the sunset. Mungo had known these views for as long as he could remember but they had never meant so much to him as they did now.

It was an unsettling kind of day with warm mists and fitful breezes; the kind of weather when the butter won't churn, his mother often said. He gave a chuckle and wondered how she was, or indeed where she was. She and James had left their wedding feast about five o'clock in the afternoon; making for Melrose to see his old mother, or so they said. It crossed his mind that he might have done better to leave the festivities at the same time. Even the brisk hilltop breezes could not clear the great weight that seemed to be resting on his throbbing brain.

All the same it had been a fine day. Every friend from ten mile round was there and many another from further afield. Two Lachlan cousins from Kilmichael had come over aboard a fishing boat from Tarbert. They brought Mungo's pay for his unfinished drove to Crieff. It was a handsome sum and Mungo was sure it was much, much more than he had ever earned. Despite his protestations, they insisted he take it. Of course the money was welcome for he had to give the bride away and pay for the feast – with her father gone it was his place to keep up the tradition, or so his mother had told him. More welcome than the money, though, was the cousins' report of the high reputation he still enjoyed amongst the good people of Mid Argyll. In prison he had fretted endlessly that he had let the drovers down and his character would be blackened.

The wedding feast had carried on until the dawn reddened the low clouds over Muirkirk way, but by that hour the fiddlers had fallen asleep and most of the guests had wandered away. He wished Margaret could have stayed longer. They had every dance together; eightsomes, foursomes and the drops of brandy. Mrs Murray was cordial, even jovial to him, but she was determined to have Margaret away before midnight. Still, Mungo was content that they were closer now, if still a long way from their passionate affair of two years before.

Everything in Mungo's life was fine except for one small but nagging exception. He was delighted that he was about to be the laird and not just the tenant of the Shaw, but he worried that the Crawfords might wish to embrace him more closely than he had expected.

"Well my boy," Sir Archie had said to him as they walked from the kirk to the blacksmith's barn, where the feast was to be held, "are you happy for your mother? James Scott is a fine man and they will do very well together."

"I'm sure you are right, they always seem very content in one another's company," Mungo replied, well aware that their new married estate was simply a solemn recognition of what had been going on for months, or years. "She'll still keep her cows and the dairy at the Shaw so I'll see her most days."

The old man smiled at Mungo's self interest and started poking in his waistcoat pocket. He fished out a parchment bearing a bright red seal.

"It's from Alistair," he said as he handed the letter to Mungo. "He seems very pleased to have a new nephew!"

Studying such an important document from the lairds second son was not easy while returning the greetings of his guests and trying to keep his footing amongst a multitude of scurrying children and dogs. As far as he could make out Alistair was now very grand indeed: the Deputy Governor of Madras, no less. He had gone to India straight after the '45 War so Mungo never knew him. It was said in the village that the old man bundled him off for fear that the family's well-known Jacobite sympathies and his eldest son's prominent support for Lord Kilmarnock might have put Alistair in danger.

"He is very kind in his remarks and even more generous with his suggestions," Mungo said. "I wonder what he means that I should have all the ground between the Shaw and the river?"

"Quite right!" said the laird, "and I agree with him. A gentleman needs his own fishings."

"But would that not take in the village too?"

"I know the folk in the Clachan can be a bit rough and ready but you'll manage fine with them, I'm sure."

Mungo handed the letter back to the laird. He wasn't too sure that he wanted to be landlord to folk he had grown up with.

"We'll have plenty of time to sort out the details when Alistair comes home at the end of the year. For now I've told Macadam to alter the deeds to include the extra land." He paused and gave a satisfied sigh. "We'll have a great ball when Alistair comes back. We can all get acquainted. It will be just like the old days," he smiled. "The Crawfords will be a force in the land once more."

Mungo had no idea what the laird meant by 'a force in the land' and he worried that there was more to this arrangement than just being good neighbours.

So it was not just a love of the landscape or even a need to clear his head that took him to the hilltop that morning. He could now see, with perfect clarity, the full extent of the grant of land that was to come his way at Martinmas. It was twice as much again as the Shaw on its own. Although he felt a little shamefaced about it, the sensation of ownership put a spring in his step. Even the remaining 'drops of brandy' began to clear from his head, but doubts remained.

If he was to pay court to Margaret Mr Murray would be keen to bring him in to the business again and Tom Murray would not do things by half. He would be quickly immersed in the many enterprises at Blairadam. This would not likely sit well with Sir Ardchie's plans to make 'the Crawfords a force in the land again' never mind his new-found duty to see to the interests of the folk of Langmuir village.

Chapter Thirty Three

When he arrived back at the farm house he had a sense that he was not alone. Mary, the dairy maid, had finished up and left before he went to the hill. He was expecting no one else. As he rounded the end of the barn a big bay horse, saddled up and sweating, was drinking greedily from the trough. The animal had surely been hard ridden. Then a vaguely familiar figure emerged from the doorway of the barn and came towards him.

"Mr Shaw?" asked the man. He was tall, fairish hair and well dressed but his bearing and mannerisms seemed familiar to Mungo. "Mr Christian sends his compliments," said the tall stranger.

"Well you'd better come in for a while," he replied, leading the way towards the kitchen door. As they walked his mind was racing – what on earth could Christian want with him?

"Have you come far? Your horse looks a bit warm. Can I bring you a drink; ale, milk?"

"I'm obliged to you; some water would be fine," he called after Mungo who had gone into the scullery. "It must be the heat that caused him to lather-up," he added. After a pause he went on, "You were not at home yesterday. Other things on your mind, I heard," he smiled as Mungo reappeared with a tankard of water.

"I trust Mr Christian is well and in a good way of business."

"He is in good humour and prospering mightily," the other replied. "The Duke of Atholl's sale of his Manx tax rights to the British government was a blow but a clever gentleman like Mr Christian is never downcast for long." Then he nodded rather sombrely and, looking up, he fixed Mungo with an earnest expression. "Mr Christian has asked me to put a proposition to you."

"I'm always open to a sound proposition," Mungo encouraged the stranger though he could hardly forget the disastrous outcome of Mr Christian's proposition, the year before.

"The Royal Society is to mount a scientific expedition to the Southern Ocean. An old collier called the *Earl of Pembroke* is to carry the scientists. She is fitting out at Whitby and should be ready for duty by next spring. The captain and first mate will be Royal Navy officers but Mr Christian has recommended you to the Society as second mate and sailing master. It is an exceptional opportunity, Mr Shaw, and Mr Christian is insistent that no one could fulfil the commission as well as your good self."

Mungo was flattered to be spoken of in this way, but he hoped his face did not show it.

"I am honoured and grateful for Mr Christian's commendation but I could not consider such an undertaking as matters stand."

As soon as he spoke his boyhood ambition to sail in a great ship to distant lands crowded into his mind. He almost wished he could recall his words.

The stranger looked disappointed at first but, perhaps sensing Mungo's reply was tactical rather than final, he countered:

"Before you make up your mind please let me tell you some details of the expedition."

The two men discussed all the facts as the stranger knew them; the size of the ship, how she was to be rigged, her itinerary, the numbers and the skills of the ship's company and of course the fee. The longer they spoke the more Mungo's objections began to melt away.

"Let me think on this a bit more," he said. "I'll make us a bite to eat."

Alone in the kitchen his interest rose further. It was not just a matter of satisfying an old ambition or even the promise of riches that drew him on. Here was a chance to make a name for himself. He could put aside all the scandal and rumour, along with memories of the privations of life on the Narrow Sea. By the time he had put a large wedge of cheese, butter and bannocks on the table he had almost decided to take up the offer. But as he poured some beer for his guest doubts and practical realities came rushing back.

"It is a very tempting proposition," he said, "but I fear I must decline."

The stranger took up a bannock and carved himself some cheese. He began to eat in silence but after maybe half a minute he looked Mungo straight in the face.

"I am sure Mr Christian understands that such a venture requires careful thought and that you must also consider the interests of others. I know he would be content to await your decision until the turn of the year."

Both men agreed without saying so that they would let matters rest there, and Mungo changed the direction of the conversation.

"You never told me your name," said Mungo.

The stranger rose from his chair and walked to the window. Then he turned and faced Mungo.

"Weston," he said, "Norman Weston."

"You must be..."

"Captain Henry's elder brother."

Both men paused and looked down, each remembering the captain's violent and untimely end. It was Norman who broke the silence.

"Mr Christian accompanied his body to Whitehaven. He even personally arranged the funeral and saw to all the family's needs. He was generous to a fault and a great comfort to our mother."

After a moment's respectful silence Mungo asked, "Did you ever find out who had attacked Captain Weston that night in Dublin?"

"We could never be sure. Maybe we should talk of other things," he said taking a swig of his ale. When he had drained his tankard Mungo brought the jug and refilled it. Perhaps the ale loosened his tongue or he sensed Mungo's need, indeed his right, to know more about Henry Weston. He resumed his narrative.

"Before he came to Mr Murray and the *Heron,* my brother had been mate on a ship called *The Friendship,* sailing in the Indies as a privateer. In an engagement near Jamaica the captain was lost and Henry took command. He was a firm disciplinarian and some of the crew turned against him and mutinied. After a prolonged confrontation he managed to talk round enough of the crew – with promises of an increased share of the booty – to regain control of the ship. He marooned the ring leaders on a small island and set sail for England."

"Was it the marooned men who made it back and attacked the *Heron* in Dublin that night?"

"No. It seems there was some trouble with the owners and the settlement was less than the men expected. A story went round that Henry had taken more than his share and was living in luxury in Scotland. I heard that the ship's carpenter, a Manxman, was determined to track him down. Maybe it was that man and his band that caught up with Henry in Dublin."

Mungo took some comfort from Norman's story. It was a logical explanation but he still wondered if Declan had been Captain Weston's murderous assailant. The silence came down again and after long seconds Mungo took up the conversation.

"How did you come to enter Mr Christian's service?"

"That is a much happier tale," said Norman. "Our family has had a chandlery in Whitehaven since my grandfather's time. I took over the business when our father died, ten years since. After Henry's funeral Mr Christian took me aside and asked if I would become his agent in Cumbria. In less than a year our little chandlery has grown fivefold on the back of Mr Christian's many commissions. I now have a good manager and that enables me to carry out special assignments, like this one, for Mr Christian."

"Mr Christian is very generous man indeed," Mungo said. "I had very little to do with him myself, except for that one voyage, but he did come to my trial you know."

Norman hesitated, as if wondering whether he wanted to pursue the matter of Mr Christian's graciousness any further. Then he continued:

"His presence at Kirkcudbright was more than just a show of support."

"How so?"

He paused again as if searching for words that would not implicate his master.

"Well if you do decide to join the voyage to the South Seas you'll have at least one good friend. The bosun is a man called Alf Garvie."

It took Mungo some little while to hoist in this dramatic revelation; Alf's failure to appear at the trial was no happy accident.

"I suppose you won't tell me how that came about," Mungo laughed.

"No, indeed; I'll leave that to Alf," his new friend smiled.

As he watched the big bay horse and its square shouldered rider cantering away down the track Mungo reflected on the possibilities facing him. It was no longer a straight choice between the landed gentry with Sir Archie and the industrial enterprise of Mr Murray. His lifelong obsession with tall ships now invaded his already crowded mind. He agonised about the best way forward but the jug of ale he had drank with Norman Weston and the after effects of his mothers wedding feast did not make the decision any easier. Soon he drifted off to sleep in Da's old chair.

He woke again in the early evening and wandered out to his usual perch on the small hill beside the house. As he watched the sun setting over the south end of Arran he began to see matters in a different light. He had lost Margaret once before and he could not let that happen again. His first aim must be to win Margaret's hand and then they could plan the future together.

Lightning Source UK Ltd.
Milton Keynes UK
UKHW032230010919
348915UK00011B/918/P